CAROLE MORTIMER

# FATED ATTRACTION

# FATED ATTRACTION

BY

CAROLE MORTIMER

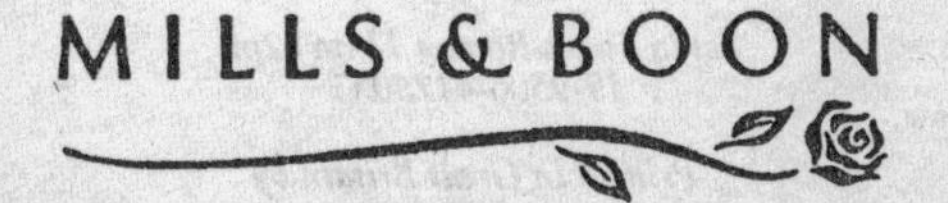


MILLS & BOON LIMITED
ETON HOUSE, 18-24 PARADISE ROAD
RICHMOND, SURREY TW9 1SR

*First published in Great Britain 1991 by Mills & Boon Limited*


*This edition 1995*

ISBN 0 263 79312 5

*Set in Times Roman 11 on 12pt.*
*19-9506-41760 C*

*Printed in Great Britain by*
*BPC Paperbacks Ltd*

## PROLOGUE

IN THE gutter.

Incredible. She, who until very recently, although she had taken it for granted at the time, had lived in the pampered, indulgent lap of luxury.

In the gutter.

Among the accumulated paper and empty cans, rainwater rushing by on its way to the drain several feet away, the rain continuing to fall heavily in the dimly lit street.

She couldn't even be bothered to get up. Her hip ached where she had landed on it heavily, and the throb in her ankle told her it was going to hurt too when she stood up and tried to put weight on it. So she wouldn't stand up, would just lie here and let the world, a world that had proved itself hard and unrelenting this last week, carry on without her. *It* didn't want her and, at the moment, *she* didn't want it!

How Jordan would laugh if he could see her now, unwanted, useless, completely defeated emotionally, and lying in the gutter while the rain fell and soaked her. It wasn't that he was a cruel man, it was just that his prediction that she would fail utterly on her own had proved correct. Even her suitcase had burst open when she had dropped it; all the beautiful clothes, that Jordan had told her time and time again that she spent too much money on, scattered over the road in the mud and the rain. So much for their 'designer labels' now!

She began to laugh, softly at first, and then more shrilly, laying back on the tarmac.

'That's all I need, a damned hysterical female!' rasped a voice that sounded more than a little impatient. 'Get up, woman, before another car comes along and finishes what I started!'

It was like having a bucket of ice-cold water thrown in her face, and she stopped laughing immediately, frowning up at the man who towered over her.

She had briefly forgotten, in her misery, the car that had turned the corner mere seconds ago, the suddenness of its appearance having been the reason she had stepped hurriedly back on the pavement, stumbling as she did so, the force of the water that sprayed over her as the wide tyres drove through puddles seeming to be the impetus needed to make her lose her balance completely, twisting her ankle as she landed heavily on her thigh.

The car had been brought to a halt some yards away, its back lights gleaming like red eyes in the darkness, the engine idly ticking over.

At least the driver had stopped.

Although there was no need for him to be so rude!

'If I could get up I would have done so,' she snapped. 'But you seem to have incapacitated me——'

'My car didn't touch you!' he bit out forcefully. 'You stepped off the pavement without looking, and when you realised there was a car coming you slipped trying to avoid it.'

It wasn't so far off the truth, but even so he didn't have to sound so arrogant about it.

'Your car hit her, anyone could see that,' a voice accused.

Amazing. Seconds ago this quiet back-street of London had been empty; now a small crowd had gathered to witness what they obviously hoped was going to be a scene.

The driver of the car glared at the man who had just spoken. 'As you were nowhere near the scene when the accident happened, I don't think that anything you have to say on the matter is relevant.'

Heathcliff. That was who this man made her think of. Dark and saturnine, with over-long hair that seemed inclined to curl, although it was difficult to tell with the rain streaming down his face—a face that was all dark hollows and shadows, his eyes glinting with anger.

Was she delirious? What did it matter who he made her think of? He was arrogant and condescending, and she had had enough of both emotions to last her a lifetime.

She moved gingerly, pain shooting through her ankle, her hip aching abominably. 'I don't think I can get up.' She gasped with the shock of the intensity of the pain.

'She's broken something.' That same accusing male voice in the crowd spoke with gloom. 'I don't think you should get up, love,' the man advised her confidingly. 'Wait until the police get here is what I say, and let them——'

'Police!' the driver echoed with scorn. 'There is no need to involve the police in this.'

'Of course there is.' The other man sounded scandalised—probably at the thought of seeing his evening's entertainment being cut short! 'You knocked this young lady down...'

'I did not knock——'

'Yes, you did!'

'No, I——'

'Oh for goodness' sake!' the 'young lady' cut in crossly, struggling into a sitting position to glare up at both of them, as no one actually seemed inclined to assist her. 'As you so rightly pointed out,' she snapped at the driver, 'if I don't soon get up off this road I'm going to be run over by other traffic and killed!'

'Here,' he bit out impatiently, his arms curiously gentle as he swung her up against his chest. 'Sorry,' he muttered as the movement caused her obvious pain. 'I will be seeing to this young lady's welfare,' he informed the crowd with finality.

Much to their disappointment, the 'young lady' noted ruefully, before she was briskly carried away to be placed on the warm leather passenger seat of the old-design Jaguar.

'My clothes!' she protested before he could slam the door behind her.

Irritation furrowed his brow once again before he glanced back at the suitcase and the strewn clothing.

'Hell!' he muttered with suppressed violence, closing her car door with the same controlled emotion.

But he did go back and pick up the clothes and push them haphazardly inside the case.

She watched his impatient movements in the wing-mirror, sure that the more delicate items of clothing—her bras and briefs were made of the finest silks—would be beyond salvation after his rough handling of them.

But the crowd had dispersed now, much to her relief, even the dogged heckler having taken himself off now that there wasn't any further fun to be had, at anyone's expense.

But, as the boot of the car was wrenched open and her suitcase flung inside, she realised how very alone she was with this man—a man who hadn't shown even a glimmer of a gentler side to his nature. He radiated barely controlled anger as he got in beside her, and she realised she couldn't get out of the car and get away from him even if she wanted to because her hip hurt her so badly and her ankle refused for the moment to support her weight, slight as it was.

If the man turned out to be some sort of kidnapper she didn't even think a ransom would be paid for her if it were demanded; she very much doubted that Jordan would pay to have her returned to him.

She might have been in the gutter a few minutes ago, filled with frustration and despair, but now she had a feeling she could be in danger!

# CHAPTER ONE

'JANE SMITH!'

She kept her head held high, although she could feel the delicate colour slowly staining her cheeks at his scepticism of the name she had given the nurse at the hospital when that lady had come to take her details before she was seen by the doctor. She had sensed the derision of the man at her side then, but he had at least waited until they were alone before expressing his scorn.

She wondered what his feelings would have been if she had calmly announced her full name.

Which she had no intention of doing.

It was quite a mouthful, for one thing. Another factor dictating his reaction would be whether or not he had heard of her family. If he hadn't it wouldn't mean a lot to him. She had also learnt during the last week that using her full name, in certain circumstances, got her absolutely nowhere.

She had to admit she had been more than a little relieved when he had driven her straight to the accident department of this well-known hospital, although she knew without seeing the doctor that she hadn't actually broken anything, that she was probably just badly bruised. Although that felt painful enough.

She was just relieved she had been wrong about the 'danger' she had sensed. The man obviously couldn't wait to get rid of the responsibility of her!

In the bright lights of the hospital waiting-room he looked even more like her image of Heathcliff than she had first thought. His hair was very dark, not quite ebony, but a rich teak-brown, inclined to curl over the collar of his shirt and ears now that it was dry, eyes the colour of grey slate made even more vivid by the dark bronze of his skin. It was a strong face, unrelenting, and the darkness hadn't deceived about the hollows and shadows, his face all angles and deep grooves; character-lines, Jordan would probably have called them.

He looked slightly older than Jordan's thirty years, possibly in his mid-thirties, and the well-worn comfort of the Jaguar he drove was also evident in the worn denims and small-checked jacket he wore. A man who seemed to care little for his appearance, and yet at the same time there was something magnetically attractive about him, his masculinity undoubted, his virility tangible.

Older than her set, out of her experience, at least fifteen years her senior, and yet she felt a certain curiosity to know more about him. Strange...

He had to be married, of course, or possibly divorced. If he hadn't been one, or both, at his age, that surely only left—— No, she didn't for one moment believe his inclinations lay in that direction. He might find her an irritant, but that didn't mean he found all women so.

What would his wife, or ex-wife, be like? she wondered. Probably tall and blonde and athletically minded, as she was sure *he* was; he certainly didn't keep as fit as he looked by the odd game of golf, as many men tried—and failed—to do. Or maybe his wife hadn't shared his interests at all, maybe that was the reason they were divorced.

Ridiculous.

She had the man married and divorced, and she didn't even know *his* name!

'A good English name,' she stoutly defended what was, after all, part of her name. She stuck out her hand. 'I don't believe we've been introduced.'

His mouth twisted at her sudden formality given the circumstances, and Jane was made to see herself through his mocking eyes. Small and pert, with a body that could easily be called boyish in the fitted denims and bulky sweater, except that the full swell of her breasts was clearly discernible beneath the woollen garment, and her hair was a long, Titian—as the Duke of York chose to call this particular shade of hair that was also the colour of his wife's!—riot of virtually uncontrollable curls that reached almost down to her waist, more tangled than usual this evening after the rough treatment it had taken from the wind and rain outside. Sparkling blue eyes the colour of sapphires dominated the beauty of her pointed face, a face bare of its usual make-up because she had felt too despondent earlier to take the usual trouble with her appearance, utterly defeated, on her way back to Jordan and his 'I told you so's.

And instead of that she was sitting in a hospital waiting-room with a man who looked as if he would like to take that 'Titian'-coloured hair, wind it around her neck, and strangle her with it!

'Raff Quinlan,' he announced drily. 'And I have never cared to look into its origins.'

And he wasn't about to start now, his tone implied.

Raff Quinlan. Even his name was different, interesting.

Her hand dropped back to her side as he made no effort to take it in his much larger one. 'Am I keeping you from something?' Her voice was tart at the obvious snub.

He returned her gaze coldly. 'Yes.'

He wasn't just blunt, he was downright rude!

She drew in an angry breath. 'I didn't choose to be run down by your car...'

'My dear Miss Smith,' he exploded, grey eyes blazing angrily. 'I did not run you down with my car. You——'

'The doctor will see you now,' a young nurse cut in firmly, giving Raff Quinlan a reproving look as she wheeled the chair he had insisted on for Jane when they first arrived through to the examination-room. 'Would you like to accompany your wife?' she offered as an afterthought.

Wife? Jane raised her eyes heavenwards; as if they looked like a married couple!

Raff Quinlan obviously thought it a ridiculous assumption to have made, too, and was on the point of giving a scathing reply.

Some devil, probably the same devil that made Jordan call her impossible, made her smile sweetly at Raff Quinlan. 'I would rather you did come with me, darling,' she told him lovingly, adopting a forlorn expression designed to make him look guilty as she suddenly looked very sorry for herself. 'I'm a little nervous,' she added in a little-girl voice.

He looked ready to tell her exactly what he thought of this supposed nervousness, but the young nurse looking at him expectantly prevented him from doing that. His mouth set tightly.

'Of course—darling,' this last was added tightly, his movements controlled as he joined them.

Jane smiled up at him smugly as they went down the corridor to the examination-room. His expression promised retribution.

It came quicker than they had both expected, and from an unexpected quarter!

'Would you like to let your husband help you to undress and get up on the couch, Mrs Smith, while I tell the doctor you're here?' the nurse suggested briskly, not giving either of them chance to answer her as she swished out of the room.

Jane had always wondered how silence could possibly be deafening, but the silence that descended over the room once the door had closed, leaving her alone with Raff Quinlan, was definitely of that kind!

She dared a glance at Raff under her lashes, not fooled for a moment by his innocently concerned expression, knowing that his anger towards her had faded to be replaced by mocking amusement.

'Well, Mrs Smith?' he finally drawled, his humour somehow making him appear younger. 'Would you like me to help you take your clothes——?'

'Out!' she ordered firmly.

'But——'

'Out!' she repeated with finality, her level gaze brooking no argument.

'If you're sure...?' He grinned at her discomfort, taking his time about leaving the room, pausing at the door. 'I'll come back after a suitable period,' he taunted. 'The nurse already has her doubts about my husbandly concern: if I just disappear she'll think I don't give a damn... What was that?' he prompted at her mumbled remark. 'Did you say something, darling? I couldn't quite hear you, my love.' He raised dark brows as her mutterings continued.

'*Everyone* in this department will hear me if you don't leave soon,' she warned audibly.

His husky laugh echoed down the corridor, and Jane knew her own teasing had been more than successfully turned back on her. Jordan wasn't capable of understanding her humour, let alone returning it; to be honest, this bantering made a pleasant change. Not that she was about to let Raff Quinlan know that—he was altogether too arrogant already.

Actually, she almost instantly regretted his having left the room, quickly discovering that the bruising to her body was so bad now every movement was an agony. Any help easing off the bulky sweater and denims would have been welcome, even Raff Quinlan's, by the time she had struggled out of her clothes and slipped beneath the sheet on top of the examination-couch, tears wetting her cheeks in painful silence.

On top of everything else, she felt sick.

Raff took one look at her when he came into the room, and picked up the kidney-shaped dish that stood on the side-table, reaching her side just in time for her to empty the contents of her stomach into it.

She fell back against the pillow once the retching had stopped. 'I'm sorry,' she groaned self-consciously.

'Don't be,' he dismissed easily, crossing the room as she closed her eyes weakly.

Jane didn't blame him for walking out in disgust; she couldn't bear to see anyone being sick, herself. She must have been more shaken by the fall than she had realised.

Her eyes opened in surprise as she felt a damp cloth against her forehead and down over the heat of her cheeks. Blue eyes looked straight into grey, so close she could see the long length of Raff Quinlan's lashes.

'I thought you had gone,' she told him huskily.

'No, I—God, you look awful!' He shook his head, frowning darkly.

She closed her eyes again, smiling faintly. 'Thanks!' she grimaced.

'I just hadn't realised——'

'Mrs Smith?' A young man with hair almost as red as Jane's came into the room, followed by the nurse. 'I'm Dr Young,' he introduced himself confidently.

Jane had already guessed that; possibly because of the badge attached to the white coat he wore that bore the name 'Dr P Young' upon it!

'I'm not *Mrs* Smith!' She was tired of that game now.

'Ah,' the doctor nodded. 'Then the two of you aren't married?'

Obviously! She was being impossible, and she knew it. If only she didn't feel so sick.

'No,' she sighed.

'Well, it doesn't matter,' the doctor dismissed briskly. 'The point is, you want Mr...? He looked enquiringly at Raff.

'Quinlan,' he instantly supplied.

'Right,' the younger man said before turning back to smile reassuringly at Jane. 'All that matters is that you want Mr Quinlan in with you during the examination.'

'But I——'

'I'm going to be here,' Raff cut in firmly, his steady gaze meeting hers with determination.

To be quite truthful, the nausea, and its subsequent result, had tired her to the point where she really didn't care any more. She very much doubted she would be the first—or the last!—woman Raff would see in her bra and briefs. She tried to remember the colour of the underwear she was wearing today, but for the moment it eluded her; she did know it would match in colour, whatever that colour was. It was one of her foibles... And extravagances, Jordan would have said. Oh, damn Jordan and his preaching! It was doing little to ease the pain as the doctor examined her ankle!

'Hm.' He frowned a little. 'Just badly bruised, I think. Although we'll X-ray it anyway,' he announced cheerfully. 'Just to be on the safe side. Your hip was the other place injured, I believe?' He briskly pulled the sheet down to examine the injured area.

Jane heard Raff's sharply indrawn breath, wondering if she could have been wrong about his having seen a woman in her underclothes before.

She looked across at him curiously, but his gaze was fixed on the area being examined by the doctor. A glance down at that spot herself told her why!

She knew her hip was extremely painful; in fact the nausea had begun in the car on the drive here from the pain of it. But she had just been concentrating on getting her outer clothing off earlier without fainting, and hadn't had the strength to actually look at her hip. She wished she hadn't bothered now either!

Her side was black and blue with bruising already, not just on the hip-bone but across her stomach and down her thigh too. It looked ghastly. No wonder Raff was staring.

Just when she thought she couldn't stand the poking and prodding into her flesh any longer the doctor straightened.

'Well, it looks as if you've been quite lucky, young lady.' His smile had gone now to be replaced by a reproving frown. 'I don't think any bones have been broken here either. You sustained the injuries in a fall, I think you said?'

'Yes,' she nodded distractedly. 'I tripped and fell over the pavement.'

The doctor continued to frown. 'The injuries seem rather—severe, for a fall of that nature.'

'Well, I——' Colour flooded her cheeks as she sensed concern behind the question. She glanced at Raff, his mouth tight now as he too sensed the scepticism. My God, the doctor didn't really think that...! She respected his concern, realised that he probably often had reason for it, but it really was unfair to Raff in the circumstances.

'I fell in the street and Mr Quinlan very kindly helped me by driving me here,' she told the doctor firmly. The last thing she wanted was to get involved with the police over what had, after all, just been an accident.

The doctor still didn't look convinced, but there was really very little he could do about the situation in the face of her insistence. 'We'll X-ray the ankle and hip just to be sure,' he told her gently. 'And decide what to do with you once we have the result of those.'

That sounded rather ominous. What did he mean, 'decide what to do with her'?

She wasn't given the chance to ask either the nurse or the doctor that question before they bustled out of the room in deep conversation together, the doctor presumably on his way to treat another patient, the nurse to organise Jane's X-rays.

Jane couldn't quite look at Raff after the implication the doctor had made about him a few minutes ago.

He crossed the room to stand next to her. 'I had no idea you were so badly marked,' he spoke quietly.

She grimaced dismissively. 'I bruise easily.'

He shook his head. 'You must have fallen very heavily. Or else I did actually hit you with the car...'

'No,' she denied as she sensed the doubt in his voice. 'I only said that earlier because I was annoyed by your bluntness,' she explained truthfully.

'Nevertheless, if I hadn't driven around that corner at speed——'

'You weren't speeding,' she cut in exasperatedly.

'But——'

'Mr Quinlan,' Jane spoke steadily. 'Believe me, my accident was not your fault.'

His mouth was tight. 'Nevertheless, I'm responsible for you...'

'I'm responsible for myself!' Her tone was a little more vehement than the occasion warranted, but she was more than a little tired of being told she wasn't capable of taking care of herself. She certainly wasn't anyone's *responsibility*. God, what an awful label to give someone! 'I'm grateful to you for bringing me here.' She spoke more calmly now. 'But there's really no need for you to delay yourself any longer.'

'I was only on my way back to my home,' he said dismissively, his gaze once again on the brightness of her hair.

'Then your wife——'

'I'm not married,' he bit out curtly.

Jane couldn't help but wonder why that was. Unless, as she had presumed earlier, he had been married and divorced. It was the most likely explanation. For a man who supposedly lived alone he had been in a hurry to get there earlier.

Something about this man raised her curiosity, possibly because she sensed there was no artifice in him—not even the one of politeness! Jordan would find him brash in the extreme, but then Jordan could be brash himself on occasion.

'Nevertheless,' she said firmly, 'the X-rays will take some time, and I really mustn't keep you any longer.'

'You——'

'Don't bother to dress, Miss Smith.' The nurse came back into the room, straightening up Jane's discarded clothes. 'We need you undressed for the X-ray, anyway.'

Jane had had no intention of even attempting to put her clothes back on in front of Raff Quinlan, even if she hadn't been hurting so badly that the nausea was never far away.

Perhaps the hospital just wasn't busy, or maybe it was the time of night, but the X-rays were completed and a diagnosis given within a matter of minutes; there were no bones broken, only the severe bruising. But even that was enough to make Jane shudder at the thought of putting her clothes on again.

Some of her distress must have shown on the paleness of her face.

'Of course, I think we should offer you a bed for the night,' the young doctor smiled encouragingly. 'If only as a precaution.'

For 'offer her a bed' Jane knew he meant admit her to the hospital, and she had no desire to spend the night in a hospital ward. But she was sure the doctor was as aware as she was that the address she had given them was that of a hotel, a hotel she had actually booked out of earlier today.

'Is that really necessary?' Far from leaving, Raff had gone with her to the X-ray department, and then stayed right by her side while the doctor gave her his verdict on her injuries. Now he spoke with a quiet authority. 'As long as Miss Smith has someone to take care of her, couldn't she be allowed to leave?'

The doctor looked slightly irritated by this interruption, obviously still not quite convinced of the other man's innocence in the affair, although he was holding a tight check on any more even veiled accusations of that nature. 'I suppose so,' he accepted slowly. 'But as she——'

'Miss Smith has somewhere to go,' Raff told him arrogantly.

Even Jane looked at him in some surprise. If that 'somewhere' was his home, then he could forget it; she may be weak but she wasn't helpless.

But if seeming to agree to that suggestion would get her out of here without too much fuss she could always make other arrangements once they were outside. After all, she didn't have to go anywhere, do anything she didn't want to do. After years of being ordered around she was finally free to make her own choices. Even if the majority of them this last week had been a disaster!

'Miss Smith? Miss Smith?' The doctor repeated his query more firmly at her wandering attention.

She looked up to find them all looking at her—the nurse kindly, the doctor enquiringly, Raff Quinlan challengingly. It was the latter that now held her attention.

'Is Mr Quinlan's suggestion agreeable to you?' the doctor persisted.

The poor man was still half convinced she had taken a beating from Raff Quinlan!

And Raff was still fully aware of the unspoken accusation.

'Yes, it's agreeable to me,' Jane finally answered, much to Raff's unspoken but felt relief, and the doctor's chagrin.

But he seemed to be resigned to her decision as he stood up to leave. 'If you have any further trouble, don't hesitate to either come back here or see your own doctor,' he advised.

'By "further trouble", I suppose he meant any more beatings from me,' Raff muttered grimly in the darkness, Jane now seated next to him in the

Jaguar, their departure from the hospital made without further incident after the nurse had carefully helped her to dress.

In truth Jane felt slightly lethargic now, the doctor having prescribed pain-killers to at least help ease some of her discomfort. The last thing she felt like doing now was sorting out a hotel for the night. But it had to be done. Raff Quinlan's ruffled feelings over the doctor's implications was the least of her worries for the moment.

She looked about her in the darkness, realising they were fast leaving town—Raff's home, wherever it was, seeming to be far from the hotels of London.

'If you pull over at the next corner, I can get a taxi back to a hotel,' she told him sleepily, those tablets, whatever they were, making her feel very tired.

He didn't even glance at her. 'I said you had somewhere to go,' he said tersely. 'And you do. You also have someone to "take care of you".'

'You?' Jane scorned, her lids becoming so heavy now she could barely keep them open.

'If necessary,' he nodded abruptly.

'It isn't,' she said drily.

He gave her a scathing glance. 'Forgive me if I disagree with you.'

Her mouth tightened at the insult. 'No.'

'My dear young lady...'

'I'm not your *dear* anything,' Jane snapped. 'And I have no wish to go to your home.'

His mouth twisted. 'You talk as if you usually expect your wishes to be carried out without question.'

Perhaps she did, but she had a feeling, from the little she had learnt of this man this evening, that he rarely considered anyone else's wishes but his own!

'I want you to stop the car immediately so that I don't have too far to walk before I can get a taxi back into town,' she told him firmly, although she was aware that her voice sounded less than convincing, and that she was feeling sleepier and sleepier by the moment.

Raff Quinlan laughed softly. 'You don't look capable of standing on your feet, let alone walking anywhere.'

'I am—capable, of doing—whatever I have to—do...'

It was the last thing she remembered saying, sleep finally overcoming her as she slumped down in the car seat.

## CHAPTER TWO

WHAT on earth...?

Where was she? Jane felt panicked as she awoke fully and didn't recognise her surroundings. She had been on her way to a hotel—but this wasn't a hotel, she felt sure of it.

God! The pain when she tried to move...

And with the pain came the return of her memory. The headlights of the car. The pain in her ankle as she turned to hurry back on to the pavement, then the terrible jarring of her hip as she made contact with the hard road.

Raff Quinlan...

She remembered everything about him too now—the way he towered over her in the darkness, his arrogance, his rudeness, the way he had insisted on bringing her to his home despite her protests...

She was almost afraid to look beneath the bedclothes, had a feeling she already knew what she was going to find. Nevertheless she closed her eyes, took a deep breath, and lifted the sheet.

Naked.

Completely.

Even the peach-coloured underwear was missing now.

There was something vaguely disturbing about the thought of someone undressing her when she was unconscious from the effect of pain-killers and tiredness because of shock—unfair somehow, and it gave Raff Quinlan an advantage over her that she didn't like. At the hospital she had been wearing no less than if she had been on a beach, but being stripped naked when she could do nothing to prevent it was—well, it was underhand.

And Raff Quinlan was responsible, somehow she felt sure of that. After all, he had admitted he didn't have a wife who could have done it.

She looked up sharply as the bedroom door opened after a brief knock.

'Ah, good morning, my dear!' A tall woman in a tailored blue dress with a pristine white collar bustled into the room carrying a silver tray that held what looked like a pot of coffee. 'I hope I didn't wake you.' She smiled brightly before putting the tray down on the bedside-table and straightening, a perplexed frown appearing between her eyes as she looked down at Jane.

'I didn't realise—— For a moment you looked so much like——' She broke off, shaking her head. 'I'm sorry, for a moment you looked so much like—someone I used to know.'

Her smile was only a little strained now. 'I haven't even introduced myself,' she scolded self-derisively. 'I'm Mrs Howard, Mr Quinlan's housekeeper.'

And she had obviously never seen Jane before this moment, confirming that she hadn't been the one to undress her the evening before!

But, remembering the evening before, Jane realised she had started a deception with Raff Quinlan that she would now have to carry on. 'Jane Smith,' she supplied gruffly.

'Cream and sugar?'

'Sorry?' She looked up with a frown, the frown clearing as she realised the housekeeper was pouring her a cup of coffee. 'Oh. Both. Thank you,' she accepted with a tight smile.

What was that saying, 'When first you practise to deceive'...?

Sitting up to actually take the offered cup of coffee wasn't as easy as it should have been, either. Every movement caused her pain, and there was her nakedness to consider. Not that she was at all shy about that, she just didn't know what explanation Raff had given this woman for her being here, and her nakedness might look a bit suspect, in the circumstances. If Raff had felt he owed his housekeeper an explanation at all! Somehow she doubted it.

'Jane Smith?'

Her frown returned as she looked up from securing the sheet more firmly about her breasts, not quite as awake as she would have liked to have been, the pain-killers seeming to have left her with a slightly muzzy feeling in her head.

She took the coffee-cup from the other woman, spilling some of the hot liquid into the saucer as her hand shook slightly. 'Sorry,' she grimaced. 'This is much appreciated.' And it was, for her mouth felt like sandpaper.

She decided to ignore the reference to her name; it had already been discussed enough, one way or another! But sipping the coffee made her realise she had a sudden *urgency* to find a bathroom!

Her suitcase was just visible behind the bedroom chair, and she had no reason to suppose any of her things had been unpacked and placed in the spacious drawers of the dresser. And, unfortunately, the last time she had seen the wrap she had brought with her it had been strewn across the road soaking up muddy water like a sponge. In fact, most of her clothes had been doing the same thing. But she could hardly stay in this bed forever!

In fact, she couldn't stay in it another minute longer, with her predicament becoming more and more desperate by the second!

'My dear?' Mrs Howard seemed to sense her discomfort, if not the reason for it.

Jane's smile was strained. 'I don't seem to be wearing a nightgown, and—well, I need to...'

'Oh, my dear, how thoughtless of me!' The other woman instantly looked contrite. 'Your things are all laundered downstairs. Mr Quinlan explained about the catch breaking on your case, and all your beautiful clothes getting muddy. I'll just pop down and get them,' she reassured her.

Jane waited only as long as it took the other woman to leave the room before struggling out of bed and into what she could see was the adjoining bathroom.

She was more than a little shaky on her legs, and each movement across the room was an agony, but she finally made it, her relief immense once she had done so.

She could think clearer now too and, although her accident the night before had delayed her returning home to Jordan, it had only done so for that one night; now she would have no choice but to go back. She had been so sure she could succeed on her own a week ago, but now she was defeated, knew he was right—that she needed him and the money to survive.

She closed her eyes in shame at the pained memories of the last week—of one rejection after another, one humiliation after another. She had been so sure she could look after and support herself, and instead she had found how ill-fitted she was to do the latter, at least. And without the qualifications and means to support herself she wasn't capable of being independent.

Of course, there were a lot of young women in London who couldn't get a legitimate job and who therefore found some other means of supporting themselves, but even going back to Jordan had to be better than that alternative. Better the devil she knew than ones she didn't know, she had decided last night when she'd packed up to go home. Much as she hated the thought of Jordan's gloating self-satisfaction in being proved right about her dependence upon him.

The housekeeper still hadn't returned to the bedroom by the time she had finished in the bathroom, and so Jane hobbled as best she could across the room, giving a gasp of horror as she caught sight of her reflection in the dressing-table mirror. Her hip seemed to have turned all the colours of the rainbow now, the bruising having spread further and deepened.

She might not want to stay in bed, but she wasn't sure she was going to be able to bear the pressure of normal clothing against her tender flesh.

She looked at her reflection critically, trying to see her body from a man's point of view. Her skin was quite tanned—it was summer, after all—and she had the usual smattering of freckles that most people with her colouring were afflicted with, although not so many that it could be thought unattractive. Firm breasts were tipped with delicate coral pink, fuller than her other slenderness would imply, but proudly uptilting. Her waist was slender, her hips boyish, her legs surprisingly long and well-shaped for her five-feet-two-inch height. Like a long, leggy filly, Jordan always said.

Jordan. Jordan. Jordan. She had never realised before quite how much notice she took of the things he said to her.

'You really are a bloody mess, aren't you?' said an impatient voice from behind her.

A voice she recognised only too well!

She gave a yelp of dismay before crossing the room to the sanctuary of the bed and the protective bedclothes, and looking accusingly at Raff over the top of the snowy-white sheet.

She hadn't heard his approach or the bedroom door opening, but there he stood, larger than life in the daylight, the fitted denims low down on his hips, the dark blue shirt he wore making his eyes look darker.

But he still made her think of Heathcliff, his dark hair tousled and inclined to curl, his skin ruggedly tanned.

'Here.' He held up the clothes that were draped over his arm, derisively taking pity on her. 'But I've seen it all before, you know,' he drawled mockingly.

In Technicolor!

Her cheeks felt hot at the thought of this man's hands on her body. Had her nakedness left him unaffected? Probably. He didn't give the impression he found her in the least attractive. It wasn't the reaction men usually had to her vivid colouring.

'In that case——' she sat up on the bed, baring her shoulders and back '—pass me my robe, would you?' She held out her hand for the garment, her gaze unflinching.

Admiration slowly darkened his eyes and, although slow in coming, he actually smiled! 'I wonder just who you are, Jane Smith?' he mused softly.

Her head went back at this direct challenge, her defensive action turning to puzzlement as his expression became harsh, and his narrowed gaze rested on the flowing fire of her hair as it fell forward across her breasts.

'I mean to find out before you leave here,' he told her curtly.

Jane felt a shiver of apprehension, instantly dismissing the emotion as being ridiculous. She didn't know exactly where she was, but she could leave any time she wanted to. Couldn't she...?

'Where did you come from last night?' Raff demanded to know. 'Where were you going *to*?'

'I don't think that's any of your business,' she snapped resentfully, well aware of what a disadvantage she was at, her robe having been placed over the back of the bedroom chair with her other clothes, way across the other side of the room. As Raff very well knew!

His eyes were still narrowed, his arms crossed in front of the broadness of his chest. 'You gave your address at the hospital last night as being a hotel, but you must have lived somewhere before staying there?'

He was being deliberately provocative, almost insulting. 'Raff...'

'Who was he, Jane Smith?' he pushed, not waiting for her to finish.

'Who was who?' Jane frowned.

'Your wealthy lover!'

'My——?' Jane choked with indignation. 'What on earth are you talking about?' she gasped.

He shrugged. 'I may not know too much about ladies' clothing——' his mouth twisted derisively '—but even I recognise some of the labels in your clothes as being designer models. Who bought them for you?'

'I don't have to——'

'It was a man, wasn't it?' he cut in forcefully. 'Silken underwear——' He held up one of the lacy bras Jane favoured, that minute scrap of expensive lace looking even smaller in his callused hand. 'Bought to please a lover. Or by him,' Raff added hardly.

In truth, each and every article of her clothing had been paid for by a man, but she had chosen the underwear to please herself, no one else, loving the silken feel of it against her skin.

She shook her head. 'You don't know what you're talking about.'

'Don't I?' he rasped, throwing the bra down disgustedly on top of her other clean clothing. 'Believe me, I know more than you think,' he told her heavily. 'But before this goes any further I think I should tell you I'm not on the lookout for an expensive mistress. Or one of any other kind, come to that,' he added insultingly.

His behaviour took her breath away, angry colour darkening her cheeks. 'If I *were* on the lookout for a rich lover, you can be sure you wouldn't even be a consideration!'

Really, the man didn't even know her, and yet he could make accusations like that!

'Then we understand each other,' he nodded with satisfaction.

'Completely,' she snapped resentfully.

'Good,' he said smugly. 'Now that we're agreed on what neither of us want, we can get around to discussing what I *do* want.'

'Sorry?' Jane shook her head, still feeling slightly muzzy. It must be those tablets she had taken the night before. Maybe she was imagining this whole conversation? It was too outrageous to be real!

'Can you type?' He sat down in the bedroom chair, uncaring that he crushed her clothes in doing so.

Jane frowned, having difficulty keeping up with the conversation now. 'Type?' she repeated dazedly.

'Yes.' His mouth twisted. 'You know, place your fingers on the keys of a typewriter and make words appear on——'

'I'm well aware of what typing is,' she snapped. 'I just don't see what it has to do with me?'

Raff looked at her consideringly. 'At a guess, I would say right now you're homeless and jobless——'

'That's a hell of an assumption to make,' Jane bit out resentfully. God, was she so transparent? Possibly, to this man, with his probing eyes and cynicism. Although he certainly wasn't a hundred per cent right about her! Just enough to have unnerved her, she admitted.

She still had no idea where she was, and although Mrs Howard had seemed respectable enough that was really little comfort right now.

Raff arched dark brows. 'But a correct one?'

'Who are *you*, Raff Quinlan?' Her head was back challengingly.

He shrugged broad shoulders. 'Rafferty Quinlan. Thirty-seven. Divorced.' The last was added bitterly. 'In charge of the running of an estate that is slowly bleeding itself—and me—dry!'

It was the very briefest of résumés, and yet Jane was able to glean a lot from it. His marriage, whether it had initially been a happy one or not, had ended badly, which might account for some of his behaviour towards her. But not all of it!

'"In charge of running an estate"?' she repeated slowly.

He nodded abruptly. 'I can't exactly claim to own it when it's mortgaged up to the hilt,' he rasped. 'My father had little interest in the place for years before he and my mother were killed in a plane crash five years ago, and he had let things deteriorate badly. My darling wife decided she didn't want to be stuck out in the middle of Hampshire struggling to make a living, let alone enjoying herself, and took what little there was left as a divorce settlement. I've only managed to keep Mrs Howard because she's run the house since before I was born, and considers it more her home than I do!'

Jane didn't believe that; she sensed a fierce pride in Raff in the estate he called his home.

And at least she knew where she was now! Not that she was too familiar with Hampshire, but she felt a little more reassured now that she was at least approximately aware of her whereabouts.

Raff's wife couldn't have loved him if she could have walked out on him for such a reason. And it would probably explain part of his resentment towards the type of woman he had decided she had to be.

But it didn't explain his conversation of a few minutes ago.

'What does all this have to do with whether or not I can type?' She frowned.

His mouth twisted. 'Well, as it seems for the moment I'm responsible for you . . .'

'You most certainly are not!' she protested indignantly. 'I'm responsible for myself,' she told him firmly.

At least, she was trying to be.

Her bank account stood at nil and, for all that she tried to deny it to this man, she was homeless into the bargain; she hadn't even thought to bring any of her jewellery—that she could have sold and lived off the money for a while—away with her when she'd left.

'You aren't doing a very good job of it,' Raff drily echoed at least some of her sentiments.

'I'm doing the best that I can!' To her chagrin she heard her voice break with emotion.

Raff looked at her closely, obviously having heard that emotion too. 'We all do that, little one,' he told her softly. 'It just isn't always enough.'

No, she acknowledged sadly, it wasn't always enough...

She didn't even want to think about Jordan sitting waiting for her to crawl back and tell him he had been right about her not being able to survive on her own.

She blinked back the tears. 'I'll make your problems one less by leaving here as soon as I've ordered a taxi.' She didn't think Jordan would mind paying the fare; it would be worth it to him to have been proved correct!

'To go where?' Raff's eyes were narrowed. 'Back to him?'

Her cheeks were flushed. 'I told you——'

'Surely working for me, once you've ceased being a walking bruise, of course—even I'm not that much of a taskmaster that I would expect you to work while you're still in pain...!' he derided what he had guessed had been her opinion of him '...has to be better than returning to a man you obviously have no desire to go back to!' he said exasperatedly.

'What do you know about how I—work?' Jane repeated slowly as all of his words sank in. 'What sort of work are you talking about?' she asked suspiciously.

His mouth twitched. 'Well, I've asked you if you can type—so I obviously want you to start cooking for me!' He shook his head. 'What sort of work do you think I mean?' he scorned.

Work. Raff was actually offering her a job! But why? He had treated her as nothing but a nuisance since he had first met her. Probably because she had been one, she ruefully acknowledged. He wasn't the type of man to take lightly having his life interrupted as disastrously as last night had done. But he also wasn't a man to shirk what he considered his responsibility either.

Responsibility. How she was coming to hate the very sound of that word!

She looked up at Raff uncertainly. 'By working for you, do you mean——?'

'I can afford to pay you a small wage, plus your room and food, if that's what you're worried about,' he cut in harshly, his eyes narrowing resentfully. 'The estate may be in difficulties, but I'm not bankrupt yet.'

And she had obviously hit upon a very raw nerve!

But the offer of a job was so tempting. Any job. It was exactly what she had been looking for, praying for. It meant so much more to her than just no longer being dependent upon Jordan. Not that she intended telling Raff Quinlan about *that*.

She looked at him quizzically. 'Why?'

He gave an impatient sigh, as if already regretting having made the offer at all. 'Don't think I would be doing you any favours, Jane Smith,' he rasped. 'I have correspondence that needs answering dating back three months or so, have been so tied up with work on the estate these last few months that I just haven't had time to tackle answering any of the mail.'

She frowned. 'You usually do the typing yourself?'

Not that he didn't look capable of coping with any problem that came his way—it was just unusual for a man in his position; she certainly couldn't see Jordan doing his own typing, no matter what the circumstances!

Raff gave a dismissive shrug. 'I have an aunt who comes down from town occasionally and does it, mainly so that she can keep an eye on exactly what's going on here,' he added derisively. 'But she hasn't found the time recently in her busy schedule.' The last was said sarcastically.

Jane wasn't the world's best typist, as the last week of job-hunting has proved, although that was mainly because it was a lot of years since she had attempted any typing at all; but if Raff didn't mind her lack of speed she was at least accurate.

My God, she wasn't seriously thinking of accepting his offer, was she?

What did she know about the man—other than the fact that he seemed to be a law unto himself? She didn't even know exactly where she was, let alone anything else.

And yet...

A job was all she needed. Just for three months. Until August the thirty-first. And there was Mrs Howard; she had seemed respectable enough...

Raff stood up abruptly. 'Think about it,' he bit out tersely.

'Oh, but——'

'I've wasted enough time already for one morning,' he continued harshly. 'Maybe when you decide what you're going to do you'll let me know?' He strode across to the door, emanating physical power, stopping to turn back to her. 'But I would advise you to consider very carefully before returning to a situation that was obviously stressful enough for you to have left it in the first place.'

And with that last, strangely gentle advice Raff left the bedroom.

Jane dropped back on to the pillows, totally dazed by this complex man. One minute so harsh and dismissive, the next almost caring. But of course he didn't care for her, just felt a *responsibility* towards her because of last night.

But did that really matter?

If she accepted his offer of a job she wouldn't be cheating him in any way, would work as hard as she was capable of, and they would both be getting something out of the situation—Raff a backlog of correspondence that was troubling him, and she—well, ultimately she would get so much more out of it.

But was this a frying-pan-into-the-fire situation? Wasn't Raff more of an enigma to deal with even than Jordan?

But it was only for three *months*, she reminded herself again. What other offers had she had?

None.

Her whole situation could be completely turned around if she just agreed to work for Raff Quinlan...

Was that too high a price to pay for proving Jordan wrong?

She had left him so confidently, so sure she could support herself. And she could—if she just took the job Raff offered her...

Pride warred with necessity—and finally necessity won. She couldn't let it bother her that Raff had only offered her the job because he felt he had rescued her like some stray from the street. She would do her job and, when the time came, leave without regret.

She hoped.

All she had to do now was let Jordan know she had succeeded. He had been sitting back, she knew, waiting for her to crawl back to him with her tail between her legs. And last night she had been so close to doing that, had never felt so miserable in her life.

The role of guardian angel sat oddly on Raff Quinlan's shoulders!

Dressing proved as difficult as she had thought it might, and by the time she had donned the thin woollen top and loose, flowered skirt the sweat stood out on her forehead and top lip, and she once again felt nauseous. But there was no telephone in her bedroom, and she had to find one. Besides, she was very curious about her surroundings, interested to see this estate Raff had talked about.

She stepped out of her bedroom into a long corridor, portraits adorning the walls, the resemblance of some of the subjects to Raff Quinlan pointing to their being his ancestors. So much for his casual dismissal the night before of his family name!

Arrogant-looking men and haughtily beautiful women seemed to follow her slow progress down the hallway, and every window she passed showed countryside, long fields, and magnificently tall trees. But there was an air of neglect about the immediate grounds, the gardens slightly overgrown, the driveway having tufts of grass growing among the gravel. Jane could see stables off to the right of the house, but the stalls looked empty of horses. Raff seemed to have been telling the truth about the lack of funds to spend on the estate, at least.

There were signs of the same lack of money in the house, too, with the bare spaces on walls where paintings other than those depicting ancestors had obviously once hung, but had probably been sold over the years in an effort to hang on to the estate at all. The carpets were old and worn too, although everywhere was obviously kept spotlessly clean by the efficient Mrs Howard.

It was a pity that such a beautiful old house couldn't be maintained in the way that it should have been, everything here in such sharp contrast to the luxury Jordan surrounded himself with.

Jordan.

He was the reason she had struggled down those stairs with her still painfully swollen ankle and stiff hip at all, her search for a telephone revealing one in the main hallway itself, her listening for Mrs Howard or Raff done almost furtively before she picked up the receiver and dialled.

The telephone rang and rang the other end. Jordan's housekeeper was finally the one to answer the call, and Jane remembered it was Henson's day off.

She asked for Jordan, knowing the call would be put through to his study at the back of the house where he couldn't be disturbed by street noise. She could even picture him as he sat behind his desk, his dark hair kept severely short, a perpetual frown between his grey-blue eyes. Poor Jordan, he never seemed to stop working.

'Yes?' he barked impatiently into the receiver, and Jane instantly knew she had been right about his being engrossed with work at his desk.

'It's Rhea-Jane,' she spoke briskly, and quickly, so that he shouldn't interrupt her. 'I'm well. I have a job. And I'm not coming home.' She quietly replaced the receiver before he could make any response.

She was trembling slightly as she straightened, committed now to working for Raff Quinlan. At least, for the moment...

## CHAPTER THREE

RAFF hadn't been lying when he'd said he 'wasn't doing her any favours' by offering her the job of typing his correspondence; most of it was pretty boring, standard stuff to do with the estate, and there was a lot of it!

Jane had waited only two days after the accident before offering to start work on the typing, having spent most of that time alone, her meals served in her room, her wanderings down to the sitting-room in the evenings revealing only an empty room bare of any human warmth because its master wasn't present.

She knew she had to do something to break out of her rut when she had actually started seeking Raff's company!

She quickly discovered where he had been on those evenings she had sat alone wishing for even his abrasive presence, for replies to the dozens of letters that were piled up on a table in his study had been curtly dictated into the machine he had thrust into her hands on the morning she had tentatively approached the room Mrs Howard had told her was his study. There had been no surprise shown at her decision to accept his offer, just a brief explanation of where she could find everything she would need to start work before he'd excused himself to go off in search of a man he had fixing a fence out on the estate somewhere.

What had she expected? Gratitude? Pleasure? Relief? She would wait a long time for any of those emotions from Raff!

She hadn't seen any more of him after two days of typing until her fingers ached, unaccustomed as they were to moving on the typewriter keys. In fact, the only contact she had had with him had been a curt note stuck on one of the letters she had typed saying 'yield' was spelt 'ie' and not 'ei' as she had typed it! There wasn't a word said about the rest of the letters that had been neatly typed without *any* spelling mistakes.

But then, she was sure Raff didn't go around thanking Mrs Howard for keeping the family dinner service free of dust, or making sure the carpets were kept clean, either. She was an employee now, and she would do well to remember that!

To Jane's surprise Raff joined her in the dining-room for dinner that evening, and she couldn't help the thrill of pleasure just the sight of him gave her.

Ridiculous. She must be getting desperate for company if she could actually be pleased to see Raff Quinlan!

He didn't sit down, just stood across the table from her scowling down at her. 'I knew you were going to be trouble the moment I saw you,' he growled impatiently.

Jane sat back with a sigh of exasperation. 'What have I done now?'

He gave an irritated movement of his hand. 'My aunt and uncle have decided to come down for the weekend,' he announced curtly.

Jane knew a little more about the Quinlan family now, having had coffee with Mrs Howard in the mornings, although the other woman was most discreet, answering Jane's questions with the minimum of information without actually being rude. Jane knew that Raff was an only child, and he himself had told her both his parents were dead. His immediate family seemed to consist of his aunt Anita and her lawyer husband, and their three offspring.

This had to be the aunt and uncle Raff spoke of now. 'That will be nice,' she said slowly, for she could tell by Raff's expression that he thought it would be far from that. A thought suddenly occurred to her to make her feel anxious too. 'Does this mean you won't need me to do your typing any more?' Having kept a job for only two days had to be worse than having no job at all! How utterly humiliating!

'Anita isn't coming down here because she's interested in doing any work,' Raff instantly scorned.

'No?' Jane frowned.

'No,' he bit out impatiently. 'My dear aunt is only interested in seeing who the woman is I have staying here with me!'

'The woman you—— You mean me?' Jane gasped.

Raff gave her a pitying look. 'Are there any other women staying here?'

Of course there weren't, but Raff had given little indication he had even noticed she *was* here, so perhaps she could be excused for showing her surprise. Although Raff's derisive expression didn't seem to agree with her.

'I'm acting as your secretary,' she frowned; he had even let her advance to taking messages from the calls he received while he was out today—promotion indeed!

Raff's mouth twisted. 'You're also female.'

She arched mocking brows, her lips tilting challengingly. 'Am I?' she taunted. 'I didn't think you had noticed!'

Raff simply looked at her, the intimate knowledge he had of her body unclothed there in his gaze, and as he continued to look at her Jane felt the heat enter her cheeks.

Had she really thought, even briefly, that she could challenge this man? He would meet her challenge every time, and better it!

'What's the matter, Jane?' he said softly. 'Are you starting to miss having a man in your life?'

Her head went back at the insult, her defiance only wavering slightly as his gaze rested fiercely on the vividness of her hair. She put a hand up to the silken tresses self-consciously.

'What's the matter?'

He moved slowly, almost predatorily, coming around the table to stand so close to her she could feel the heat of his body through the black trousers and grey shirt he wore. His hand moved, almost against his will it seemed, the movement made jerkily as he gathered up a handful of the fiery hair.

'I should never have let you stay here,' he rasped, although he didn't seem to be speaking to her, but to himself.

The touch of his hand made her tremble, though she did her best to try to look unmoved by the intimacy.

'Red hair,' he muttered harshly. 'Damned red hair!' His hand clenched in her hair now, and in doing so it pulled her closer towards him.

Jane looked up at him with pained eyes, but he didn't seem to realise he was hurting her, staring at her hair as if it were about to catch fire in his hand.

She had noticed his reaction to her colouring in the hospital and then again the following morning in her bedroom upstairs. Oh, God, it would be just her luck if the wife who had walked out on him had been a redhead! It would certainly explain his behaviour now.

It didn't even begin to explain her own reaction towards him!

The man had been rude to her, insulted her in ways that no one else ever had, and yet she was more aware of him than she had been of any other man, could feel her pulse racing now, her breathing shallow, as if she was almost afraid to break the spell that held him captivated.

And yet, in a way, she knew he didn't even see her, that his thoughts were miles away...with some other woman, probably. Jane knew a sudden desperation to know more about the wife who had deserted him when he had apparently needed her the most.

But she was given no opportunity to voice her curiosity as Raff's mouth came crashing down on hers, arching her neck back painfully.

Her pulse leapt at the unexpectedness of his kiss, her first instinct to pull away from the anger that emanated from him. But then the anger seemed to leave him, the kiss suddenly slow and searching, his lips moving sensuously against hers.

She was lost, had never felt so helplessly out of her depth in her life.

It was only a kiss, she tried to convince herself.

But it was so much more.

She had never felt so totally weakened before, knew that if Raff decided to make love to her, here and now, she would be able to do nothing to stop him.

She looked up at him with darkened eyes as he at last raised his head from hers. 'Raff, I——'

'I wondered if——'

An embarrassed Mrs Howard stood in the doorway, her face colouring as she took in how close Raff and Jane were to each other.

'Erm—I'm sorry,' she attempted awkwardly. 'I only wanted to see—I'll come back later.' She turned to beat a hasty retreat.

'Mrs Howard,' Raff stopped her harshly. 'I was just on my way to see you anyway,' he announced, although it must have been obvious to all of them that that hadn't been his immediate plan.

Jane wasn't sure *what* his immediate plan had been! She would probably never know now, either.

Was she stupid? This man, despite having just kissed her, despised her too, and she was still living in his house only because she needed this job very badly, and for no other reason. To even imagine there could ever be anything between herself and Raff Quinlan was just asking for trouble.

When had she ever avoided trouble?

She dismissed this thought immediately. Raff Quinlan wasn't the man for her. Then why did her legs still feel weak and her arms ache to arch up about his neck and draw him back down to her?

'My aunt and uncle are coming down for the weekend,' he told the housekeeper abruptly. 'Could you make up a room for them?' He strode forcefully from the room without waiting for her reply.

Mrs Howard looked completely dazed. 'Miss Anita and her husband . . .?' She frowned. 'Why, I can't remember the last time they both——' She broke off, shaking her head, focusing slowly on Jane. 'I'm really sorry about just now, I didn't realise—I only wondered if Raff would be joining you for dinner,' she explained lamely.

Jane had come to like this woman very much over the last few days, and she respected her deeply for her unwavering loyalty to Raff and his family, guessing that the Quinlan family had become almost her own after her husband had died of a heart attack only a few years after they had been married.

She couldn't help but regret being partly to blame for the other woman's embarrassment now.

'It would appear not,' she shrugged ruefully. 'But I'll help you prepare the room for Raff's aunt after I've finished my meal if you would like me to?'

'Oh, I couldn't let you do that.' The older woman shook her head.

'Why not?' Jane instantly dismissed. 'I work here too, you know, and I'm well aware of the amount of work involved with clearing away after dinner.'

Mrs Howard seemed to run the household completely single-handedly, and while that was admirable she wasn't a youngster any more. And, in the circumstances, helping to prepare the bedroom seemed the least Jane could do; after all, if she weren't here she doubted Anita and her husband would be coming down to Quinlan House at all!

Anita Barnes turned out to be a female version of Raff when she arrived with her distinguished-looking lawyer husband the following afternoon—possessed of a regal elegance with her dark hair caught in a neat coil at her nape, the grey tailored dress suiting her tall slenderness.

She looked Jane up and down critically after Raff had introduced the two women, her eyes narrowing as she looked into Jane's face.

'Nice to meet you,' she greeted Jane off-handedly. 'You remind me of someone,' she accused without preamble.

Jane's eyes widened, feeling almost as if she had been attacked. 'Do I?' she returned with a politeness the other woman lacked. Anita Barnes, like her nephew, was someone who didn't suffer fools gladly. What a family! Jack Barnes seemed innocuous enough; he probably had to be with a wife like this!

'Hm.' The other woman still looked at her through narrowed lids. 'I'm not sure...'

'Anita, leave the poor girl alone,' Raff derided in a bored voice. 'Her name is Jane Smith, and she's a secretary. Leave it at that, will you?' he instructed tersely.

Neither statement was strictly accurate, but Jane wasn't about to argue with him.

'Hm, it will come to me soon, I'm sure.' Anita Barnes remained undiverted, although she turned her attention to her nephew now. 'I hope you don't mind, darling, but Bobby will be down some time before dinner.' The affectionate smile she gave completely transformed her face, making her look almost beautiful. 'The poor darling needed a little break from London; he's been working terribly hard.'

'Bobby's idea of working hard is getting up before ten o'clock in the morning,' Raff muttered as his aunt and uncle left the sitting-room to go upstairs and rest in their bedroom before dinner.

'Who is Bobby?' Jane asked, completely in the dark about his identity.

'Anita's oldest offspring,' Raff explained scornfully, 'and the apple of her eye. Bobby can do no wrong as far as Anita is concerned,' he added disparagingly.

Bobby Barnes. It sounded like a name of a football player, or maybe a boxer.

'He's an actor.' Raff instantly shattered that idea, his contempt for anything as frivolous as acting for a career evident in his expression. 'Unfortunately, Bobby is one of the ninety-five per cent of actors who are always out of work!'

'With a name like Bobby Barnes I'm not surprised!' Jane made a face.

'Hm, on the subject of names...' Raff's mood suddenly changed, his attention all centred on Jane now.

She was instantly wary, bracing her shoulders defensively. 'Yes?'

He nodded slowly. 'I telephoned the hotel you gave at the hospital as your last address——'

'You had no right!' she gasped, horrified that he had thought to do such a thing; it had never even occurred to her that he might do so. But she was living in his house, working for him; she had been a fool to think he would just accept her on face value alone. And now he had caught her completely off-guard!

'I had every right,' he rasped, moving closer to her. 'Do you know what they told me at the hotel?' he queried softly, his manner no less ominous for that.

That they had no Jane Smith registered the night she had claimed to be there...

She swallowed hard. 'No, what did they tell you?' she delayed, trying to think of some sensible remark she could possibly make to the question she knew had to be coming. There wasn't one!

Raff eyed her mockingly. 'That they aren't at liberty to tell me who may or may not have been guests at the hotel,' he drawled, dark brows arching as he watched the colour flood back into cheeks that had been pale with tension a moment ago. He gave a derisive inclination of his head. 'A pity, but there you are.'

Jane gave an inward sigh of relief, glaring up at Raff with resentful eyes. He had done that deliberately, had hoped to knock her off balance into possibly admitting something she otherwise wouldn't have done. Thank God she hadn't completely lost her nerve and done just that!

'Yes, isn't it?' she returned sweetly, completely insincere—as he was! 'I think I'll follow your aunt and uncle's example, and go up to my room for a rest before dinner,' she told him lightly, her head high as she crossed the room.

'Yes, do that,' Raff murmured from behind her. 'But, Jane...?'

She turned reluctantly, having no choice but to do so, although she made no verbal response.

'I'll continue searching and probing until I find out exactly who you are,' he warned softly, all mockery gone now. 'Just because I don't make an issue of it every time I see you, it doesn't mean I don't think about it.'

'I could be a criminal of some kind,' Jane challenged; she was shaken by his persistent interest, she couldn't deny it. She had been a fool to think even for a moment that he wouldn't pursue the subject.

'I don't think so,' he returned consideringly. 'But I hate mysteries,' he warned again.

Jane left the room more hurriedly than she would have liked to have done, stopping in the hallway to heave an exasperated sigh.

Raff could ruin everything for her with his 'searching and probing'...

Raff wasn't present when Jane entered the sitting-room later that evening; only Anita and Jack Barnes were there, the latter, as Jane had guessed, wearing a dinner-suit and snowy-white dinner-shirt. Jane had thought dinner with the Barneses present wouldn't be the casual affair she had been used to, which was why she had put on the royal blue cocktail dress, its design simple, but comfortable to wear on her still bruised body, the bodice fitted, the skirt flowing silkily about her shapely legs.

Anita Barnes had swapped one tailored dress for another—black this time, but just as expensively cut.

Bobby Barnes didn't seem to have put in an appearance yet, unless he too was still changing for dinner.

Jane couldn't help feeling curious about how Raff would look in a dinner-suit. Devastatingly attractive, she decided defeatedly. She was becoming altogether too interested in Raff Quinlan, the memory of the kiss they had shared the evening before having kept her awake long into the night. It had been no casual kiss, and had seemed almost against Raff's will. Her lips still tingled from the touch of his, and she looked about her guiltily as she knew her conflicting emotions must have shown in her face. Fortunately Anita Barnes didn't consider she had to make polite conversation with the 'hired help', and her attention was centred on her husband as she talked to him in her imperious voice. Jane took the opportunity to get her wandering thoughts firmly under control.

'Miss Jane Smith, I presume?'

She swung round at the sound of that mocking voice, a voice that was more than vaguely familiar, her breath catching in her throat as she looked up at the dark-haired young man with his classical good looks and laughing blue eyes.

Robert Barnstable!

And he knew damn well she wasn't 'Miss Jane Smith' at all!

## CHAPTER FOUR

JANE closed her eyes, willing him to disappear, but he was still standing mockingly in front of her when she opened them again.

She had been so deep in thought she hadn't been aware of anyone having entered the room, but now she looked up at Robert with disbelieving eyes. Why *him*? Was nothing going to go right for her?

'Bobby Barnes, I presume?' she returned softly, although inside she was quietly panicking.

For, by a process of elimination, in the same way he had probably realised she was 'Jane Smith', she knew this had to be Raff's cousin Bobby.

It was just her luck that 'Bobby' had turned out to be one of the group of young actors she knew well in town.

Unfortunately she hadn't known Robert well enough to realise Barnstable was a stage-name!

It *was* just her luck.

He grinned down at her, wickedly good-looking, wearing his dinner-suit with a natural elegance. But then he did have natural grace and charm, especially charm. She had been out to dinner with him herself at least once, and had found him very good company, not at all inclined to want to talk about himself all evening, the way some actors were.

But she would never, in a million years, have guessed that he and Raff were cousins!

'If you ever tell any of that crowd in London that my family call me Bobby. . . !' He groaned at the embarrassment of it.

Jane didn't return his smile, looking up at him intently. 'I'm more concerned with whether or not you intend telling your family, especially Raff, what the crowd in London call me!'

'Ah,' he said more soberly. 'Well, I must admit to being slightly baffled by what you're doing here?'

She shrugged. 'Raff seems to think I could be on the look-out for a rich protector.'

Robert's splutter of laughter caused his parents to look at them curiously, Anita Barnes instantly displeased to see her son talking to Jane at all, let alone actually enjoying her company.

It was also the moment Raff chose to enter the room, his steady gaze narrowing on them as they stood so close together across the room from him.

As Jane had rightly surmised, he wore his dinner-suit and snowy-white shirt with complete disregard for their formality, his hair curling damply over the collar of the latter, revealing that he had recently taken a shower.

'Yes, well, he would, wouldn't he?' Robert remarked drily, meeting the other man's gaze challengingly. 'My cousin's estimation of women isn't very high. Mind you, with an ex-wife like Celia that isn't surprising,' he grimaced.

Celia. At last Jane knew Raff's wife's name. Not that it did any good to know it, it only made her seem more real, more someone who had meant something in his life. And, somehow, that was painful to even think of.

'Maybe I remind Raff of her?' she suggested, hoping Robert wouldn't pick up on the intense curiosity she had to know more about the other woman, to try to understand what sort of woman it was that had made Raff as cynical as he was.

'You?' Robert frowned down at her. 'No.' He shook his head. 'Celia was tall and willowy.'

And she was short and skinny! 'I thought possibly my hair...?' She curled one of the flowing strands around her fingers, Raff's attention having been momentarily claimed by his uncle, who seemed completely unaware of Raff's interest in Jane and his son. Or his wife's!

'Your hair?' Robert looked even more puzzled now. 'What about your hair?' His frown deepened.

'I thought—— Wasn't Celia a redhead?' It was Jane's turn to look unsure now.

Robert laughed softly. 'Blonde, brunette, black, every colour you can think of, but I don't think she was ever—— Wait a minute.' He paused thoughtfully. 'Yes, I think she may have been a redhead when she and Raff first got married. Hm, I'm almost sure she was.' His brow cleared. 'But it wasn't for long,' he dismissed. 'Celia seemed to change the colour of her hair to match the clothes she wore!' he told Jane ruefully.

But she had been a redhead when Raff first married her...

It was one explanation for the way he seemed to dislike the colour of her hair, the way it seemed to make him more angry with her. But he couldn't blame every other woman with red hair for the way his initially red-haired wife had let him down!

She shrugged. 'Maybe it's just me he distrusts,' she sighed. 'He gives the impression no man is safe with me.'

'I should be so lucky!' Robert looked at her admiringly.

He had never made any secret of the fact that he found her attractive, and Jane knew that tonight she looked better than she had done for some days, the pallor from her accident having faded, made more so by the application of a light make-up, her blue dress flowing silkily over her body, her hair like a bright, shimmering flame as it cascaded down over her bare shoulders.

Raff was looking at her again now, but if *he* found her in the least appealing he didn't show it, glaring at her coldly while remaining in conversation with his aunt.

Looking at the two men, it was clear which one was the more obviously attractive, and yet, despite all Robert's charm and good looks, Jane knew that of the two she was more attracted to Raff.

Strange... until recently she had never thought of herself as a masochist!

'I believe we're about to go in to dinner now that my dear cousin has finally decided to join us,' Robert said drily. 'You still haven't enlightened me as to what "Jane Smith" is doing here acting as Raff's secretary, so I'll have to get back to you again later. You know, Raff might change his attitude a little if he knew who you really are,' he mused.

Jane eyed him sceptically. 'Do you really think so?' She thought of the life she had previously led, and knew it wouldn't find favour in Raff's eyes at all.

'Maybe not,' Robert acknowledged with a grimace. 'Actually,' he added conspiratorially, 'I'm more than a little curious to find out how Jordan feels about your working here?'

'It must be obvious he has no idea.' Jane frowned her irritation.

'Hence "Jane Smith", I suppose?' Robert nodded. 'Hm, I'm sure Jordan would be very interested to learn of your whereabouts.'

'Don't even think about——'

'Have to go, Rhea—er—I mean, Jane.' Robert grimaced. 'Better not make a mistake like that again, had I? I'll talk to you again later,' he promised.

'Oh, but——'

'My mother is waiting impatiently for me to escort her in to dinner.' He patted Jane's arm reassuringly in a distracted way, his attention already transferred to his mother as she glared at him disapprovingly from across the room, obviously furious at the amount of time he had spent talking to Jane.

She didn't envy him his mother's wrath, sure that Anita Barnes was a force to be reckoned with when angry, if she was anything like her nephew; and Jane felt sure, even on so brief an acquaintance, that that woman could be very like him. Even being 'the apple of his mother's eye' wouldn't save Robert from her displeasure, Jane was certain.

As the only other female in the room Jane should really have been escorted in to dinner by Jack Barnes, but he seemed to be taking his cue from his wife, obviously knowing better than to anger her any further where Jane was concerned, strolling in to the dining-room at his wife's other side.

There was an awkward silence as Jane and Raff realised they had no choice but to go in to dinner together.

And Raff looked far from pleased about it!

Maybe she shouldn't have joined them for dinner at all this evening; she was, after all, only an employee, and Anita Barnes didn't give the impression she usually ate with the 'hired hands'.

But Raff should have told her earlier if that was the case; she couldn't not go into dinner with the family now!

Raff made no effort to offer her his arm. 'What do you think you're doing?' he rasped.

She blinked up at him. 'I——'

'Stay away from my little cousin,' he warned harshly.

She drew in a sharply angry breath. 'He came over and started talking to *me*,' she bit out indignantly. 'What was I supposed to do, be rude to him?' She glared up at Raff. 'I suppose then I would have been reprimanded for *that*,' she added impatiently. 'I can't seem to win with you!'

With that, she turned on her heel and walked into the dining-room without him, uncaring of how odd that must look.

Robert raised questioning brows at her flushed cheeks and glittering eyes.

'Are you working at the moment?' she asked him as she took her seat at the table down the opposite end to Raff, as he pulled his own chair out and sat down with the minimum of movement, his body stiff with anger. 'Raff tells me you're an actor,' she smiled encouragingly at Robert, determined not to be completely unnerved by Raff's contemptuous attitude.

Robert nodded, more than happy to pour fuel on the tension he sensed between Jane and Raff. 'I'm rehearsing a play,' he said with satisfaction.

'That must be fascinating,' she prompted, studiously ignoring Raff, although she knew his angry gaze was still on her.

Robert gave her a look that told her he knew exactly what was going on, and he was more than willing to help her annoy Raff. In fact, anyone listening to him over the next couple of hours could be forgiven for believing that goading Raff was what Robert lived for!

Jane could perfectly understand why that was—the two men being complete opposites, Raff taking life so seriously, Robert treating everything as if it were a game.

Raff's manner got frostier and frostier, his eyes colder and colder, as the evening wore on.

Anita Barnes didn't look too thrilled by her son's apparent interest in her nephew's secretary either, any comments she made to Jane being waspish, to say the least.

By the coffee stage of the meal Jane just wanted to escape from the situation she had helped to create because of her annoyance with Raff. Anita Barnes was just watching her with narrowed eyes now, and Raff himself looked ready to commit murder—with Jane as his obvious victim!

'You know, Raff,' Anita Barnes spoke slowly, her head tilted thoughtfully as she looked at Jane, 'I've finally remembered who your secretary reminds me of. I knew it would come to me if I just gave myself a little time,' she added with satisfaction.

'Yes?' Raff sat stiffly erect in his chair.

'Yes,' his aunt turned to him with narrowed eyes. 'It was that woman your father was involved with.'

Raff's mouth tightened. 'I'm sorry, I don't know what you mean,' he bit out tersely.

Neither did Jane; as far as she was aware Raff's parents had been together when they died in the plane crash and, if that were so, how could Raff possibly know any woman his father had been involved with previous to his marriage? Raff wouldn't even have been born!

She watched the aunt and nephew curiously, Raff seeming not at all pleased with the turn the conversation had taken.

'Of course you do,' Anita said dismissively. 'She was your nanny at the time.' She turned to her husband. 'You remember her, Jack,' she encouraged. 'What was her name? I'm surprised you don't remember it, Raff; you were so very fond of her. I remember how heart-broken you were when she left so suddenly,' she derided.

'I——'

'It was Diana,' Raff put in softly. 'And I don't care to have personal family business discussed just now,' he warned his aunt coldly.

Because of Jane's presence, she knew. But he needn't have worried; she wasn't at all interested in any skeletons in this family's closet. Except that the conversation had set off little alarm bells in her own mind; her mother had been a nanny before she'd married her father, and her first name was Diana...

But it had to be a coincidence. Good grief, the Princess of Wales herself was named Diana, and she had worked with children before her marriage too!

Nevertheless, it was slightly unsettling...

'Busy?'

Jane looked up at Robert as he stood framed in the doorway of the small sitting-room where she sat.

And it must have been obvious, as she sat on this small chintz-covered sofa, idly flicking through a magazine she had no real interest in, that she wasn't doing anything in the least important!

She put the magazine down on the seat beside her. 'Extremely,' she drawled sarcastically.

He grinned down at her as he entered the room. 'That's what I thought.'

She grimaced. 'Actually, I am busy—staying out of everyone's way!'

She had made her excuses as soon as she possibly could once the meal had finished the previous evening, and had managed to avoid any further contact with the family today by going for a walk as soon as she'd got up, and taking some sandwiches with her so that she didn't have to join the family for another tension-filled meal.

Unfortunately the Barneses' BMW and Robert's more flamboyant sports car were still parked in the driveway next to Raff's old-style Jaguar when she'd returned late in the afternoon, and so she had taken refuge in this small sitting-room that was rarely used. Robert must have actually been looking for her to have found her in here.

'The parents have just departed,' he told her with a grin, perching on the wooden arm of one of the chairs that matched the chintz sofa.

Jane wasn't at all surprised that the couple hadn't felt it necessary to actually say their goodbyes to her; she was only an employee, after all.

'My mother having settled herself you aren't after the family silver,' Robert continued mockingly, dressed casually today in denims and a loose white cotton top.

'After the——?' Jane spluttered indignantly. 'Surely if that were what I was after I would have taken it and run by now?' As far as she was aware the family didn't *have* any silver!

'Oh, I didn't mean silver of the precious metal kind...' Robert arched meaningful brows.

'Then what——?' She broke off, her eyes widening as she thought Robert's meaning was becoming clear. 'You don't mean *Raff*?' She was incredulous at the mere idea of it.

Robert nodded. 'Mother has it in mind for Raff to remain unmarried, and for me to one day inherit all this.' He waved his arms about pointedly.

But could Anita and her family, even if this preposterous idea were true, not see the financial difficulties the estate was in, and just how little there would be for Robert to inherit as Raff's heir? Although the other couple were obviously rich in their own right, so perhaps this didn't worry them unduly. Jane had no doubt that even if the Barneses were in a financial position to help him, Raff would never ask them for it; he was a proud man, determined to make it—or not, whichever it turned out to be!—on his own merits.

'One look at Raff and I together, and your mother knew I was no danger to her aspirations,' Jane said drily.

Robert grinned. 'Raff has always been blind where women are concerned.'

She felt a little uncomfortable discussing him in this way—even with Robert, who had been something of a personal friend in London.

'Maybe he has good reason to be,' she dismissed, thinking of his broken marriage.

'Maybe,' his cousin acknowledged uninterestedly. 'His father wasn't too lucky in love either. None of the male members of this family seem to have been, now that I come to think of it.' He frowned.

'But Raff's parents must have been married over thirty years.' She was intrigued in spite of herself at the mention of Raff's father twice in as many days.

'Married, yes,' Robert said drily. 'Happily, no. Aunt Helen, Raff's mother, was something of a bitch. She and Celia were the best of friends,' he added, as if that said it all.

And maybe it did. But how sad that both the Quinlan men, father and son, had been so unhappy in their marriages.

But it still left the question of the woman, Diana, whom *she* reminded Anita Barnes of.

'Who was Diana?' she asked curiously.

Robert shrugged. 'I don't really know. Before my time, I'm afraid. I didn't actually come here to talk about Raff or the rest of the happy family,' he asserted. 'I'm still agog to know what you're doing here playing at secretaries?' he taunted.

'I'm not playing at it,' she protested indignantly. 'I'll admit I'm not very good at it, but I work fast enough for Raff, which is what matters. And it *is* a job,' she shrugged.

'But why do you need one?' He still looked puzzled.

As well he might. Much as she disliked having to do it, she knew that nothing less than the complete truth would appease Robert. And maybe she owed him that much for keeping quiet what he knew about her.

She looked at him warningly. 'This is in the strictest confidence.'

He sat forward on the arm of the chair. 'I'm all ears,' he encouraged confidingly.

Jane gave him a censorious glare. 'This isn't funny, Robert.'

He held up his hands defensively. 'I'm not laughing.'

'You aren't taking it seriously, either.' Jane stood up impatiently, striding over to the window, staring out at the rolling hills while she tried to collect her thoughts together. Finally she turned back to him.

'In just under three months' time I shall be twenty-one,' she began slowly. 'If by that time I have managed to stay in useful employment—a job where I actually earn a wage rather than the charity work I have been involved in so far—I inherit the money my father left for me.' She gave a grimace of disgust at her father's obvious lack of trust in her.

She had never had an easy relationship with her father, and had been away at finishing-school in Switzerland when he had died just over two years ago. She had come back to England to take over running the houses he had all over the world, and become so caught up with that that it had been increasingly difficult for her to do anything else, although charity work had also featured largely in her busy life.

But Jordan had known of the stipulation in her father's will if she was to inherit the full fortune which had been left to her; indeed he was one of the trustees who would decide whether or not she should inherit.

'Jordan doesn't believe I can do it,' she added hardly.

'It's incredible!' Robert breathed softly. 'It's like something out of a Victorian novel.'

Jane sighed. 'My father had little belief in women's capabilities.'

'Your mother...?'

'Died when I was born,' she rasped sharply. 'But you see why I need this job so badly?' She frowned. 'At the moment I'm totally dependent on Jordan except for my allowance, and I want more than anything to be free of the financial hold he has over me.'

Robert looked troubled. 'I had no idea...'

'No one does,' she sighed. 'And I would much rather it stayed that way.'

'It's awful for you,' he agreed. 'But I've always thought Jordan was a decent sort, even if he can seem a little unapproachable at times.'

'Oh, Jordan is—well, he's just Jordan,' Jane shrugged. 'A law unto himself most of the time,' she accepted ruefully. 'But I—I want to do something else with my life other than be the social butterfly everyone seems to think I am. I'd like to start up a business of my own.'

The enthusiasm she had kept firmly in check bubbled to the surface, and her eyes glowed. 'Despite what Jordan might think to the contrary,' she said drily, 'I've discovered over the last weeks that I am qualified to do something. As a social hostess

I have no rivals,' she grinned. 'With the money from my inheritance I could set up an agency. There must be dozens of people who would value my help and advice for their social functions.'

'Oh, dozens,' Robert echoed wryly.

She looked at him sharply. 'You don't think so?' she said uncertainly.

It was an idea that had been formulating in her mind over the last few days, none of the plans concrete yet, the idea just slowly fermenting and growing. Why not? She was more than qualified, and it would be something she had always wanted—to be able to run her own business, to be an independent woman.

He shrugged. 'If anyone can make it work I'm sure you can. It seems a pity you have to put up with grim old Raff to get your inheritance, though. Although,' he added consideringly, 'I don't suppose he's any grimmer than Jordan. Why hasn't he caused an uproar about your just taking off like that?' Robert mused.

'Pride,' she answered without hesitation. Jordan would never admit he wasn't in complete control, of any situation. 'Besides, what could he really tell anyone? I've over eighteen, and there is no reason to presume I'm actually missing.'

'But you used the name "Jane Smith" just to be on the safe side?' Robert taunted.

Her cheeks were flushed at the gibe. 'How do you think Raff would have reacted if I had used my full name?' she said defensively.

'Hm,' Robert nodded. 'I see your point.'

'Don't think it wasn't tried and tested,' Jane added ruefully. 'I went after a dozen or so jobs in town before I got this one, and at the ones where I used my full name the reaction was always the same: what did I want a job for at all? Raff already distrusts me enough without that added complication.'

'Because you're female,' Robert acknowledged matter-of-factly.

'Possibly.' Although Jane still wasn't a hundred per cent certain about that, and wondered if her similarity to this woman, Diana, who had been in his father's life might have something to do with it. She would probably never know.

'Hm, well, I don't envy you explaining things to Jordan when you finally resurface. But I take it from all this you don't want me to say hello to him for you?' he teased with a grin.

'Over your dead body!' She could just imagine the embarrassing scene that would ensue if Jordan were to come here in search of her!

Robert quirked dark brows. 'What's it worth?'

'Mandy Padbury,' she returned instantly, reminding him of an embarrassing relationship she was sure he wouldn't want his family, now that she had met them, to know about!

'Unfair!' he grimaced in defeat.

They laughed softly together, but Jane's humour faded as soon as Robert had gone; she still had Raff to face after last night...

# CHAPTER FIVE

WHAT was that strange noise?

It wasn't a loud noise, just persistent, despite being irregular. Or maybe it seemed persistent because it was irregular? It was like waiting for the dripping of a tap, listening for the sound of the next tapping noise.

It hadn't woken Jane; she hadn't been to sleep yet. The meeting with Raff that she had dreaded still hadn't taken place. Immediately after his guests had all left he'd gone out on estate business, and Jane had long been in her bedroom when she'd heard the sound of his car returning.

Perhaps it hadn't been estate business at all? Maybe his family were all wrong about him, and he had a girlfriend somewhere in the district? Although from the little she had come to know of him over the last few days she didn't think he was the type of man to kiss one woman—no matter how provoked he had felt at the time!—while having a relationship with another. And he had most definitely kissed her!

It was while she was in the library looking for a book to read because she couldn't sleep that she had first heard those faint tap-tapping noises.

Maybe it was burglars, trying to break the glass in a window without actually rousing the household? She wouldn't have heard the noise herself if she hadn't already been downstairs.

She tentatively followed the sound of the tapping noises, her sky-coloured nightgown and wrap floating silkily about her ankles as she crept along soundlessly in the matching coloured mules.

The sound seemed to be coming from inside Raff's study, the door being slightly ajar, a light visible inside, despite it being almost two o'clock in the morning.

Who could be in there this time of night? Raff had gone to bed hours ago. At least, she had presumed he had gone to bed...

Endearing was not a word she had ever thought to associate with that arrogantly autocratic man, and yet it was the only word she could use to describe seeing a thirty-seven year old man wrestling with the keys of a typewriter as if it were almost a foreign object. But it probably was to him!

He had obviously been bent over his task for some time now, his brow furrowed into a frown of deep concentration, the sheet of paper inside the typewriter only half covered with print. And at the speed he was typing it must have taken him hours to do. No wonder he appreciated her slow but accurate efforts if this was the best he could do!

But what was he doing typing for at all? That was what she was still here for. But perhaps he didn't want her to see what he was typing. The question now was, should she let him know of her presence, or just sneak away to her bedroom unseen?

Even as she posed the question to herself Raff's head rose and he looked across the room at her.

He didn't actually seem to see her standing there for several seconds, but blinked suddenly, slowly focusing on her as his mind cleared slightly. As he did so, the harshness entered his eyes. 'What are you doing down here?' he rasped.

She had never met a man who could make her feel so uncomfortable!

But this scene—the desk scattered with business papers in the middle of the night, and even the furrowed brow of the man behind the desk—was an all too familiar sight to her.

'Can I get you some coffee and buttered toast?' she offered, having no idea whether he had eaten dinner while he was out or not. But she had learnt from experience that coffee and toast this time of night usually had the effect of reviving Jordan.

Raff sat back in his chair. 'You shouldn't be awake this time of night.' He ignored her offer.

'I couldn't sleep,' she explained.

He frowned, looking at her critically. 'Are you in pain?'

Except for the odd twinge from her ankle and a slight soreness to her hip her injuries no longer troubled her. They certainly didn't keep her awake at night. Thoughts of this man managed to do that quite successfully!

'I ache sometimes,' she admitted truthfully. 'But there's no real pain any more,' she assured him, noticing that Raff instantly looked relieved.

'Actually, I was looking for a book in the library when I heard you typing,' she calmly answered his earlier accusatory question. 'Although I didn't realise it was typing at the time; I thought it might have been a burglar,' she ruefully admitted her folly.

Raff shook his head. 'But you came looking for the source of the noise anyway?' he derided drily. 'You seem to be making a habit of walking into trouble because you don't practise caution.'

'I wouldn't have tackled the burglar myself!' she returned heatedly.

'He would have been wasting his time anyway.' Raff gave a weary smile. 'There's nothing left in the house worth stealing.'

'Coffee and toast,' Jane decided firmly, knowing from nights like this with Jordan that when he was hungry and over-tired his defences were down.

Raff gave her a scathing look. 'You don't look as if you've ever done more than simply appear decorous in that outfit. Are you sure you know where the kitchen is?' he scorned.

She held her tongue with effort, smiling tightly before leaving the room; she hadn't expected her offer would sweeten his temper.

It was just as well, because she would have been disappointed!

She not only knew where the kitchen was in this huge house, she also knew where everything was kept in it. It took her very little time to make a pot of coffee and a plate of hot buttered toast.

She could hear Raff typing determinedly again as she approached his study in the still quietness of the rest of the house. But, for all his derision of her, he got up quickly enough when she entered the room, and made a space for the tray on top of the desk.

'Black for me,' he requested gruffly as she poured the coffee into two mugs. Even these seemed to have come as a surprise to him, as if he expected her to drink coffee out of nothing but the best china cups.

But somehow coffee tasted better in mugs at this time of night. Raff obviously thought so too, downing the strong brew with obvious pleasure, and eating several of the half-slices of toast, too.

He looked better already; the lines of strain eased about his mouth, slight colour came back in his cheeks, making her doubt again that he had actually had any dinner earlier. He was a big man, and not eating proper meals couldn't be good for him. Neither could working in here until this time—not when she knew he was up and about the estate by seven o'clock most mornings.

'Can't that wait until tomorrow?' she prompted gently, nodding towards the half finished typewritten sheet.

He groaned at the reminder of the typing he had been doing when she'd entered the room. 'As I told you when I asked you to stay on here and help with my correspondence, I just don't have the time to do this during the day.'

'As you've just pointed out, I thought that was what I was here for.' Jane frowned.

He shook his head. 'This file is too...confidential for me to trust it to anyone else,' he said.

And she couldn't be trusted was what he didn't say. He didn't even know her real name yet—although he would continue to work on it!

'Who could I tell, Raff?' she scorned.

He shrugged, watching her through narrowed eyes. 'You tell me.'

She sighed. 'All right, struggle on alone, if that's what you want!' She stood up to leave.

'You're very touchy tonight,' Raff drawled mockingly. 'Have some toast.' He pushed the plate towards her. 'It's just about the best toast anyone has ever made for me,' he added gruffly. 'Not too much butter, but not too little either. And perfectly melted into the toast.'

As olive branches went it could use a little work, but coming from Raff Quinlan she knew she wouldn't get any more than that.

As for the perfect toast, that had come after much practice on Jordan; he was probably as much a taskmaster as Raff was. He could be so stuffy at times, although his fussiness over how his toast was buttered seemed to have actually paid off for her.

The two men were alike, not only in their looks, but their manner was very similar too. Although perhaps Raff had a little more humour to him than Jordan; Jordan would never have let 'little Jane Smith' stay on in his home when he was almost certain that wasn't her real name. He wouldn't see it as the challenge Raff obviously did.

Jane took half a slice of the toast—not really because she was hungry, but more out of an effort to show she wasn't going to bear a grudge because he didn't trust her enough to let her do some very private typing for him; there would be no point in such childish sulks.

'Just like mother used to make,' she returned lightly.

Raff's mouth twisted. 'I doubt my mother ever made me toast,' he said drily.

'No boiled eggs and toast soldiers when you were ill?' she teased, almost able to imagine him as a little boy, all dark tousled hair and big grey eyes. He would have been adorable.

'No,' he laughed derisively.

'Mine neither,' Jane said wistfully. 'My mother died when I was born,' she explained at his questioning look.

He frowned. 'I'm sorry.' He obviously genuinely meant the emotion, and wasn't just paying polite lip-service.

'I'm not so sure *she* was.'

Jane wasn't even looking at Raff now, talking almost to herself as she became lost in memories.

'My parents' marriage was reputedly very rocky, and had been for some years. I was apparently a last-ditch attempt on their part to bridge the ever-widening rift. I don't think my father ever forgave me for the fact that my mother died having me and left that particular riddle undone. He was a very methodical man,' she added without bitterness, her voice flat now.

Jane didn't realise that she had revealed in those few brief sentences all the lonely years of her childhood when she had first tried to win her father's love by being so good he couldn't help but be proud of her, and when that failed becoming an out-and-out rebel so that he at least had to notice her!

He had noticed her all right, instantly placing her in a boarding-school—which she had promptly got herself expelled from. And then another boarding-school. And another. All of her school life had been spent going from one boarding-school to another because she was so rebellious, until at last she was old enough to leave.

Only her father hadn't even wanted her back home then, arranging for her to go to Switzerland to a finishing-school. Being a rebel and getting herself noticed had become such a part of her life by then that she had continued to be unçooperative until her father had died two years ago.

Even as she'd stood at his graveside watching them lower his coffin into the ground she had wondered if there had been *anything* she could have done to make him love her? The answer had been a resounding no; she had merely been a means to an end as far as her father was concerned—one that was no longer necessary with the death of her mother. She had simply been a reminder that he didn't even want in his sight.

And she had never before talked to anyone about—or even hinted at—the rejection she had felt from her father from birth.

She looked dazedly across the desk at Raff, wondering why it should be this man she allowed to see her pain beneath the veneer of sophistication?

He seemed to be aware of her sudden uncertainty, her vulnerability from what she had unwittingly revealed.

'My own parents' marriage wasn't any recommendation either,' he admitted ruefully. 'They lived apart for a lot of my early childhood, and I only have sketchy memories of my mother being involved in my life after that.' He grimaced. 'Hence my aunt's indiscreet remark yesterday about my father's involvement with another woman.'

Diana. The nanny. *Raff's* nanny.

Jane swallowed hard. 'Did you like her? This other woman? Diana, wasn't it? Your aunt said she looked after you——' she shrugged as his mouth suddenly became tight '—that I reminded her of this woman...'

'Rubbish,' he bit out harshly. 'Oh, I'll grant you there's a surface similarity in the colouring and your build, but that's all it is, a similarity!'

'Mrs Howard said I reminded *her* of someone too the first morning we met,' Jane remembered slowly. She was sure now that this woman Diana had to be the one the housekeeper had meant that morning. And after realising Raff had once been married *she* had assumed it had been Celia she reminded everyone of.

Diana. A nanny.

Her mother?

The only way she could actually be sure would be to reveal her own identity and ask Raff outright if Diana's surname had been Holmes. And she wasn't ready to give up her job here yet.

Besides, this Diana, the other Diana—if it had been another Diana!—had been involved with Raff's father. It couldn't have been her mother.

Could it...?

'I told you, a surface similarity,' Raff dismissed again. 'If it weren't for your hair no one would even think twice about it.'

In all of the photographs of her mother she had seen, her hair had been as long and red as Jane's own . . .

'Look, it's late now, Jane.' Raff stood up to come round to her side of the desk. 'We're both tired, and need some sleep.'

She wasn't sure she would be able to sleep after this!

Raff put up a hand to the paleness of her cheek, shaking his head reprovingly as she swayed slightly.

'You shouldn't be up this late,' he murmured, swinging her up into his arms. 'You were very badly bruised only a few days ago. Don't struggle,' he warned softly when Jane began to squirm as he carried her out of the room and up the wide staircase.

He carried her with ease, but he was too close, his warmth enveloping her, her arms clinging about his neck.

He made her feel small, and feminine, and utterly defenceless.

She began to struggle again as they entered her bedroom.

'Don't——' His chiding reprimand broke off abruptly as he looked down at her, grey eyes looking deeply into dark blue. 'Jane!' He gave a strangulated groan as he lowered his lips to hers.

Jane slid slowly down the length of his body as he lowered her feet to the floor, the kiss seeming to go on forever, and yet it wasn't enough for either of them.

Their mouths moved together hungrily, Jane giving a husky gasp of pleasure as one of Raff's hands moved to cup her breast, its tip straining forward, hardened with longing.

And her ache was of a different kind now; Raff's thighs moulded against her own, telling her of his need too.

Raff's hands cupped either side of her face now as he rested his forehead on hers, his breathing ragged. 'I'm supposed to be taking care of you, not——'

He shook his head with self-disgust, straightening. 'Put this down to the lateness of the hour,' he advised harshly. 'It couldn't be anything else,' he muttered as he abruptly left the room.

Jane sat down heavily on the bed, her eyes huge blue pools of vulnerability.

'Telephone?' She frowned up at Mrs Howard the following morning as she sat bent over the desk she worked on, doing her best not to even think about what had happened the previous evening. As she was sure Raff was!

She sensed the other woman's interest in the fact that this was the first private telephone call Jane had received since she had come here almost a week ago.

And who could blame her?

'For me?' Jane blinked her surprise. 'Are you sure?'

She wasn't sure of anything herself any more, and didn't see why anyone else should be!

'Of course I'm sure!' The housekeeper was slightly put out that Jane should doubt her word.

'Thank you,' Jane accepted heavily, getting slowly to her feet to go and take the call in the hallway.

Robert—it had to be; he was the only one who knew she was here. Well, the only person who would know to ask for 'Jane Smith'!

She only hoped he wasn't about to make a nuisance of himself because of that. She didn't need him popping in and out of her life—not now. She already had too many other complications to deal with.

Consequently, when she lifted up the receiver she wasn't feeling kindly disposed to Robert's being a disruptive presence in her already turbulent life. 'Yes?' she prompted tersely.

'It's Jordan,' came the harshly unexpected reply. 'I'm well, too—in the circumstances! But I want to know more about this job of yours. I'll be waiting for you in our favourite restaurant tomorrow at one o'clock. Be there.'

The receiver was put down at the other end with a decisive click.

Jane was too stunned to even move for several minutes.

She had been partly right, for it had to have been Robert who'd told Jordan of her whereabouts!

And if she didn't meet Jordan tomorrow for lunch as he had instructed she knew he was capable of coming here instead.

Which would cause all sorts of problems.

Damn Robert!

## CHAPTER SIX

*'Moi?'* Robert questioned with exaggerated innocence when Jane telephoned him to tell him exactly what she thought of his betrayal.

'Mandy wasn't enough of a deterrent, hm?' Jane said coolly.

'It wasn't that,' he wheedled, all bravado gone. 'Of all things to happen to me, when I got back to town on Sunday night I bumped straight into Jordan. He was in the foulest temper imaginable, and I knew that if he ever found out I had known where you were and hadn't told him...! Put yourself in my place, Rhea,' he pleaded.

Jane could do that all too easily; Jordan could be formidable. But it didn't make her situation here any easier. Because of Robert she now had to try to get tomorrow off so that she could go into town and meet Jordan.

She had to accept that there was little more she could say to Robert on the subject, although she left him in no doubt about how annoyed she was with him.

It was asking Raff for the day off that was going to be so difficult; she hadn't even worked for him a full week yet.

He had fallen back into the habit of not joining her for dinner since the departure of his aunt and uncle, and so she had no choice but to seek him out in his study after she had finished her own meal. There was a tray with empty plates put to one side of his desk to show that he had at least eaten.

But he looked more tired than ever tonight, and there was a wary look on his face as he glanced up and saw her.

Jane knew the reason for that wariness, knew he was unsure how they were supposed to behave towards each other after last night.

For a man like Raff the emotion must be galling!

Well, if he thought she had assumed anything after their kisses the previous night he was mistaken; she didn't think it would ever pay to assume anything where this man was concerned.

'I just brought coffee for us both tonight.' She held up the two cups as she entered the room.

'Thanks,' he accepted abruptly, taking one of the cups before sitting down again behind the desk.

Jane hesitated, and then sat down in the chair opposite him. He didn't have the typewriter on the desk in front of him tonight, just long, hand-written pages.

Raff saw her gaze on them. 'I—er—decided to write the report out again by hand, and thought I would accept your offer of last night.'

God, how that cost him!

'Why?' she prompted softly.

He shrugged. 'The report is pretty urgent,' he bit out curtly, obviously hating having to change his mind like this after what he had said to her yesterday. 'I'd like you to start work on it as soon as possible.'

'Of course,' she nodded. 'I'll start typing it straight away if you have some of it already completed?'

He gave a slight smile. 'There's no need to do that, tomorrow will do.'

Now it was her turn to look uncertain. 'I—er—I know this might seem a bit cheeky, but I wondered if I could have tomorrow off?' The last came out in a rush, and she looked at him ruefully.

'Why?' he returned, as she had seconds earlier, his eyes narrowed searchingly on her flushed face.

'I—need to go into London for the day,' she explained with a grimace of reluctance. But she couldn't just swan off for the day without asking Raff. She may not be used to being employed by someone, but she did at least know that!

'Your days off are Saturday and Sunday,' Raff told her harshly.

'I'll work on Saturday instead of tomorrow to make up for it,' she promised.

He gave a deep sigh, sitting back in his chair. 'I know I don't have the right to interfere in your life——'

'No, you don't,' she put in firmly.

Raff shook his head. 'You became my responsibility the night you stepped off the pavement in front of my car.'

She stood up abruptly, moving across the room to pick up the typewriter from the table where she usually worked. 'I release you from that responsibility,' she told him hardly. 'Now, if you'll give me the sheets of notes you've already completed, I'll get to work on them.' She supported the typewriter on her wrist while holding out her hand for the sheets of paper.

Raff gave them to her. 'Where are you going with that?' He nodded at the typewriter.

'To work on the dining-room table, if that's all right with you,' she replied.

'You won't disturb me if you stay in here,' he assured her.

Maybe not, but he would disturb her! She couldn't be in the same room as him and not be deeply aware of him, would never be able to work with him sitting just behind her.

'I would rather go in the other room,' she said stubbornly, turning to leave.

'Jane.' He stopped her huskily.

She turned slightly.

'Don't do anything foolish,' he warned gruffly, his expression harsh.

He believed she was meeting her ex-lover in town tomorrow!

Well, if he thought she was going to be tempted back to the life she had led in London, he was mistaken. It was strange really, she didn't miss her life there at all. Oh, she missed Jordan, wished there weren't this rift between them, but she didn't miss any other part of the life she had had with him.

She didn't want to even think about how much part her growing attraction for Raff played in that.

If she were about to do anything foolish, it was here with Raff, not in London! Falling in love with him would have to be the most foolish thing she had ever done in her life.

'I won't,' she assured him now.

'And that report is highly confidential,' he reminded her again.

She frowned at his persistence in repeating those words, as if she were going to run out into the street and shout it to all and sundry!

But the reason for Raff's persistence in the need for complete confidentiality became clear to her in the very first paragraph of his report.

Raff was proposing to turn the house into a hotel, the grounds into a sports complex, part of it given over to a golf course!

Jane avidly read through the rest of the report, realising from its content that Raff was putting together a package to present to the banks in the hope of securing the financial backing he would need for such an ambitious idea.

And it did sound very ambitious indeed, although Jane didn't doubt that if anyone could make a success of it Raff could—she was sure he had the ability to make anything he set his mind to succeed. But he had to get considerable financial backing first. And that could be the problem.

And how would the rest of the family feel about having the estate turned into a luxury resort?

'They don't know about it yet.'

Jane looked up sharply at the sound of Raff's softly spoken words, her hair moving silkily against her spine, loose tonight, although the black dress she had on was worn more for comfort than effect, despite the fact that the dark colour made her hair look like flame.

Raff stood framed in the dining-room doorway, although he moved further into the room and closed the door firmly behind him as she looked at him, running a hand through the already tangled thickness of his dark hair. 'I knew as soon as you had read even a part of that report that you would begin to wonder about the rest of the family,' he explained heavily.

Jane moistened her lips. 'It all sounds wonderful.' What else could she say?

He gave a humourless smile. 'But not quite what my dear aunt has in mind, hm?'

She doubted it very much. It would seem slightly vulgar to a woman like Anita Barnes to have the estate turned into a hotel complex, even if it were of a most luxurious standard!

Raff shook his head. 'I'm running out of ideas of how to hold on to this money-gobbling pile.' He looked about him as if, at that moment, he felt he was a prisoner of circumstances.

'Don't your aunt and uncle have money?' Jane suggested tentatively.

His mouth twisted. 'Not enough for the money-monster,' he dismissed. 'No, the estate has to be turned around so that it can begin to support itself. Farming the land doesn't work, and we certainly don't own enough properties to keep things going.' He gave an impatient shrug. 'I don't even know if this idea is viable really, I'm leaving it to the banks to decide that.'

Oh, it all sounded viable, was just the sort of place that had become so popular with her London crowd the last few years, all of the facilities in one place for the 'idle rich' to play with. But if Raff went through with making the estate into a leisure complex it would no longer belong solely to the Quinlan family, and the privacy here would be gone forever.

'Is it what you want?' she probed gently.

'It isn't a question of what I want,' he dismissed irritably. 'My choices are limited.'

Jane chewed on her bottom lip, remembering the conversation about the estate she had had with

Robert at the weekend. 'How do you think the rest of the family will feel about this?'

Raff frowned. 'You mean Anita and Co?'

She repressed a smile at this description; it wasn't really a time for humour. 'That's who I mean,' she nodded.

He sighed. 'I'm not blind to the aspirations Anita has towards the estate, I just don't intend obliging her by popping off before I've had at least my "three score years and ten", and in the meantime the estate has to survive—in any way that it can,' he added grimly. 'The same way I do.'

Jane nodded. 'The leisure complex would be one way of doing that.'

'What do you think of the idea?' He watched her with narrowed eyes.

'Me?' She looked startled. What did she know about such things—more to the point, what did *he* think she knew?

He shrugged. 'I just thought you might have had more experience of places like this than I have.'

Jane's mouth twisted. 'With my designer-label clothes, silk underwear, and rich lovers, you mean?' she said drily.

Raff looked irritated. 'Perhaps I was a little hasty in those assumptions,' he muttered.

Amusement darkened her eyes at this begrudging almost-apology. 'Were you?'

'To tell you the truth——' he crossed the room to her abruptly '—I'm getting to the stage where I don't really care any more!'

Jane looked up at him with wide eyes, knowing he was going to kiss her again. And each time he did her defences got a little weaker. She was falling in love with this man. And it seemed as inevitable as that very first night they had met. Almost a fated attraction. The chances of their meeting any other way had to be extremely remote.

His hands were gentle as he raised her face for his kiss, their mouths moving together in gentle exploration until hunger took over, her hands entwined in the dark thickness of his hair as she held him close to her.

Raff's eyes glowed darkly as he looked down at her. 'A few centuries ago you would have been burnt as a witch,' he murmured gruffly, his face relaxed in languid passion.

The only time he seemed to relax at all!

'Why?' Jane prompted. But she knew, she knew... But she just needed to hear from his lips that he was as affected by their kisses as she was.

His mouth tightened, as if he regretted kissing her at all, and he moved away from her abruptly. 'Will you have dinner with me tomorrow night?' he asked abruptly.

There was no reason why she shouldn't have returned from town by then, but it was the unexpectedness of the invitation that made her hesitate.

'Why?' she said again.

'Oh, for God's sake, Jane!' He strode away impatiently. 'Does there have to be a reason?'

She looked at him consideringly, knowing he didn't like having his motives questioned like this. But she was so uncertain...

'I think so, yes,' she nodded.

He scowled. 'Why don't you just accept before I come to my senses?'

That was partly what she was afraid of. It also seemed too much of a coincidence to her that he should want to take her out tomorrow evening, when he more than suspected she was meeting a man during her trip into London. The last thing she was going to feel like after a lunch with Jordan was answering yet more questions, about him this time!

'Ask me again after tomorrow,' she told Raff wearily.

He frowned, thrusting his hands into his trouser-pockets. 'What will your answer be?'

'Yes. Probably.' She grimaced.

'Then answer me now,' he instructed abruptly. 'Either you do want to come out to dinner with me or you don't. I'm not about to repeat the invitation.'

Ever, he left unsaid. But the implication was there all the same.

'Yes,' she said abruptly, hating this feeling of manipulation, knowing that if she didn't feel so attracted to him that he would never get away with it. As she dared not let him think that he had this time either! 'But not tomorrow,' she added firmly. 'Wednesday, instead.' She named the day after tomorrow, her head held high in challenge as anger darkened his features.

'Why is that?' he derided. 'Expecting to be too tired to go out to dinner when you get back tomorrow?'

His insult was clear, and it took all Jane's effort of will not to tell him exactly what he could do with his dinner invitation, knowing that if she did there might never be another one. And she was too attracted to him to want to do that...

She met his gaze unflinchingly. 'I expect to be less than good company after the drive and a little shopping in town, yes,' she nodded.

His eyes blazed, and Jane knew he wanted to rant and rave at her about the stupidity of meeting Jordan at all. But he didn't, although anger emanated from every pore of his body. 'Wednesday night,' he bit out coldly. 'Eight o'clock,' he added sharply before slamming out of the room.

Jane sat back weakly, feeling emotionally drained.

She had just never met a man quite like Raff before. And that was the problem.

The man who most closely resembled Raff sat across the restaurant table from her, had already been seated at their usual table when she arrived ten minutes late for their one o'clock luncheon appointment.

She knew Jordan would have arrived precisely on time, been shown to the table by Henry, who knew them both so well, and she also knew that Jordan had made a great pretence of looking at the menu, all the time his anger burning coldly under the surface as the minutes ticked away, signalling her tardiness.

For Jordan had known she would come, that although she might be late she would definitely meet him here.

Jordan had changed little in the two weeks since she'd last seen him. And he should have looked different, his hair should have grown longer—something, anything to show that time had elapsed for him too. But Jordan always looked the same, always neat, always impeccable, never a hair out of place, that rich dark hair always kept the same short length, although Jane had never been able to work out when he fitted these visits to the hairdresser into his busy working schedule. He probably paid someone to visit his office and cut his hair while he continued to work!

After Raff's unkempt look, his hair over-long and certainly not kept in any particular style, Jordan looked even more austerely impeccable than ever!

But she loved him anyway. Had always loved him.

She still wasn't sure how she felt towards Raff.

'Well?' Jordan barked, his patience—what there was of it!—finally at an end.

Jane smiled at him brightly; she had never been cowed by him the way other people seemed to be. And he knew it. 'I was glad you telephoned,' she told him lightly. 'I have something I want to talk to you about.'

'*You* have——'

'Jordan, please.' She mockingly interrupted his explosion. 'People are staring,' she taunted.

'I don't give a damn what other people are doing,' he grated fiercely, although it was noticeable that he had lowered his voice slightly, grey-blue eyes glittering angrily at being goaded into losing the strict control he usually kept over his temper. 'I want to know what you think you're playing at?'

Her eyes widened innocently, on her own territory now, supremely confident among the other rich patrons of this exclusive restaurant, dressed in the 'designer label' clothes Raff had so scorned.

Strangely enough she had a feeling Raff and Jordan would actually get on well together, despite their differences in lifestyle and the seven or eight years' difference in their ages. They were very alike in so many other ways; maybe that was one of the reasons she found Raff so rakishly attractive.

She sobered at the thought. 'I'm not playing at all, Jordan,' she said softly. 'I have a feeling my game-playing days are over,' she added ruefully.

His eyes narrowed suspiciously. 'What do you mean by that?'

She shrugged off the importance of her statement—maybe because she didn't want to admit what the answer really was.

She drew in a deep breath. 'What can you tell me about the chances of success at turning a substantial manor house and its grounds into a going concern as a hotel and leisure complex?'

Jordan's mouth twisted sardonically. 'A little premature, aren't you?'

'Hm?' She gave him a vague frown, still deep in thought, barely noticing as the drinks he had ordered arrived at the table, the menu still closed in front of her.

'Spending your inheritance already?' he mocked. 'There's still ten weeks to go to your birthday.'

Jane gave him an impatient look. 'I'm not asking for myself.'

His frown turned to one of puzzlement. 'Then who?'

She sighed at his persistence. 'A—friend.' Telling Jordan to mind his own business would just result in her not getting any answers from him at all, and if anyone could advise her as to the viability of Raff's proposal it would be Jordan.

'Who owns a country residence he wouldn't mind converting?' Jordan mused shrewdly.

'I don't believe I said it was a he,' she bristled defensively.

Jordan gave her a scornful look. 'Would you bother to ask at all if it were a she?'

Now it was Jane's turn to frown. 'I'm not sure I like your implication.'

'No?'

His cool mockery annoyed her immensely; she hadn't been as selfish in the past as he was implying...had she? If she had, meeting Raff had changed all that!

'Jordan, just answer my original question,' she said irritably.

'This job you have,' he spoke thoughtfully. 'It's at the Quinlan house, a large manor house with thousands of acres of land attached. This "friend" you're talking about wouldn't be Rafferty Quinlan, would it?' Jordan's eyes were narrowed.

Jane gave a start of surprise—couldn't help herself—although she didn't know why she should feel in the least surprised that Jordan should know about the house and Raff; she should have realised that in the two days since Jordan had found out her whereabouts he would have found out everything he could about the house and its occupants. Nevertheless, she felt slightly disconcerted, and she certainly didn't want to get into a lengthy discussion about Raff.

'Do you have to know everything?' she attacked.

'Yes!' Jordan bit out forcefully.

Jane sighed. 'Why can't you just answer a straightforward business question?'

'Maybe because "business questions" are the last thing I expect from you,' he snapped. 'You've never shown the slightest interest before.'

She grimaced at the truth of that. And maybe it wasn't a good enough excuse that *he* had never shown the slightest inclination to discuss business with *her*. It was just possible, she could see in retrospect, that Jordan might not have spent so many nights closeted alone in his study if she had been willing to listen and talk to him about any problems he may have had. Raff had certainly done so when she had given him the opportunity, and how much closer her relationship with Jordan than it had ever been with Raff!

'I'm sorry for that.' She put her hand over his much stronger one as it rested on the table-top, his fingers long and tapered. 'But won't you help me now?'

He looked at her searchingly, as if this were the last thing he had expected of her. And maybe it was. Jane began to wonder just how selfish she had been over the years. And to wonder at the reason for the change in her...

Jordan drew in a deep breath. 'If it is the Quinlan house you're talking about—let's just theoretically say that it is...' he added drily at her stubbornly defensive expression.

Despite all the odds, Raff had trusted her with a confidence, and she couldn't go breaking that now.

The only trouble with that was that to be able to help Raff in the way she would like to she had to at least discuss this with Jordan, his knowledge of these things being so much more superior than either Raff's or her own.

'... The size of the building, the considerable grounds,' Jordan continued firmly. 'The right location—not too far from London, basically—I think it would stand a very good chance of success as a leisure centre, with the right backing. I think it could succeed very well,' he nodded thoughtfully.

Jane was satisfied with that answer, confident in Jordan's opinion; anything he touched seemed to turn to gold, and if he thought the venture could succeed then it would.

'As you don't appear to be going to enlighten me any further on that subject,' Jordan continued harshly, 'perhaps we had better get back to the original one.'

Jane removed her hand from his. 'Which was?' she prompted wearily, only too familiar with his stubborn determination.

He impatiently waved the waiter away from taking their order, which was probably the third time he had done so in the last fifteen minutes or so; the way things were going they wouldn't get to actually eat at all!

'What did you think you were doing,' Jordan attacked as soon as the waiter had gone, his voice so controlled it was dangerous, 'just taking off like that?'

She turned from giving the poor, downcast waiter a sympathetic smile, the smile fading. '*You* told me I had to get a job and prove myself capable of doing so before I was twenty-one,' she reminded him accusingly, 'or you would have no choice but to advise the trustees of Father's will to hold my money over until I'm twenty-five!'

'You weren't supposed to just take off like that after I'd issued the challenge,' he rasped.

'Wasn't I?' she shrugged. 'I thought I was.'

'You could have let me know where you were. *How* you were,' Jordan snapped.

'But I did,' she reasoned.

'A week after you'd disappeared!' he said impatiently. 'Good God, you could have been kidnapped for all I knew of your whereabouts.'

Jane smiled as she remembered she had thought that might be a possibility herself that night she had met Raff and he had just taken her off so arrogantly—and how she had doubted Jordan would pay any ransom demand.

'It isn't funny, damn it!' Jordan misunderstood the reason for her humour, his expression full of anger. 'Not when you consider who you are.'

Who was she? The last few weeks she hadn't really been sure from one minute to the next!

Oh, yes, Rhea-Jane Somerville-Smythe.

As if it weren't ridiculous enough that she had been blighted with one double-barrelled name, her father had chosen to burden her with two!

'You're heiress to a considerable fortune,' Jordan reminded tautly.

Oh, yes, she was that, too.

*If* she could prove before she was twenty-one that she was capable of being responsible for all that money.

'And you're my sister,' Jordan added forcibly.

Oh, yes, she was that, too...

## CHAPTER SEVEN

'As you realise, I'm not using my full name,' Rhea-Jane told her brother drily.

'"Jane Smith"!' Jordan said disgustedly.

She glared at him. 'You should try getting a job, any job, with a name like Rhea-Jane Somerville-Smythe. It isn't just difficult, it's impossible! If Father's will hadn't——'

'I've told you already, I'm not responsible for Father's will, only in seeing that his wishes are carried out,' Jordan dismissed. 'He would be very upset if he knew that clause in his will had resulted in what it has.'

Rhea-Jane shrugged. 'He didn't leave me much choice. But then, he never did, did he?' Her tone edged on bitterness, although it was an emotion she had always shied away from where her father was concerned; he just hadn't liked her, and there had been nothing she could do about it.

Her brother sighed. 'You were a rebellious little madam.'

'And he never forgave me for Mother dying when I was born,' she defended heatedly.

Jordan's hard face softened slightly. 'He was never any different, Rhea.' He used that first part of her name affectionately, as most people did who knew her well. 'I had to prove myself time and time again as being worthy to carry on after him.'

And it hadn't embittered him. Or had it? Jordan was even more difficult to know than Raff was, and he had no confidants, talked to Rhea if he talked things over with anyone. She had never thought about it before, but perhaps that too was as a result of having the father they'd had.

Jordan looked at her sympathetically. 'But I suppose I did have the advantage of having a mother who loved me unquestioningly for the first eight years of my life,' he realised gently.

Rhea-Jane gave a regretful smile. 'I wish I had known her.' She frowned as she recalled several conversations she had had lately that had disturbed her, conversations that she had so far been unable to confirm as being about her mother. 'She was a nanny before she married Father, wasn't she?' she probed as lightly as she was able.

'Rhea.' Jordan looked at her warningly. 'You're just trying to divert attention from yourself; we haven't talked about Mother and Father for years.'

'But I never knew Mummy——'

'Rhea, it's almost twenty-one years since she died,' Jordan cut in impatiently. 'I barely remember her myself!'

'But do you know if she ever happened to work for the Quinlan family?' Rhea-Jane persisted exasperatedly.

'The Quinlans?' he frowned. 'Why on earth should she have worked for them?'

She shrugged irritably. 'It's just that I seem to remind several members of the family of someone they used to know, and someone came up with the name of Raff's old nanny. It was Diana.' Her eyes darkened.

She had just enough doubt in her mind that it could actually have been her mother for her to need to find out positively; it was going to look very odd to Raff if her mother should turn out to be the woman who had once been involved with his father! He wasn't likely to believe that she hadn't known of the relationship, judging by the way he already distrusted women so badly.

'That's ridiculous,' Jordan dismissed scornfully. 'Why on earth should that Diana have been Mother?'

Why indeed? And yet she had this nagging doubt at the back of her mind that wouldn't let her rest easy about the subject. But she didn't think Jordan would welcome any suggestion from her that their mother might once have had a relationship with Donald Quinlan, especially as the other man had been married at the time; Jordan had absolutely idolised their mother.

'I don't suppose it's really important,' Rhea-Jane told her brother lightly. 'I only mentioned it in passing. The important thing is that you think this leisure-complex project could succeed...'

'I said it stands a very good chance,' Jordan corrected firmly. 'With the right backing. I would need to know a lot more about it before I gave my considered opinion.'

'I'm typing up a report on it for Raff right now—— What's so funny?' she demanded as she saw Jordan begin to smile.

His mouth quirked. 'So that expensive finishing-school is starting to pay off at last,' he derided. 'What's your typing speed?'

'Very funny, Jordan,' she snapped. 'Don't worry, I'll never be any threat to Glenda.' She mentioned his secretary's name.

'I would never employ you, anyway,' he told her bluntly. 'I don't believe in nepotism. But I would be very interested in seeing a copy of that report.' He looked at her steadily.

She sighed her indecision. 'It's a very confidential report...'

'You've told me most of the details already,' he reminded her. 'So you may as well let me have a look at the rest of them,' he encouraged.

'Well...' She hesitated.

'I give you my word it will go no further.'

When Jordan put it like that...! She knew that when he gave his word he meant it.

She nodded. 'I'm going to finish typing it when I get back this afternoon; I'll try and get a copy off to you before the last post.'

He looked at her consideringly. 'You seem very concerned that this Raff Quinlan should succeed?'

'Just give me your opinion on the report, and stop trying to make something out of nothing,' said Jane, her cheeks flushed.

'Is it nothing?' Jordan probed.

Her head went back defensively. 'Yes!'

But she knew that it wasn't, knew without doubt that she was teetering on the edge of falling in love with Raff.

'Where exactly did you go yesterday?' Raff rasped, his eyes narrowed to steely slits. 'Or did you just get bored with the present company, and feel a need to see your rich boyfriend again?'

He had been dying to throw that accusation at her since she had first asked for the day off! Of course, she could just tell him that Jordan was her older brother, but if she did that she would have to tell him everything, and if she did *that* he was sure to ask her to leave, clause in her father's will or not!

And how could she help Raff if she was forced to leave? Because she was sure, once Jordan had read the report she had sent off to him the previous evening, that she would be able to offer Raff firm advice about the conversion of the estate into a leisure complex, albeit if that information had come from Jordan.

But Raff wasn't likely to let Rhea-Jane Somerville-Smythe stay on here and offer him that help.

Her family was well-known in the City, Jordan even more successful than their father had been, their business acumen notorious, their wealth even more so. The Somerville-Smythes were an 'old' family, part of the 'establishment', and Jordan was a worthy successor as head of that family, was highly respected, and would be furiously angry to learn he had been called any woman's 'rich boy-friend' in that condescending way! If there were any women in Jordan's life he was extremely dis-creet about them.

Rhea-Jane had known Raff's mood was suspect when she'd met him earlier to go out, but he had said nothing on the drive to this country res-taurant, nor while they'd perused the menu and ordered their meal. What conversation he had made had been polite in the extreme. She should have become wary as soon as she'd realised that!

Instead, as they'd waited for their food to be served, Raff's question had come straight for the jugular.

She was still reeling slightly from her meeting with Jordan, her brother wanting to know every detail of her job before he would let her go, his 'Goodbye, Jane Smith' a timely reminder as she left that he would be keeping a close eye on her in future, that he wasn't about to put an end to what she was trying to do just yet, but that he reserved the right to do so if he deemed it necessary.

'I wasn't bored at all,' she answered Raff's question calmly enough.

His expression was stony. 'Mrs Howard tells me that you had a telephone call before you felt this sudden need to go into London.'

She shouldn't really be surprised that the housekeeper had told Raff about the call, knowing that the other woman had probably felt honour-bound to do so; Jane was, after all, an employee in Raff's house, and they knew so little about her that the telephone call had probably seemed important to the other woman. Nevertheless, things would have been much easier if Raff had never known of the telephone call.

But, then, when had life ever been made easier for her?

'I did receive a telephone call, yes——'

'From the man you ran away from in the first place?' Raff cut in harshly.

She blushed. 'I didn't run away from him——'

'All right, the man you left so abruptly that you had to stay in a hotel because you had nowhere else to go!' he altered impatiently. 'It all adds up to the same thing; you had left the man, but as soon as you received a telephone call from him you rushed off to London to see him.'

'I had a good reason for meeting him,' she defended, deciding it was pointless to waste time arguing with him over what Jordan had, or had not, been in her life.

His mouth twisted with distaste. 'I'm sure you did.'

Rhea-Jane gave a rueful smile. 'Careful, Raff,' she murmured. 'Your prejudice is starting to show.'

He took a large swallow of the whisky and water that had just been delivered to him, not even wincing as the fiery liquid passed down his throat.

Rhea-Jane sipped at her own glass of white wine, looking at Raff over its rim. 'Actually,' she added softly, 'I wanted to talk to him about you.' She deliberately avoided using any names, sure that Raff was just as capable of making enquiries as Jordan was—and, if he did, that he would discover who she was and throw her out.

'Me?' Raff looked at her suspiciously. 'You talked about me?'

'I didn't mention your name,' she told him truthfully; after all, Jordan had been the one to actually introduce Raff's name to the conversation.

'Why the hell did I come into your conversation at all?' Raff burst out impatiently. 'I don't think I care to be discussed by you and your friends!'

He made the latter sound like an actual insult!

'You weren't discussed at all,' she bristled. 'I believe I said you were mentioned.' She made this sound deliberately insulting, too.

Raff's mouth tightened ominously. 'But in what context?'

'In the context of my employer,' she snapped, goaded into being defensive, giving up any idea of discussing Jordan's opinion with Raff this evening. 'What other context is there?' she scorned.

'Just what, exactly,' he spoke in a level tone—too level, 'did you *mention* about me?'

He was likely to explode with temper if he thought she had discussed his personal business with anyone, even if it had been with good intentions. And from the look of him it wouldn't do any good to assure him Jordan could be discretion itself when he chose to be; she could tell from Raff's mood that he wouldn't believe she had acted out of a desire to help him.

'I told you——' her gaze was evasive, but she couldn't help it, hating having to lie '—I told him you were my employer.'

'For what purpose?' Raff grated.

'For *no* purpose,' she said exasperatedly.

His eyes were narrowed. 'Then why talk about me at all?'

Jane gave a weary sigh. 'I think perhaps it would be better if we just forgot about dinner and left now.'

He looked at her intently, grudging respect slowly entering his eyes as he did so. 'You mean it, don't you?' he said in some surprise.

'Of course I mean it,' she snapped impatiently. 'I didn't exactly enjoy my lunch out yesterday.' They had finally got around to eating, but by that time

Rhea-Jane didn't feel like it, merely picking at the salad she had ordered. She didn't think she was going to fare any better this evening after the conversation they had just had!

'But I would like to enjoy my dinner, and it looks as if I have to go back to the house to do that!' she finished.

The grudging respect turned to amusement as Raff began to smile. 'Wouldn't you rather enjoy the steak you have just ordered here?'

'Yes, I would rather,' she mimicked mockingly. 'If I'm allowed to?'

Raff held up his hands defensively. 'I'm hungry too, so how about a truce?'

She couldn't be bothered at this moment to point out to him that to call a truce they both had to have been at war—and *she* certainly hadn't been intending to fight with anyone this evening. Intentions, and what actually happened, when this man was about, were two entirely different things, as she had already learned too well.

She gave a weary shrug. 'A truce it is—as long as I can eat my dinner in peace!' Her eyes flashed warningly.

He relaxed visibly. 'Dinner in peace it is,' he conceded teasingly.

Actually, she had been let off the hook easier than she had hoped after his anger of a few minutes ago; she had expected Raff to pursue the subject of her luncheon with this unnamed friend of hers until he had the answers he sought.

The least Raff and Jordan knew about each other the better!

Strange really, because she was sure, despite their differences, that the two men would at least respect each other.

But she very much doubted they would ever get to meet each other, for ten weeks from now she would just be an unpleasant memory for Raff!

As it was, they had an enjoyable evening after all; a lovely meal, pleasant conversation, both of them seeming to want to steer clear of any subject that might prove volatile. Which seriously limited the things they could talk about, but at least there were no more arguments!

'What do I tell Mrs Howard about our dinner out this evening?' Rhea-Jane asked on the drive back to the house, having left it to Raff earlier to tell the other woman they wouldn't be at home for the meal. But she didn't think she would escape so easily tomorrow morning when she had coffee in the kitchen with the other woman as usual.

Raff glanced at her as he sat behind the wheel of the car. 'Maybe we should just tell her that I invited you out tonight because I just couldn't keep my hands off you any longer.'

Rhea-Jane's mouth quirked at his mockery. 'That's hardly true.'

'The evening isn't over yet!' He raised those dark brows suggestively.

She laughed softly at his teasing, the laughter dying in her throat as he didn't return the humour, but simply met her gaze steadily for several seconds before returning his attention to the road.

The car was suddenly charged with tension, a sexual awareness that made Rhea-Jane shiver with anticipation.

Except for a single light left on outside the front door, and another in the hallway, the house seemed to be in darkness when they got in, Mrs Howard obviously having retired for the evening.

Raff refused Rhea-Jane's offer to make them both coffee.

She didn't know what she was supposed to do now. Should she just go to bed? She wasn't sure.

'Let's go into the lounge for a few minutes,' said Raff, instantly solving her indecision for her, entering the darkened room ahead of her to switch on the two side-lamps that gave off a warm glow.

Rhea-Jane eyed him a little apprehensively, not altogether sure she should be alone with him like this. If he should kiss her again...! But apart from that remark in the car just now he had given no indication during the rest of the evening that he wanted to do any such thing, she chided herself.

'I enjoyed tonight.' He broke the silence.

'Don't sound so surprised,' she scolded mockingly. Really, to listen to him it sounded as if there was something wrong with enjoying her company! They had had a bumpy start to the evening, but it had certainly progressed smoothly after that.

He sat down next to her on the sofa. 'Do you have any idea how long it is since I actually enjoyed a woman's company?'

She would hazard a guess at it being some time ago, judging from his instant distrust of women, and yet he must have had *some* happy moments with his wife.

'In any capacity,' he added gruffly.

Rhea-Jane swallowed hard, not sure she wanted to hear this. The thought of him with another woman—in any capacity!—suddenly made her feel ill. Oh, she knew he wouldn't have been celibate before his marriage, or after, and yet she felt an overwhelming resentment towards any other women who had been in his life.

It was quite frightening to realise how jealous she felt.

'Why do I find *you* attractive?' Raff entwined his fingers in her hair, staring at it as if fascinated. 'I wish I knew more about you,' he frowned darkly.

'The little you do know, you dislike,' she reminded him lightly. She had avoided being trapped into revealing who she was once tonight, she wasn't going to fail now.

'I've never said that,' he rasped, his fingers tightening.

'Lust can be a great incentive to memory lapses,' Rhea-Jane scorned hardly.

His mouth firmed. 'I wish it were only lust I were talking about.'

She frowned at him, her gaze searching his face. 'What do you mean?'

He shook his head, pulling her slowly towards him.

*This* was what he meant, this instantaneous attraction that neither of them seemed able to control!

Rhea-Jane trembled in his arms, her senses reeling as the warmth of his lips claimed hers.

Every time she was with him like this it was as if she had come home after a long journey.

Raff groaned low in his throat, deepening the kiss, caressing her back with restless hands.

It was Rhea-Jane's turn to groan as one of those hands moved to cup her breast, desire coursing through her body, her limbs filled with a melting warmth that quickly spread through her whole body.

The pad of his thumb moved rhythmically across the tip of her breast, causing her to gasp as the hardening of her body betrayed her—if her response hadn't already done that!

'Raff...!' She drew in a sharp breath.

'I know, I know,' he muttered, laying her gently back on the sofa, his lips moving down her throat to the sensitive hollows below, his tongue caressing the smooth skin there erotically.

His hair was silky-soft beneath her fingers, her body arching against him as his lips closed over the hardened tip of her breast through her dress, the sensation of that rasping tongue through the silk material unlike any pleasure she had ever known before.

Raff half lay across her, his body hard with desire, a desire that shook his body as she moved against him, entwining her legs with his, letting her shoes drop to the floor, curving herself against him, wanting to be closer still.

Raff looked down at her with dark eyes. 'I can't make love to you here.'

She blinked up at him, the spell broken. She was stupid, or naïve; it hadn't occurred to her that Raff would want to make love to her.

'Mrs Howard might walk in.' He misconstrued her silence as disappointment, attempting to explain his reluctance in case she should misunderstand him.

Raff wanted to make love to her.

What would he say when he discovered the assumptions he had made about her morals were completely wrong?

It wasn't that she was a prude, or even that she had never been tempted. A couple of years ago she had been very tempted, but the man in question had decided she was too young at eighteen to know what she was doing. He had been forty-two, and already married; in fact, his own daughter had been one of her friends, her contemporary, so the infatuation had died a death several weeks later.

Almost three years later she was still a virgin.

Because there hadn't been a single man in all that time she wanted to make that sort of commitment to.

Was Raff that man?

Oh, yes...

'Jane?'

She looked at him dazedly. She *loved* this man, loved Raff Quinlan.

'Jane, I——' He broke off as a knock sounded on the door, getting quickly to his feet and standing slightly in front of Rhea-Jane so that she could compose herself as Mrs Howard came into the room.

'Yes?' he prompted tersely, and Jane felt sorry for the other woman; she couldn't possibly have known what she was interrupting—again!

And it was just as well they had been interrupted; she might have ended up babbling her love for this man otherwise!

Poor Mrs Howard looked flustered. 'I heard you come in, and I thought you might like some coffee...' she trailed off awkwardly.

Rhea-Jane stood up, smiling reassuringly at the other woman. 'That sounds like a lovely idea,' she encouraged.

The housekeeper turned to leave thankfully, hesitating only slightly before turning back to Raff.

'There were a couple of telephone calls for you while you were out, I left the numbers for you to return the calls on your desk.' She frowned. 'One man seemed rather insistent, although he wouldn't leave his name.'

Raff looked as if business calls were the last thing he wanted to deal with right now!

But Rhea-Jane needed a little time to collect her thoughts together! 'I'll come and help you with the coffee while Raff makes his call,' she told the housekeeper, deliberately avoiding Raff's gaze as she followed the other woman out of the room.

'There's really no need,' Mrs Howard protested.

There was every need, if she were to end this evening with any degree of decorum. Besides, she felt she owed the other woman some sort of explanation. After all, she had been so insistent that she was only an employee, like Mrs Howard herself, this last week, and tonight she had calmly been out to dinner with her 'boss'!

'I would like to help,' she smiled, walking ahead to the kitchen.

Mrs Howard still seemed flustered as she moved about the room preparing the tray while Rhea-Jane filled the percolator. 'I really didn't mean to intrude just now,' the housekeeper burst out, obviously uncomfortable with the whole situation.

'You didn't.' Rhea-Jane touched her arm, giving it a little reassuring squeeze. 'Raff and I were just discussing business.' Surely she could be forgiven that lie, for the sake of this woman's embarrassment?

'I don't know,' she began uncertainly. 'Raff didn't seem at all pleased, and—— Raff?' Her shocked gaze focused over Rhea-Jane's left shoulder. 'What on earth has happened?' she gasped.

Rhea-Jane understood the other woman's concern as soon as she herself turned to look at Raff, his expression like thunder. And it was, she realised, directed straight at her!

'I want to talk to you, Jane. Alone,' he grated forcefully. 'Now!'

'Really, Raff——'

'It's all right, Mrs Howard,' Rhea-Jane softly reassured her as she left the kitchen, her gaze never leaving Raff's pale, angry face.

Although she felt far from reassured herself as she followed Raff to his study, his back rigid with fury. What had she done now? How could he have changed so much in just a few short minutes?

He sat down abruptly on the front of his desk as she closed the door behind her, just looking at her for several long, tension-filled moments. Rhea-Jane could feel the moisture making her spine sticky, sensing the violence within him that was barely held in check.

What had *happened*? Had he, somehow, realised who she was, and wanted an explanation?

She drew in a ragged breath. 'Raff——'

'The "rich friend" you met yesterday...' his voice was dangerously soft when he at last spoke '...It wouldn't have been Jordan Somerville-Smythe, would it?' His eyes narrowed.

She paled. How could he possibly——?

'I can see by your face that it was,' Raff bit out contemptuously, his mouth twisted with disgust. '"In the context of being my employer",' he mimicked grotesquely. '"What other context is there?"' he continued challengingly. 'The context of my private business, that I had *entrusted* you with!' he accused heatedly, sitting forward now, his hands clenched into fists at his sides.

He *knew* she had discussed the possibility of the estate's being turned into a leisure complex with Jordan! But how——?

Jordan himself, she realised with a sick feeling in the pit of her stomach. *He* had been the man who'd telephoned Raff earlier this evening and hadn't given a name.

But he had given one now!

He had read the report she'd sent him, and not wasted any time after that in trying to talk to her, but had contacted Raff directly.

Oh, Jordan...

## CHAPTER EIGHT

JANE moistened dry lips, realising she was in serious trouble this time, feeling hot and cold at the same time. 'Raff——'

'I *trusted* you, damn it!' His fist landed heavily on the desk at his side. 'I trusted you, and you took the first opportunity you could to run off and tell your rich boyfriend every damn detail!'

'I——'

'Don't even attempt to deny it,' he warned coldly. 'I know it had to be you who talked to him because the report I sent the bank hasn't had time to reach them yet!'

She realised that, and the only thing to Jordan's credit in all this seemed to be that he hadn't betrayed the very vital confidence of just exactly who she was and what she was to him.

But it wasn't much of a credit, because it no longer seemed so very important; Raff was going to want her to leave after this, anyway.

'He actually telephoned here,' Raff continued incredulously. 'Had the audacity to offer me a business deal!'

That sounded like the Jordan she knew and loved! Although she could cheerfully have strangled him at that moment. But he wouldn't really have thought about the damage he could be doing, she knew that; Jordan functioned on a business level only most of the time. And he obviously thought the leisure complex a good business venture.

She looked at Raff curiously. 'What was your reply?'

'What was——? Jane, you broke a confidence!' Raff stood up furiously.

Rhea-Jane held her ground. 'I did it with good intentions. Jordan is an excellent business-man——'

'I'm well aware of who he is,' Raff cut in coldly.

*Exactly* who he was? Did he know Jordan was Diana's son?

She shrugged. 'Then you must realise how competent he is. I actually only asked him about the viability of a leisure complex, I had no idea he would be interested in investing in it himself.'

Although possibly she should have done; Jordan was first and foremost a businessman. 'What *did* you tell him?' She frowned.

Grey eyes glittered glacially. 'He's coming here tomorrow so that we can discuss it,' Raff revealed defensively, as if he wished he could tell her he had told Jordan to go to hell. But, thankfully, good sense had prevented him from doing that.

Only one thing mattered to Rhea-Jane at that moment; Jordan was coming *here*. Not as her brother, but as a prospective business partner for Raff, by the sound of it.

'Is he the one, Jane?' Raff asked tautly.

She looked at him dazedly; the one what?

'The one you were running away from that night?' he explained harshly.

Colour heated her cheeks. 'I wasn't running away from him,' she asserted. Although she was aware it wasn't so far from the truth. She had been trying to escape the life she had made for herself with Jordan; she just hadn't realised it at the time.

Raff clearly saw the indecision in her expression. 'Running *to*, then,' he almost accused.

Her eyes flashed at the insult intended. 'I wasn't running *to* him either!'

'But you did live with him?'

She sighed at his persistence. 'Yes. But not in——'

'He doesn't know about us?' Raff's eyes were narrowed, his hands thrust into his denims pockets.

'Us...?' she echoed dazedly. 'Raff——'

'I don't think Somerville-Smythe is a man ruled by his emotions,' he cut in coolly, 'so I'm expecting our meeting tomorrow to be purely of a business nature. I would prefer it if anything the two of you have to say to each other you do in your own time, and not in mine!'

Rhea-Jane looked at him searchingly. Did that mean he didn't want her to leave immediately, as she had expected he would?

He was right about Jordan, though; he certainly wasn't ruled by his heart, and if he thought the leisure complex was a good investment then it almost certainly was. She couldn't have been happier for Raff. Although it certainly hadn't helped her own situation with him. But, knowing her brother as she did, she didn't even think he would see any of this as a problem; he always saw his personal and business life as completely separate things, and functioned accordingly.

She moistened her lips. 'What time are you expecting Jordan to arrive?'

'Mid-morning,' Raff supplied tersely.

She would make sure she was nowhere in sight at that time, had no wish to make the situation any more taut than it obviously already was.

And any relationship she might have thought was delicately forming between herself and Raff was definitely at an end. She didn't need Raff to tell her that, she could see exactly how he felt about her now in his face.

Jordan couldn't have known just how untimely his intrusion had been, but if he thought he was going to get away with doing what he had without being told exactly what Rhea-Jane thought of him, no matter how innocent his motives, he was mistaken!

'What kept you?' he drily received her call a few minutes after she had awkwardly excused herself from Raff, leaving him staring after her broodingly in his study.

Rhea-Jane counted to ten before answering her brother—although it didn't actually seem to cool her anger very much! 'What do you think "kept me"?' she finally challenged.

'I have no idea—Quinlan?' he realised slowly.

'Don't sound so surprised, Jordan,' she scorned. 'How did you expect him to react to me after you had just told him you knew all the details of a report he believed to be completely confidential, and calmly offered him a business deal?'

'In a businesslike manner,' her brother instantly dismissed—as she should have guessed he would!

She wished she could convince Jordan of just how insensitive he had been, but she knew she would be wasting her time and her breath even trying; he just wouldn't understand.

Perhaps it was enough that he realised she was very angry about what he had done.

'You've made my position here very awkward.' She stubbornly hung on to her outrage.

'I don't see——'

'Jordan, I'm your sister!' Her impatient outburst started out high-pitched, and lowered drastically on the last word as Rhea-Jane looked about the hallway guiltily in case anyone should have overheard her. Which was ridiculous. Raff had stormed past her a few minutes ago on the way upstairs to his bedroom, and Mrs Howard would have retired for the night long ago, knowing better than to expect any explanation from Raff for his earlier behaviour.

'I'm well aware of who you are, Rhea,' Jordan began in a bored voice.

'But Raff isn't!' she reminded frustratedly.

'It's time that particular deception came to an end anyway,' Jordan dismissed. 'You've proved your point, Rhea, and I'm more than happy to advise the other trustees of Father's will to release the money to you on your twenty-first birthday.'

She should feel triumphant. Over the moon. It was what she had wanted, what she had entered into this charade for. Her independence. The means to make a life for herself.

But she would have to leave Quinlan House. Leave Raff...

'What if I'm not ready for the "deception" to come to an end?' She tried to make light of it, but knew she had failed miserably!

'Don't be ridiculous, Rhea.' All complacency had left Jordan's voice now, so that he sounded almost as arrogant as Raff himself! 'I can hardly have my sister working as a secretary to my new business partner!'

No, that wouldn't do at all, as far as the Somerville-Smythe pride was concerned, Rhea-Jane acknowledged wryly.

'Has it even occurred to you that he may not want to be your business partner?' she pointed out drily.

'He will,' Jordan returned confidently. 'If he has any business sense at all!'

No arrogance from Jordan this time, just an assurance of his own capabilities. But he hadn't met Raff yet, couldn't quite know what he would be up against, had already antagonised Raff by telephoning in the first place. It was sure to be a case of 'the irresistible force meeting the immovable object' when these two men met!

It might be fun, at that.

It was certainly inevitable.

And if it couldn't be avoided there was no point in trying to run away from it. She certainly wasn't going to make herself scarce tomorrow now, as Raff wanted her to do.

'Although I can't be sure that he does,' Jordan added mockingly. 'After all, he did employ *you* as his secretary!'

'Very funny,' she replied sarcastically. 'We'll see tomorrow, shall we?' she taunted.

'You may as well have your things packed so that you're ready to leave with me after I've spoken to Quinlan,' Jordan advised uninterestedly before ringing off.

Rhea-Jane frowned at the receiver frustratedly as the disengaged tone came on the line.

Jordan had spoken, so it had to be so!

No wonder she had come close to strangling him several times in her life!

But even so, he was probably right about the packing. And she certainly didn't think she was going to sleep, anyway...

She felt as if she were walking on hot coals all morning, unable to even think about concentrating on work, aware of Mrs Howard giving several curious looks in her direction, as she didn't eat anything for breakfast, but poured herself several cups of coffee instead. The other woman obviously misunderstood her nervousness, and put it down to the sudden strain that seemed to be back in Rhea-Jane's relationship with Raff. If only it were that simple!

Rhea-Jane was standing at the day-room window when she saw Jordan's new-style Jaguar turn into the driveway at exactly ten twenty-five, knowing he would have driven the pale blue car himself, hating to give anyone control over his life, even in so small a way.

She felt a certain sisterly pride in him as he stepped out of the car on to the gravel driveway; he was an incredibly handsome individual, completely fit, his dark suit perfectly tailored—as were all his clothes.

He would be an extremely attractive man if he relaxed a little and didn't take life so seriously all the time.

Rhea-Jane's first instinct was to run out into the hallway and open the door to him herself. That would appear strange enough in itself to Mrs Howard, she was sure, but if she launched herself into Jordan's arms, as she longed to do, the other woman was likely to be scandalised, especially as Jordan had supposedly come here to see Raff.

If *Raff* himself were to witness such an affectionate display, the tenuous hold he had over his self-control was likely to break completely!

She could hear the voices out in the hallway, knew Jordan would be asked to wait there while Mrs Howard went to Raff's study to tell him his visitor had arrived, if he weren't already aware of the fact.

The housekeeper had been full of the fact, while she'd poured Rhea-Jane's coffee that morning, that for once Raff hadn't gone straight out to work on the estate after his breakfast.

Rhea-Jane couldn't resist the temptation, while the other woman was absent, of just making Jordan aware of her presence in the house.

Her brother's mouth quirked mockingly as she strolled so confidently out of the day-room. 'Quite an impressive place,' he drawled appreciatively.

She gave an inclination of her head. 'And it could be made even more so.'

'That's what I'm here for,' Jordan nodded.

It wasn't quite what she had meant, but she knew Raff's idea of a leisure complex was the last chance he had to hang on to his estate at all.

'Jordan, I haven't had a chance to tell Raff I'm your sister yet, and I would appreciate it if you didn't do it either.' She looked at him pleadingly, genuinely intending to tell Raff herself who she was, but at a time she thought was right. If ever such a time existed...

Jordan looked sceptical too. 'I don't think——'

'Mr Quinlan will see you now, Mr Somerville-Smythe,' Mrs Howard spoke softly behind them, and Rhea-Jane was slightly shamefaced as she turned to face the other woman, wondering just how much of their conversation she had overheard.

Poor Mrs Howard must be confused by a whole series of events that had taken place at the house lately—first Rhea-Jane's unexpected arrival, then the Barnes family deciding to descend on them out of curiosity, and now Jordan. The poor woman must wonder what on earth was going on!

But it was just like Raff to let his housekeeper show Jordan to his study rather than coming out to greet the other man himself, it would put him at an advantage she was sure Jordan was fully aware of; he used these same tactics himself whenever he could!

'I'll talk to you later,' Jordan told her mockingly before following Mrs Howard down the hallway.

Rhea-Jane was even more restless while the two men talked in Raff's study than she had been while waiting for Jordan to arrive. The two men were too much alike, she acknowledged, to actually like each other, but she had a feeling they would respect each other. As long as Raff's prejudice, because of what he believed Rhea-Jane's relationship to be with the other man, didn't jeopardise the interview. If Raff would just give Jordan a chance...

This was ridiculous; neither man would thank her for worrying over him like a mother hen!

But she couldn't help her concern, and the longer the meeting went on the more worried she got, finally going down to the kitchen in the hope that she could be of some help there to take her mind off the two men talking in Raff's study.

When she saw that Mrs Howard was setting up a tray for coffee, Jane knew she had to offer to take the tray up to the two men herself.

'You know Mr Somerville-Smythe, do you?' Mrs Howard made the query casually enough, although she was obviously deeply curious to know exactly what all the unusual happenings were about.

But it wasn't up to Rhea-Jane to enlighten the other woman. 'From London, yes,' she answered economically. 'So I would be pleased to take the tray up for you.' She smiled brightly.

Mrs Howard tilted her head questioningly. 'Shall I put on a third cup?'

Hardly! 'Er—no.' Rhea-Jane did her best to keep a straight face, but it was difficult when she could so easily envisage Raff's fury if she should dare to presume to sit down and drink coffee with himself and Jordan. 'I—they're discussing business,' she added dismissively.

The other woman's curiosity was really aroused now, but Rhea-Jane knew there was no way the other woman would actually ask her what 'business' the two men could be 'discussing'.

She would have liked to be fair, and tell the other woman, but she knew it was up to Raff to tell Mrs Howard if there were to be any changes made on the estate.

There was no guarantee, knowing Raff as she did, that he would agree to Jordan's financial proposals.

It was difficult knocking on a door when holding a tray in one's hands. Jane had never quite appreciated the problem before now, finally resorting to a gentle kick against the polished wood, and hoping Mrs Howard would forgive her for the faint mark her soft leather shoe had left on the wood.

Raff's eyes narrowed as soon as he opened the door and saw it was her standing outside with the laden tray.

'Coffee,' she announced brightly, raising the tray pointedly.

He had no choice but to stand back and let her enter to put the tray down on his desk-top.

Well, that wasn't strictly accurate; he *did* have a choice, but even *he* wouldn't be that rude to her with a third person present in the room!

'Shall I pour?' she offered lightly, smiling at no one in particular, knowing that if she looked directly into Raff's face that he would look furious, and that Jordan would more than probably look amused by her tactics.

'Why not?' Raff closed the door behind her with a firm click. 'I'm sure you know how we both take our coffee.'

Her hand shook slightly as she lifted the coffee-pot; she could tell Raff was more angry than she had ever seen him before, more furious even than he had been the previous evening after talking to Jordan on the telephone.

'And, of course,' Raff continued hardly, 'there's no need to introduce the two of you either, is there?'

'It would be a little ridiculous, in the circumstances.' Jordan was the one to drily answer him as Rhea-Jane seemed to be momentarily struck dumb.

Rhea-Jane swallowed hard, not liking the look of the pulse that beat so angrily in Raff's tightly clenched jaw. Maybe she shouldn't have brought the coffee after all...!

'I'll leave the two of you to continue talking,' she told them hastily, turning to leave.

'That won't be necessary,' Raff grated, his eyes glacial when she at last chanced a look at his face, and she turned quickly away again from the antagonism she saw there. 'We've finished talking business, there only remains the question of...you.'

She raised startled eyes to his. 'Me?' she echoed dazedly, looking questioningly at Jordan, wondering what he had said to the other man about her, receiving only a puzzled shrug in reply; he no more knew what the other man had meant than she did.

And then Rhea-Jane knew. Of course, Raff still believed she and Jordan were lovers...!

'Yes?' she prompted tensely, her head held back proudly, the hair that so troubled him like a flame down her spine.

'Rhea-Jane will be leaving with me, of course,' Jordan announced arrogantly.

Raff's eyes glittered dangerously as the other man at last revealed her full first name to him. 'Surely that is for—Rhea-Jane to decide?' he challenged softly.

She looked at the two men, realising that they might have come to terms over business—at least, she hoped they had!—but that she, obviously as far as Raff was concerned, was another matter entirely.

She suddenly realised what a bone, that was being fought after by two dogs, must feel like!

Jordan shook his head. 'There can be no question of her staying on here now.'

Raff's mouth tightened at the other man's arrogance, his eyes icy as he looked across at Rhea-Jane. 'Do you want to move back in with him?' he rasped.

What was the alternative? What was Raff offering in its place?

Jordan stood up restlessly, his eyes narrowed. 'Just what has been going on here the last couple of weeks, Rhea? I thought you said this was just a job?'

Her cheeks felt warm, but she was filled with confusion over Raff's behaviour. 'I don't——'

'Do you want to live with him?' Raff cut in harshly, his whole body taut with tension. 'Or stay here with me?'

With him? Was he serious? He looked very serious indeed!

'I don't need saving from myself, Raff, no matter what you may have assumed to the contrary,' she assured him, unable to think of any other reason for his offering to let her stay on here. 'You see, Jordan is——'

'Very wealthy, very influential,' Raff acknowledged grimly. 'But is that really what you want, a rich lover?'

'You know it isn't——'

'I don't have the wealth—yet,' Raff told her grimly. 'Although if the leisure complex venture turns out as profitable as Somerville-Smythe believes it will, that will change in the future. I don't know if you love me, but I do know, from your responses to me, that you aren't in love with *him*.' He nodded in Jordan's direction. 'And I'm willing to offer you marriage, Rhea,' he added challengingly.

*Marriage?* He wanted to *marry* her?

She looked at him searchingly; he didn't look like a man who had just proposed marriage to her.

Because what he was doing was dangling a gold ring in front of her nose, because he believed it was the one thing Jordan had never offered her!

'Rhea,' Jordan spoke harshly. 'You haven't answered my question.'

And he wanted to know *exactly* what had been 'going on' while she had been staying here, she could tell by his tone of voice that he wouldn't be satisfied with anything less.

'Stop trying to intimidate her,' Raff warned softly. 'She can make her own mind up.'

Jordan looked at him coldly. 'My dear man——'

'I'm not your "dear" anything,' Raff rasped.

'All right—Quinlan,' Jordan bit out in a barely controlled voice. 'I don't know what Rhea has told you about the two of us——' he frowned darkly at Rhea before continuing '—but you seem to be under some misapprehension about our relationship. I am not, nor have I ever been, some sort of rich protector for her. I am, in fact——'

'Jordan, no!' she groaned, knowing everything would change once Raff knew who she really was. And she hadn't answered his suggestion of marriage yet!

Her brother gave her an angry scowl. 'If there was some sort of problem here you should have corrected it before I arrived this morning,' he criticised harshly. 'I told you last night——'

'Last night?' Raff echoed suspiciously. 'You telephoned Somerville-Smythe after we talked last night?'

She grimaced. 'Yes. But I——'

'Just what sort of hold do you have on her?' Raff turned angrily on the other man.

'No hold, Quinlan,' Jordan told him calmly. 'Just one of the closest relationships possible between a man and a woman. Are you going to end this ridiculous farce, or am I?' he prompted Rhea-Jane impatiently.

'The two of you are—married?' Raff said disbelievingly.

'Hell, no,' Jordan denied derisively. 'If we were I would have put her over my knee and given her a good hiding by now! I may still do so,' he added, looking at her challengingly.

She gave him a dismissive movement of her hand, moving to stand in front of Raff, putting her hand on his arm as she looked up at him. 'Do you really want to marry me?'

'I would hardly have asked you if I hadn't meant it,' he grated.

Now probably wasn't the time to point out to him that he hadn't actually *asked* her, just offered her an alternative to living with Jordan!

'I hope you know what you're doing, Quinlan,' Jordan muttered. 'I wouldn't wish this hellion on any man, let alone one I intend having as a business partner. This would be a one-way transition,' he added warningly. 'No trying to give her back once you realise how difficult she is to live with.'

'I'm not difficult to live with——'

'Damned impossible most of the time,' Jordan acknowledged impatiently. 'But maybe she'll make you a better wife than she has me a——'

'Careful, Somerville-Smythe,' Raff warned harshly.

'—sister,' Jordan finished drily.

'Oh, Jordan!' She turned to him, knowing by the way Raff had instantly tensed that he was deeply disturbed by the revelation, that he was more bothered by this than his first assumption about their relationship. 'Raff, I was going to tell you.' She looked up at him imploringly.

He wasn't even looking at her, but staring steadily at Jordan. 'Did you say "sister"?'

'There's little likeness between the two of us, I'll admit,' Jordan nodded. 'Rhea looks like our mother, and I—well, I suppose I must take after my father's side of the family,' he shrugged, because apart from his height he really looked little like their father either; Jordan's colouring was much darker. 'But yes, Rhea is definitely my sister.'

At last Raff looked down at her, and there was such cold disdain in his eyes that Rhea-Jane felt almost as if he had struck her. 'Rhea-Jane

Somerville-Smythe.' The name sounded obscene on his lips.

She swallowed hard. 'If you would just let me explain...'

He pushed her sharply away from him as she would have reached out to him. 'There's nothing to explain,' he told her glacially. 'Whatever little game you've been playing here is over.'

'Raff——'

'I want you to leave here. Now!' he grated harshly, his fury barely leashed, the move to sit down behind his desk seeming to be made more out of a need to put distance between himself and Rhea-Jane than actually to sit down. 'Both of you,' he added flatly.

'But——'

'Rhea, I think it's best if we do go,' Jordan put in quietly, obviously able to gauge the other man's mood as being dangerously close to breaking-point. 'Get your things together, and we'll leave.'

A sob caught in her throat. 'But, Jordan——'

'Now isn't the time, Rhea,' he comforted her, glancing at the stony-faced man who sat so still across the room. 'Definitely not the time,' he repeated with a pointed grimace.

It had all gone so terribly wrong. If she could have just explained to Raff... But Jordan was right, he didn't want to listen now. Maybe when he had calmed down she could just start to explain why she had behaved the way she had. Although looking at his face now, she had a feeling it could be a long time before she could do that.

She felt numbed, and collected her case from her room as if in a dream. Jordan was waiting in the hallway for her, with no sign of the other man, and so she could only assume he was still in his study. Rhea dared not even risk trying to make her goodbyes to Mrs Howard, sure she would break down if she didn't go now; she would have to telephone the other woman once she felt a little stronger.

Saying goodbye to Raff was something she couldn't even think about.

Jordan didn't say a word, just put her case in the back of the car before getting in beside her.

He reached out and squeezed her hands as she clenched them together on her lap. 'You can't blame the man, Rhea,' he soothed. 'At the moment Raff is feeling very humiliated by your deception. Just give him time.'

She just nodded wordlessly, too choked up to speak just yet.

But Jordan's own air of calm was to desert him a few days later!

## CHAPTER NINE

'HE'S taking this too far!' Jordan stormed into the house, throwing his briefcase down with little regard for the expensive leather, and going straight over to the drinks cabinet to pour himself a glass of whisky, something he rarely did.

Rhea-Jane watched him warily, looking up from the details of property she had been going over for the last few days in an effort to find somewhere suitable for opening up her agency. It didn't look as if it was going to be as simple as she had first thought.

Not that that would stop her; she was determined to do something with her life.

Besides, she had to keep herself busy. So that she didn't dwell on thoughts of Raff.

She was too afraid to let herself even *start* to think about the way they had parted, knew she would break down completely if she did.

She sat back in her chair now, looking across at Jordan. 'What's wrong?' she prompted as he threw the whisky down his throat, his expression grim.

'Quinlan,' he grated.

Rhea-Jane tensed at the mention of his name. 'Raff?' she questioned lightly. 'What has he done to upset you?'

'I instructed my lawyers to send Quinlan all the legal paperwork needed for the business partnership,' Jordan bit out furiously. 'They arrived back today,' he added harshly.

'Yes?' She had tensed expectantly.

'Unsigned!' her brother burst out disgustedly. 'With a terse letter attached to them saying he had changed his mind and decided not to accept my offer after all.' Jordan shook his head. 'The man is a fool. He knows damn well my terms were more than fair.'

But at the time Raff had agreed to the business deal he hadn't known Rhea-Jane's name was Somerville-Smythe too, that she was Jordan's sister. That had to be the reason why he had changed his mind.

And he would lose the estate completely if he didn't do something about his situation soon.

Did he really think it was worth paying that price not to have anything further to do with *her* family?

He had to. God, how he must hate her for her subterfuge!

But she couldn't let him make such a sacrifice out of disgust for her behaviour, she had to try and talk to him.

'*Now* is the time.' She stood up decisively, looking at Jordan challengingly as he realised she meant to go to see Raff. 'He needs this business deal,' she attempted to justify her actions. 'He may regret he ever knew me, but that's no reason to sacrifice everything he's worked for for so many years. I'm going to see Raff now, Jordan,' she stated firmly. 'And don't try and stop me because——'

'I wasn't about to,' he drawled, sitting down in one of the armchairs. 'I put through several telephone calls to Quinlan House today, and each time the housekeeper told me Raff was away.'

'And you don't believe that,' Rhea-Jane sighed.

Jordan raised dark brows. 'Do you?'

No, she didn't; she was sure Raff wouldn't go anywhere at a crucial time like this.

But there was one way to find out, one person she could talk to who might know if Raff was away or not.

She left Jordan in the lounge, and put a call straight through to Robert.

'Well, well,' he began. 'If it isn't Rhea-Jane Somerville-Smythe returned to the fold!'

She groaned. 'You've heard about that?'

'About what?' The frown could be heard in his voice.

'You haven't spoken to Raff?' Rhea-Jane said cautiously, sure, now that she thought about it, that Raff wouldn't have told his family about her.

'Not recently,' Robert drawled. 'One of the crowd said they had seen you in town the other day,' he said carelessly.

'So you wouldn't know if Raff was away at the moment?' she sighed.

'Of course he isn't away,' Robert instantly scorned. 'Raff never leaves his beloved estate.'

She frowned. 'Are you sure?'

'Raff isn't away, believe me.' He sounded hurt by her lack of faith in him. 'Mother would be down there caretaking the place if he was,' he assured her. 'But "the silence has been deafening", to quote a phrase,' he added drily. 'Has Jordan finally agreed to let you have your inheritance, is that why you're back in town?' he continued interestedly.

'Something like that,' she avoided. 'It's just that Raff doesn't seem to be taking calls,' she added worriedly.

'Oh, he often does that,' Robert dismissed unconcernedly. 'Especially if Mother is in one of her bossy moods. But you can depend on it, he's there all right.'

That was what she had thought, she had just wanted it confirmed before driving all the way to Quinlan House.

'What have you done to upset my dear cousin?' Robert probed mockingly. 'Don't tell me, he found out who you are and threw you out!'

She couldn't exactly blame him for his curiosity, but she had no intention of satisfying it!

'You'll have to talk to Raff about that,' she answered evasively again.

'He's as tight-lipped as the proverbial clam, always has been,' Robert grumbled. 'I would be wasting my time asking him anything!'

'You're wasting your time with me, too,' she told him in a bored voice. 'I've got to go now, Robert, but I——'

'Hey, wait a minute!' His hurried protest interrupted her dismissive goodbye. '"One good turn deserves another", and all that.'

'When did you start talking in clichés, Robert?' she taunted. 'It's very boring!'

'That isn't nice, Rhea-Jane,' he complained in a slightly sulky voice, having been convinced for years that he was such a fascinating individual no woman could resist him.

'I'm in a hurry, Robert.' Rhea-Jane sighed her impatience. 'And anyway, you *owed* me a favour after the way you let me down with Jordan,' she reminded him.

'I've explained why I did that,' he wheedled. 'For goodness' sake, Rhea, I only want you to come to a party with me on Saturday night.'

'Why me?' she prompted warily.

He laughed softly, his bad humour gone as quickly as it had arrived; one thing about Robert, he was never in a bad mood for long. 'Do I sense suspicion in your voice?' he taunted.

'In all probability,' she said drily.

'I've invited you out dozens of times in the past, Rhea——'

'I hadn't worked for your cousin then,' Rhea-Jane derided.

'If I promise not to even mention Raff's name, will you come to a party with me on Saturday?' he cajoled.

He was good company when he wanted to be, and he *had* kept quiet about her identity to the rest of the family, much as it must have been a temptation to him not to be... 'Oh, all right,' she conceded without much enthusiasm for the idea.

'You are a love!' Robert's grin could be heard in his voice. 'I'll pick you up about nine o'clock on Saturday night.'

Rhea-Jane rang off, not wasting any more time even thinking about Robert. She could more than handle him, and she had more important things to think about.

Like hoping Raff would be at Quinlan House, as Robert seemed so sure he was.

'I'm going out for a while,' she told Jordan briefly. 'Do you think you could take a look through those?' She pointed at the estate agents' lists on the table. 'You probably know what to look for better than I do.'

And it would help take his mind off Raff!

'But——'

'I have to go, Jordan.' She waved vaguely in his direction, her thoughts already miles away.

Jordan probably knew exactly where she was going, but he wasn't about to deter her!

The two of them had got on a lot better together the last few days, Rhea-Jane having learned a new respect for Jordan and how hard he worked, Jordan seeming to at last accept that she had grown up. They had never mentioned Raff's unexpected offer of marriage, and what Rhea-Jane's answer to it might have been. But the knowledge was there, anyway. They both knew what she would have liked her answer to be.

She and Jordan had never got on so well together, but it was a pity that understanding had come only because she had loved and lost Raff.

She hoped, time and time again, on that drive down to Hampshire, that Robert was right about Raff's being at the estate but just not receiving calls; especially ones from Jordan, Rhea-Jane's brother!

But Raff's actions to her appeared to be a case of 'cutting off his nose to spite his face', and—God, she was getting as bad as Robert with his clichés!

But Raff *was* just being stubborn as far as she could see, was achieving nothing by it, except the possibility of losing the estate to the creditors. And he couldn't really want that, no matter how stubborn he might be feeling at the moment.

Mrs Howard looked surprised to see her when she opened the door to Rhea-Jane's knock, which wasn't surprising, considering the abrupt way she had departed only a few days earlier.

Rhea-Jane hesitated in the doorway. 'Is Raff at home?'

The housekeeper's expression suddenly became evasive. 'Er—well—he is,' she finally admitted awkwardly. 'But——'

'He isn't receiving callers,' Rhea-Jane finished drily, sympathising with the other woman's embarrassment, but so thankful to know that Raff was in the house. 'Don't worry, Mrs Howard——' she touched the other woman's arm reassuringly '—I'll tell him I let myself in,' she promised her as she entered the house.

'But—but——'

'And I'll let myself out again,' she offered, smiling brightly before walking quickly down the hallway towards Raff's study, sure he would be in there, and not wanting to give Mrs Howard time enough to collect her scattered wits, and try to stop her, and forewarn Raff. Forewarned was the last thing she wanted him to be!

She knocked briefly on the study door before entering, having several seconds to look at him before he became aware that it was she who had entered the room, and not Mrs Howard as he had assumed.

The intense feelings of love were quickly followed by anger. He was still working too hard, his face more strained than ever. There was no reason, except his own stubbornness, for him to be pushing himself like this.

'Why have you changed your mind about going ahead with the leisure complex?'

His head had snapped up at the first sound of her voice, his gaze becoming more and more glacial as he looked at her.

He didn't answer her immediately, just sat back in his chair and looked at her.

Rhea-Jane's first impetus had passed, and the longer he looked at her the more uncomfortable she became. And she knew that was exactly what he was hoping to achieve.

But she hadn't taken the trouble to change before coming out, had left immediately the decision was made, before self-doubt could make her change her mind, still wearing the jeans and casual top she had put on that morning to spend the day working at home.

The longer Raff continued to look at her the more she wished she had taken the time to change into one of her 'designer-label' outfits; at least she would have felt more confident in them. Although she didn't think Raff would have found her appearance any more pleasing in the clothing he had been so contemptuous of when they'd first met.

'What,' he finally spoke softly, dangerously so, 'makes you think I've "changed my mind about the leisure complex"?'

Rhea-Jane blinked, frowning. 'But—Jordan said——'

'That I've decided not to follow through on his offer, after all?' Raff finished slowly. 'But that doesn't mean I'm not willing to go into business with someone else.'

Her cheeks had become flushed at the contemptuous way he had said 'his' offer, but her frown deepened at his last remark. 'You're still going ahead with the complex?'

'Of course.' He gave a slight inclination of his head.

He just wasn't interested in going into business with *her* brother, was his unspoken comment!

She moistened her lips. *Now* what was she supposed to say? 'But Jordan's deal,' she finally attempted. 'Surely it was——?'

'I would prefer not to discuss any of that with you,' Raff cut in with cold dismissal.

It was meant as a slap in the face—and it felt like one!

'Now, if you have nothing else to say...?' Raff looked down pointedly at the work on his desk.

'Raff, why won't you at least listen to me?' She went forward pleadingly. 'I know you think I was playing some silly sort of game while I was here, but—but—— Well...'

'Yes?' he prompted hardly.

She swallowed hard. 'I needed a job——'

'With all the Somerville-Smythe millions?' he snorted disbelievingly.

'That's just it,' Rhea-Jane nodded frantically. 'I had——'

He stood up abruptly. 'I'm really not interested, Miss Somerville-Smythe,' he told her coldly. 'And please don't come here trying to interfere in my private business again.' His eyes were narrowed. 'Because it is *my* personal business.'

'You asked me to marry you!' she reminded him out of desperation.

He remained unmoved. 'We all make mistakes.' He began looking through his work, obviously dismissing her.

It was like a physical blow. She knew she had hurt him, but now he was trying to deliberately hurt her. And, although she had half expected it, he was still succeeding.

'It wasn't a mistake, Raff,' she told him with quiet dignity. 'And just for the record——' she paused at the door '—my answer would have been yes.'

She left the room, taking several deep breaths once out in the hallway before walking to the front door, her head back proudly. She might feel like skulking from the house in utter desolation, but she wasn't about to do it.

She managed to leave without bumping into Mrs Howard, which was probably just as well; her emotions were under very tight control, only relaxing slightly once she reached the sanctuary of her car.

And then the tears began to flow, as she acknowledged to herself that she had hoped—and prayed!—Raff would make some attempt to stop her leaving.

She should have known better.

Jordan was still up when she got in and, much as she didn't feel like being seen by anyone just now, she knew she at least owed Jordan an explanation.

He was still in the lounge, although he had obviously eaten his dinner in her absence. He looked up at her expectantly.

Rhea-Jane sighed. 'I failed to talk any sense into Raff—you will have gathered that's where I've been?' She grimaced.

Her brother shrugged. 'I guessed it might have been, yes.'

'He didn't even want to begin to listen to me, I'm afraid,' she revealed dully.

'Rhea——' He broke off as the doorbell rang, and the two of them frowned at each other.

It was ten o'clock at night; who on earth could be calling at this time?

'I'll get it.' Jordan stood up. 'I told Henson we wouldn't need him any more tonight,' he explained before leaving the room.

Rhea-Jane was glad of the respite which gave her the opportunity to gather her shattered emotions. Jordan wasn't stupid, he could easily guess at all the things she hadn't yet told him about her visit to Raff.

She turned as she heard him enter the lounge again. 'Jordan, I——' The words froze in her throat as she saw the man standing at Jordan's side.

Raff...

# CHAPTER TEN

RHEA-JANE, who had been home only a few minutes, couldn't believe Raff was here now. He had to have left Quinlan House almost immediately after her to have got here so quickly.

He was looking at her intently, a nerve pulsing in his cheek, his body filled with nervous energy.

Nervous? *Raff?*

She frowned her puzzlement at his behaviour. What was he *doing* here? Not two hours ago he had left her in no doubt as to how he felt about seeing her again.

'I came to accept your offer,' he finally said, his voice strained. 'If it still stands,' he added uncertainly.

She shrugged. 'I'm sure Jordan is still interested in——'

'I'm not talking about the leisure complex,' Raff cut in harshly. 'A short time ago you told me you would have accepted my marriage proposal if I had let you give me an answer. I've come to accept your acceptance.'

Jordan gave a brief laugh, shaking his head at the two of them. 'I think I had better leave you two alone to talk; it all sounds a little complicated to me.' He turned to leave.

'Oh, but Jordan,' Rhea-Jane stopped him, frowning. 'Don't you want to talk to Raff?'

He glanced at the other man. 'I believe it can wait. It's already waited this long, a few more hours isn't going to make a lot of difference. Besides,' he added teasingly, 'I think the two of you had better sort out this marriage proposal before either of you changes your mind again!'

There was an awkward pause after Jordan had left the room, neither Raff nor Rhea-Jane seeming to know what to say to each other now they were alone.

But Raff had followed her, after all!

It had taken him a little longer than she would have wished, he had put her through fresh heart-break, but he was here.

'I want it clearly understood,' Raff suddenly rasped, 'that I won't touch a penny of your money. You can do what you like with it, but I never want it said I married you for your money.'

'Raff——'

'Because I'm *not* marrying you for your money. In fact——'

'Raff, the way things stand, at this moment in time I don't *have* any money,' she cut in firmly, relieved to see she at last had his full attention. '*That's* why I needed a job, why I—— Oh, God, it's a long story,' she frowned, and then proceeded to tell him of her father's will and the conditions attached to it.

'Damn fool,' Raff muttered, hands thrust into his trouser-pockets.

'Not really.' She grimaced. 'I was a headstrong little madam until I reached eighteen, which was when my father died.'

Raff gave a wry smile. '*Was* a headstrong little madam?' he taunted.

Rhea-Jane returned his smile, a bubble of happiness starting to rise inside her. 'If you think I'm bad now you should have known me three years ago!'

'I would have liked to.' He spoke gruffly. 'Rhea, did you mean what you said earlier, about marrying me?' He stood in front of her, his eyes dark with emotion.

'I meant it,' she nodded.

His hands came up to cup each side of her face. 'Will you do me the honour of marrying me?'

'Oh, yes!' She threw her arms up about his neck, feeling as if she had come home.

They kissed with a thirst that seemed as if it might never be assuaged, over and over again, desire licking through their bodies, both of them trembling with need as they moved slightly apart.

'I've missed you so much these last few days,' Raff admitted gruffly.

'I've hated it.' Rhea-Jane shook her head at the unnecessary suffering they had both been through.

'I just felt such a damned fool,' Raff sighed, grimacing. 'There was I telling this rich and powerful man that I wanted to marry you and he couldn't have you, and you turned out to be his *sister*, and just as rich and powerful!'

'But——'

'I know you aren't really like that, darling,' he smiled down at her. 'If you were, you would have told me several times in the last few weeks exactly what I could do with my job. I know you said you needed the job, but you didn't need my insults too,' he realised self-derisively as she would have protested. 'Once I realised who you really were I——'

'No more self-recriminations.' Rhea-Jane's fingertips on his lips stopped him. 'We're together now. And nothing else will drive us apart, will it?' she added a little anxiously.

His arms tightened about her. 'I promise to try not to behave like a stubborn fool again,' he derided himself.

'And I promise—— Oh, dear!' She gave a sudden frown. 'Now I don't want you to be cross, but I—well, I've agreed to go to a party with Robert on Saturday evening.' She smiled grimly.

Raff's brows rose. 'In that case, I take it he knew all along exactly who you were?'

'I'm afraid so, although I swore him to secrecy,' she hastened to explain.

Raff's mouth quirked. 'Then by all means keep your date with him on Saturday night; it will be a case of "your fiancé came too"! It might be a good idea if Jordan accompanies us as well,' he added thoughtfully.

'Isn't that being a little too cruel?' Rhea-Jane protested laughingly. 'One of you Robert might be able to cope with, two of you just wouldn't be fair!'

Raff shrugged. 'The party he is taking you to is undoubtedly Anita and Jack's anniversary bash; it will be the ideal time to announce our engagement and introduce you and Jordan to the rest of the family,' he explained.

'Your aunt isn't going to be pleased,' Rhea-Jane said soberly, remembering the other woman's coldness towards her.

'Anita's opinion has never been of importance to me before, so I don't see why I should change the habit of a lifetime,' Raff dismissed.

But none of them was quite prepared for Anita Barnes's reaction when she discovered exactly who Rhea-Jane was!

Robert arrived exactly on time to pick her up for their date on Saturday evening, coming to an abrupt halt when she showed him through to the lounge and he came face to face with the other two men.

Raff had more or less moved in over the last couple of days, most of their time having been spent together, Raff more relaxed now, the strain gone from his face, Rhea-Jane knowing that her own face glowed with happiness.

The three men together were enough to take any woman's breath away, all so tall and handsome, and very attractive in their dinner-suits and white shirts. Rhea-Jane felt privileged to be escorted by three such dashing men.

Although Robert still wasn't aware of the fact that she *was* going to be escorted by all three of them! Poor Robert.

'Er—Jordan,' he acknowledged abruptly. 'Raff...' he added in a puzzled voice.

Raff glanced at the plain watch on his wrist. 'I see you can be punctual when a beautiful woman is involved,' he drawled.

'Do you want a drink first or shall we be on our way?' Jordan offered politely, looking at them enquiringly.

Robert's eyes widened. 'We? But——'

'I don't think it's safe to let my fiancée out alone with you,' Raff told him lightly.

'And just to make sure, I'm coming along too,' Jordan explained mockingly.

Raff and Jordan had become a formidable duo the last few days.

From a business angle the partnership was moving along nicely, and, to Rhea-Jane's surprise, on a personal level the two men were becoming the best of friends. Poor Robert didn't stand a chance when they joined forces.

'Fiancée?' Robert looked totally stunned by this piece of information. 'But you didn't say anything the other night when I——'

'Oh, we weren't engaged then,' Raff informed him dismissively, his arm going gently about Rhea-Jane's shoulders as he drew her to his side. 'Rhea had already agreed to go out with you when she consented to be my wife. Of course, she didn't want to let you down at such short notice,' he continued, 'but in the circumstances I don't——'

'Oh, I'll be only too happy to have you accompany us,' Robert assured him hastily, obviously reconciling himself to the situation, perhaps even coming to enjoy it a little; after all, there was his mother to tell the good news to yet! 'You too, Jordan, of course,' he added with largesse.

By the time they reached the Barneses' home Rhea-Jane could see Robert was clearly aware of all the possibilities the next few minutes could bring, and that he was greatly looking forward to the upset the announcement of Raff's engagement to Rhea-Jane was going to cause the rest of the family.

Robert had always known he would never be any more than a friend to Rhea-Jane himself, so she certainly hadn't expected him to be upset on that count, and now he was over the first shock of realising she was going to be his cousin-in-law he was enjoying himself immensely.

The driveway to the Barneses' house was full of Mercedeses, BMWs, Jaguars, and there was even one majestic Rolls-Royce.

'Just a few family friends,' Robert teased as he parked his sporty car out on the road.

'Now you know why I usually avoid these affairs,' Raff muttered to Rhea-Jane as he opened the door for her to step out of the car beside him on the pavement.

'Never mind——' she put her arm through the crook of his, reaching up to kiss him lingeringly on the lips '—the next party you'll have to go to is our wedding.'

'Next month?' he urged gruffly.

They had talked over possible dates for the wedding, and as far as Rhea-Jane and Raff were concerned it could be tomorrow, but Jordan insisted Rhea-Jane should have a proper wedding, with the right amount of notice given to family and friends. He was also adamant that it should be a church wedding, and that he would give her away. Rhea-Jane had teased him about the latter, claiming he would probably force Raff to take her if he could!

'As soon as it can be arranged,' she promised.

'Come on, you two,' Robert urged them impatiently. 'You'll have time for all that later.'

Rhea-Jane laughed softly as they followed him to the house. 'You can hardly wait to make the announcement, can you?' she taunted.

He turned to grin at her. 'No!'

'He's honest, anyway,' Jordan drawled as he brought up the rear.

Raff gave him a meaningful glance. 'You haven't met my aunt Anita yet,' he warned.

'I'm looking forward to it,' Jordan muttered as the door was opened by a young girl of about sixteen who, with her cascade of dark hair, bore a distinct resemblance to Robert.

'So am I,' Raff murmured with amusement.

Anita Barnes was at the centre of what Rhea-Jane could only describe as a 'glittering' crowd of people, the glitter mainly coming from the jewels the middle-aged women were adorned with.

But as soon as Anita saw Robert she excused herself and crossed the room to greet him.

The older woman looked almost pretty tonight, a happy glow to her austere features, an affectionate smile curving her lips as she reached up to kiss her only son. 'Thank you for the beautiful flowers you sent, darling,' she told him warmly. 'Your father is about somewhere...' She gave a dismissive gesture in the direction of the crowded sitting-room behind her.

'I'll see him in a minute,' Robert nodded. 'Right now, Mother, I'd like to——'

'Raff!' Anita had finally seen him standing slightly to one side behind Robert. 'How lovely of you to come,' she added in a rather puzzled voice, as if seeing him here was the last thing she had expected. As it probably was! 'I had no idea you knew——'

'Raff came with me, Mother,' Robert cut in firmly, obviously slightly put out at having his announcement interrupted.

'He did?' Anita looked even more puzzled, knowing the two of them had never really been close.

'And his fiancée,' Robert added softly.

'His——?' Some of the gaiety left Anita Barnes's face, her eyes widening as she saw Rhea-Jane standing at Raff's side. 'But—but you're——'

'Rhea-Jane Somerville-Smythe,' Robert told her with relish.

'No...!' his mother protested weakly, paling.

'And this is her brother——'

'Jordan,' Anita finished faintly, what little colour had been left in her face after Rhea-Jane had been formally introduced fading rapidly as she looked disbelievingly at Jordan. 'How—what—how did you find out? Did she leave you a letter or something like that? And after telling me no one would ever find out!'

She turned accusingly to Rhea-Jane. 'And how dare you sneak into the family home in that way? Jane Smith, indeed!' she snorted. 'And I even commented that weekend on how like Diana you were,' she added self-disgustedly. 'How you must have laughed at me. What did you do it for, that's what I would like to know? There's no money, you know.' She gave a harsh laugh. 'Good God, with the Somerville-Smythe millions why should you be interested in the little there is in the estate? You——'

'Anita!' Jack Barnes cut in forcefully, keeping a tight smile on his lips for the benefit of the audience to this conversation his wife's outburst had aroused, and taking a firm hold of her arm. 'Keep your voice down,' he muttered. 'If there's some problem let's all go into my study and discuss it.'

'But——'

'I think Jack is right, Anita,' Raff put in harshly, his narrowed gaze on his aunt's face.

Rhea-Jane was still stunned by the vehemence of the attack, trembling slightly as Raff's arm moved protectively about her waist. A little outrage on the other woman's part, on account of her deceit, was to be expected, but this was something else!

Jack Barnes's study bore little resemblance to either Raff's or Jordan's, being meticulously tidy, decorated in blues and greys probably of his wife's choosing.

Anita waited only long enough for the door to be closed behind her before turning on, of all people, Jordan this time. 'You have no claim on the family estate, you know,' she scorned. 'Not without running the risk of losing all that Somerville-Smythe left you. And——'

'Anita!' Raff's quietly authoritative voice silenced the tirade. 'Jordan is about to become my brother-in-law.'

'The damned irony of it!' his aunt scoffed disgustedly. 'But then, I suppose for respectability's sake it couldn't have worked out better,' she scorned, turning flashing eyes on Rhea-Jane. 'I should have known you were *her* daughter. The likeness...' She shook her head frustratedly. 'You seem destined to make fools of the men in this family, no matter what the barriers might be!'

Raff moved forward, a nerve pulsing in his cheek. 'Anita, I want you to tell me what the hell you're talking about.'

Her gaze swept scathingly over Rhea-Jane and Jordan. 'Why don't you ask them?'

His gaze didn't waver. 'Because I'm asking you.'

'The little fool was pregnant when she left Quinlan House,' Anita announced distastefully. 'Such an innocent, she got herself pregnant!'

Raff stiffened at Rhea-Jane's side. 'Rhea-Jane is not pregnant,' he said with certainty.

'I'm not talking about *her*,' Anita dismissed scathingly.

'My mother,' Jordan put in huskily. 'She's talking about my mother.'

'You see, he knows what I'm talking about,' Anita pounced triumphantly. 'The little fool didn't want to get rid of it, but by this time Donald's responsibilities lay with Helen, seriously injured after a car accident, and so I offered to help Diana out.'

'How?' Raff demanded harshly.

'Financially,' his aunt snapped. 'Until she could decide what she was going to do about the baby——'

'She kept it,' Jordan put in softly, looking as if he were made of stone, he stood so still.

'She kept *you*, yes.' Anita glared at him. 'What do you want from us now?' she demanded to know. 'You have more now than you would ever have got with Donald as your father!'

It was all so incredible.

It couldn't be true, could it, what Anita Barnes was undoubtedly saying?

Jordan was Raff's *brother*...?

Because that was *exactly* what the other woman was saying.

'They've made a fool of you, Raff,' Anita told him scornfully. 'Little Miss Smith here coming to live in Quinlan House pretending she needed a job, when all the time——'

'Mrs Barnes,' Jordan cut in coldly. 'Fantastic as it might seem, Rhea is a complete innocent in all this.'

'You don't really expect me to believe that?' Anita said scathingly.

'I expect you to believe,' Jordan's voice was at its most dangerously soft, 'that until a few minutes ago neither Rhea nor myself, nor indeed Raff—if his stunned expression is anything to go by—had any idea that Donald Quinlan was...my father.' For all his hauteur, Jordan was obviously dazed by the knowledge, too.

As well he might be—it was incredible!

Anita looked at the three of them, really looked at the three of them for the first time, seeing the truth of Jordan's words there in their faces. 'Oh, God,' she breathed weakly. 'You mean, if I hadn't said anything——'

'As you appear not to have done all these years,' Raff put in harshly.

'—none of you would ever have known,' Anita realised heavily, all the fight seeming to have gone out of her at this realisation. 'Oh, God,' she groaned, grasping the back of the chair that stood in front of the desk. 'When I saw the three of you together I thought you must have somehow found out the truth and come here to confront me with it.'

'I think,' Raff stated firmly, 'that now you have gone this far you had better tell us exactly what that truth is!'

Anita closed her eyes briefly. 'The two of you are really going to be married?' She looked at Rhea-Jane and Raff.

'As soon as it can be arranged,' Raff nodded tersely.

Anita sighed, moving to sit down. 'Then you'll have to know the truth, won't you?' she accepted dully. 'You know, for years Diana and I would avoid being at the same social occasions.' She shook her head. 'And now this!'

Rhea-Jane moved to Raff's side as Anita began to tell them what had happened thirty years ago.

Donald and Helen Quinlan were separated when Diana went to the house as Raff's nanny, Helen having left some months previously with the family chauffeur, claiming she had had enough of the boring life to be had there.

Rhea-Jane felt Raff tense at this, and her hand caressed his arm to show him she understood the dismay this conversation was giving him.

The inevitable had happened. Donald and Diana fell in love.

It was obvious, from Anita's scornful attitude, how she had felt about that!

'You would have approved of that, I dare say?' Anita accused Raff.

'And obviously you wouldn't?' he rasped.

Anita's turned back with derision. 'Diana was even more unsuitable as mistress of Quinlan House than Helen had been!'

'In whose opinion?' Raff challenged.

'You know how I've always felt about Quinlan House,' his aunt defended.

He nodded. 'To the point where no one was good enough to own the estate but you!'

Anita's face was flushed. 'I have as much right——'

'I don't think there's any point in getting involved in personalities, Anita,' Jack Barnes cut in quietly, obviously as stunned by his wife's revelations as the rest of them. 'Just stick to the facts,' he encouraged uncomfortably.

'Very well,' she accepted snappily. 'Helen was injured in a car accident, paralysed from the waist down. Her young lover deserted her without a qualm, apparently,' she added distastefully. 'What could poor Donald do in the circumstances?' she shrugged. 'He suddenly had a wife, the mother of his son, who needed him very badly.'

'And Diana was expecting his child,' Raff bit out, glancing at Jordan, who stood so white-faced and still across the room.

'Donald never knew about that——'

*'What?'* Raff demanded incredulously.

'Diana hadn't had a chance to tell him, when Helen's accident happened,' Anita explained impatiently. 'Donald would never have ignored the existence of his son if he had known about him,' she defended.

'*You* knew,' Raff accused.

'Only because I had seen Diana being ill one day and guessed at the truth,' his aunt told him defensively. 'But she swore me to secrecy...'

'A secret you were only too happy to keep,' Raff taunted harshly.

'Raff!' Jack Barnes cautioned. 'This isn't helping the situation.' He glanced pointedly at Jordan.

'No,' Raff accepted impatiently.

Anita drew in a deep breath. 'Diana decided she had to leave, and because of Helen's presence back in the house Donald had no choice but to accept her decision. I felt almost sorry for Diana, offered to help her out if I could. Then by some fluke she met Somerville-Smythe,' she said disgustedly. 'He couldn't have children of his own, Diana was pregnant but alone; it was a perfect match,' Anita dismissed scathingly.

'But—but that can't be possible,' Rhea-Jane protested that claim. 'There's me!'

Anita looked at her assessingly. 'So there is,' she drawled speculatively. 'And undoubtedly Diana's daughter.'

'And James's daughter, too,' Jordan assured Rhea-Jane calmly, the first time he had spoken since

Anita had begun her explanation. 'I can still remember his behaviour when you were born.' He shook his head. 'There was grief that he had lost Mother, but at the same time he went around the house ranting and raving about it "only being a damned girl after all these years of trying". It didn't make sense to me at the time, but it does now.'

And Rhea-Jane realised now that her father had never forgiven her for 'only being a damned girl'. She had been his first legitimate child, and not the boy he had hoped for! It explained so much of his behaviour towards her.

In fact, all of this explained so much...

'And my father and mother lived the rest of their married life in armed neutrality,' Raff sighed. 'What a damned waste!'

'But your Rhea-Jane wouldn't have been born if Donald and Diana had stayed together all those years ago,' Anita pointed out mockingly.

His arm tightened about Rhea-Jane's shoulders. 'Then for our sakes I can only be glad it worked out the way that it did. But——'

'Mummy!' The young brunette who had originally opened the door to them entered the room after the briefest of knocks. 'Your guests are getting a little restless at your disappearance. After all, it *is* your anniversary party!'

'We're coming now, Chelsea,' her father assured her firmly. 'Anita, Robert, I see it's time we rejoined the party.' He turned to Raff, Jordan, and

Rhea-Jane. 'I think the three of you need to be alone to talk.'

'But, Jack——'

'Anita, I think your silence all these years has caused enough damage,' he reproved his wife in an uncharacteristic show of strength where she was concerned. 'The least we can do now is leave these three young people alone to become accustomed to their change of relationship.'

Anita followed her husband disgruntledly, Robert giving Rhea-Jane an encouraging smile before exiting himself.

Raff and Jordan simply stared at each other once they had been left alone in the silence of the study, and Rhea-Jane recalled all the times she had compared the two men and found them to be so much alike. There was a similarity in their looks too, she realised now, although she had obviously never looked for such a likeness before.

Raff was the first to speak. 'Despite her designs on the Quinlan estate I can't believe Anita kept all that to herself for thirty years.' He shook his head a little dazedly. 'If Rhea-Jane and I hadn't met...'

'But we did,' she reminded him firmly.

'Fate.' Jordan finally spoke. 'It had to happen,' he added convincingly. 'And I have a feeling that Mother would have been very happy about it.'

'Jordan——'

'Would the two of you excuse me?' Jordan interrupted Rhea-Jane in a strained voice as she would have gone to his side. 'I—I need time to be alone and—think about all this.'

'But——'

'Let him go, Rhea.' Raff softly stopped her, watching the other man as he crossed to the door with jerky movements. 'He needs time on his own,' he advised gently after Jordan had left. 'Time to think, as he said. Time to reassess his own position.'

'Oh, Raff.' Rhea-Jane buried her face against his chest. 'I can't believe all this.'

'Then how do you think Jordan feels?' he cajoled. 'Hey, come on, Rhea, it will all work out, you'll see,' he soothed as she trembled.

'How could Anita have kept such a thing to herself all these years?' She shook her head disbelievingly.

'At a guess I would say I was just about right when I suggested she didn't want another child on the scene ruining Robert's chances of one day inheriting the estate,' Raff drawled.

Rhea-Jane looked up at him. 'You know about that?'

'Of course,' he dismissed, some of his own shock starting to fade. 'And until I met you there was never any chance of her plans being foiled.' He smiled down at her.

'And they're foiled twice over now that Jordan knows he's your—brother.' She shook her head. 'That's going to take a little getting used to! And we could have children of our own. I'd like that,' she added wistfully.

'So would I.' Raff's arms tightened about her. 'Maybe once we have a child, whom we can all share in, Jordan included, this change of relationship won't seem so strange to us.'

'Let's hope not,' she said worriedly, knowing what a blow the last half-hour had been to Jordan; in a sense he had lost his own identity. He was going to need all the loving support they could give him over the next few months.

'We'll support each other.' Raff accurately read her concern. 'It will work out, Rhea.'

And when he spoke as positively as that she couldn't doubt him!

## EPILOGUE

'MY MOTHER still isn't pleased,' Robert told her drily.

Rhea-Jane smiled up at him as they danced together in the main salon of the house, the furniture cleared from the room to allow for the fifty or so guests invited to celebrate her twenty-first birthday with her. 'She looks a little happier than she did at the wedding last month.' She glanced across to where Anita Barnes was at least trying to look as if she were enjoying herself—even if she was convincing very few people of the fact!

It had been a busy month, work due to begin on the estate directly after this party, Raff and Jordan partners in the venture, their relationship known only to close family. After all, the marriage between Rhea and Raff had made the two men brothers-in-law, and it had been accepted as natural that the two men should go into business together.

'"Family silver", and all that,' he reminded her.

Rhea-Jane laughed softly. 'She's going to be even more upset when she knows about the baby.'

'My God, you aren't—you don't mean——?' Robert stopped dancing to stare down at her. 'Already?'

'Already,' she glowed up at him, ecstatic with the news. 'Raff is absolutely delighted,' she added happily.

'You certainly didn't waste any time!' Robert looked admiring.

The first night of their honeymoon, to be exact...

Diana's grandchild would be born into the Quinlan family, surrounded by the love of its mother and father.

'If you aren't going to dance with my wife, then I will,' Raff told the younger man, whisking Rhea-Jane away among the other couples dancing before Robert could even think of raising any objections.

She smiled up at him lovingly. 'I think Robert is going to enjoy telling his mother about the baby,' she said with relish.

Raff grinned. 'I wouldn't be at all surprised. I've just had the pleasure of telling Jordan. He wants to know if he's going to be known as Uncle Uncle Jordan, as the baby will make him an uncle twice over?'

'I never thought of that!' she laughed.

Raff sobered slightly. 'He's going to be just fine, you know.'

She looked across to where Jordan was in polite conversation with one of Raff's elderly maiden aunts. There could be no doubting that finding out that Donald Quinlan was his father and not James Somerville-Smythe, as he had always thought, had knocked him for six, but he slowly seemed to be adjusting to the fact.

'We'll make sure he is,' Rhea-Jane agreed warmly.

'God, you're lovely.' Raff looked down at her darkly. 'Do we have to stay here? Can't we just slip away and be alone together?'

She moved closer to him. 'We've been "slipping away to be alone together" the last nine weeks,' she reminded him ruefully. 'We really should make an effort to behave ourselves tonight.'

Marriage suited both of them; theirs was a loving relationship, a true partnership, because although Raff refused to touch any of her money they were, in fact, working together with Jordan on the leisure complex, would run it together once everything was completed: Rhea-Jane had found her niche in life, after all.

'We've made an effort—and failed,' Raff coaxed. 'Come on, Rhea,' he encouraged. 'It *is* your birthday today, darling. I think reaching the age of twenty-one deserves to be celebrated—privately.'

'Later,' she promised.

'Now,' he insisted softly.

Rhea-Jane looked up at him, loving every hard contour of his face, recognising the desire she could see there, knowing that same desire herself.

'Now,' she agreed huskily, knowing that their fated attraction had turned into something so much more special, that it would last a lifetime.

"We'll make sure he is!" Rhea-Jane agreed warmly.

"Are you, really?" Matt looked down at her darkly. "Do we have to stay here? Can't we just go away and be alone together?"

She moved closer to him. "We've been allowed away to be alone together the last three weeks," she reminded him naughtily. "We really should make an effort to behave ourselves tonight."

Marriage, those two of them knew, was a loving relationship, a true partnership. Because although Matt refused to touch any of her money they were in fact working together with Jordan on the leisure complex, would run it together once everything was completed. Rhea-Jane had found a niche in life after all.

"We've made an effort, and failed," Matt teased. "Come on, Rhea," he encouraged. "It is your birthday too, darling. I think reaching the age of twenty-one deserves to be celebrated—privately!"

"Later," she promised.

"Now," he insisted softly.

Rhea-Jane looked up at him, loving every hard contour of his face, recognising the desire she could see there, knowing that same desire herself.

"Now," she agreed huskily, knowing that their [illegible] attraction had turned into something more special, that it would last a lifetime.

# SAVING GRACE

# SAVING GRACE

BY

CAROLE MORTIMER

MILLS & BOON

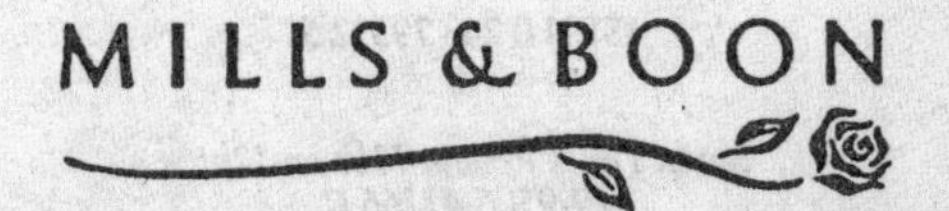

MILLS & BOON LIMITED
ETON HOUSE, 18-24 PARADISE ROAD
RICHMOND, SURREY TW9 1SR

*All the characters in this book have no existence outside the imagination of the author, and have no relation whatsoever to anyone bearing the same name or names. They are not even distantly inspired by any individual known or unknown to the author, and all the incidents are pure invention.*



*First published in Great Britain 1992 by Mills & Boon Limited*


*This edition 1995*

ISBN 0 263 79312 5

*Set in Times Roman 11½ on 12pt.*
*19-9506-41166 C*

*Made and printed in Great Britain*

## PROLOGUE

'OUCH, Tim,' came the wounded cry. 'I told you not to do that!'

Silence followed the protest, and the man who had unwittingly stumbled upon the two hesitated among the undergrowth and bushes that shielded them from his view. And him from theirs.

Jordan had stopped his car and got out on to the roadside on impulse, drawn by the perfect blanket of snow in the field, the fine horse-chestnut trees in the middle of it all still weighed down by their bounty of conkers.

He wasn't even sure what had made him stop, didn't normally notice his surroundings that much. But even the most hardened cynic—and some would say he was one!—couldn't remain untouched by the beauty of the Lake District, even in November, and Jordan had finally succumbed to the perfection of this snowy-white field, pulling his car over to the side of the road before crossing over the verge and walking across the crunchy snow.

'Tim, if you do that again, we're going home,' that voice complained huskily.

He certainly hadn't expected to stumble across a pair of lovers in the snow! Surely they could have chosen somewhere a little more comfortable—and dry!—for their meeting?

So much for his impulse. What was that saying—he couldn't remember it exactly, but something to do with 'stopping along the way to smell the roses'? The season was all wrong but, even so, the first time in years he had done something so completely out of character, and he almost fell over a couple of lovers in a passionate tryst!

He decided to chance a glance at the couple, trapped as he was among the foliage. He didn't want to be caught here if the couple decided to go any further in their lovemaking!

Identical red bobble-hats were pulled low over their ears to keep out the cold, blue duffel coats buttoned up to the throat, blue jeans tucked into black wellington boots.

The two *boys* might almost have been twins except that the one on the right was taller by at least a foot. But the faces beneath the red woollen hats were both finely drawn, almost delicate-looking, a smattering of freckles across small pointed noses. Obviously the two of them were brothers. The village of Grasmere wasn't too far from here, so they had probably escaped up here to play.

As the taller of the two boys held out a conker suspended on a piece of string, the reason for his earlier protests became obvious: his opponent, now wielding a slightly larger conker, didn't pull his punches!

Jordan felt a constriction in his chest, a yearning for—for what? he scorned himself. How could he possibly feel wistful for something that had never been his?

The larger of the brothers had his conker smashed into pieces with the first forceful strike this time, shaking his head when the younger suggested they thread another conker on to his string and have a re-match. From the look of the broken conkers at their feet, the older boy had suffered a humiliating defeat.

He pocketed the knotted string before bending down to pick up a handful of snow, quickly moulding it into shape before launching it at his unsuspecting brother.

The snowball fight that followed was fast and furious, with both opponents collapsing into each other's arms in a fit of the giggles after five minutes, their clothing, hats, and faces covered in melting snow, mittens protecting their hands from the worst of the cold.

Once again Jordan felt that tug inside, these two young boys' pleasure in each other's company evoking feelings of deprivation inside him, feelings he had tried so hard to fight over the last two years, but which were becoming more and more difficult, rather than easier, to dampen down as time went on.

If he was honest, and it seemed he had to be, that had been one of the reasons he had wanted to get away for a while. Rhea-Jane and Raff were wonderful, couldn't have made him feel more wanted, but he was still a third person, who had to be an intrusion into the intimacy of their lives.

So he had chosen to come away on this business trip himself rather than sending one of his assistants. It was probably going to be a waste of his time, but it was a valid excuse to get away at least. He had even felt guilty about needing the excuse, knowing it was ridiculous, but Rhea-Jane, his well-meaning young sister, tended to be overprotective of him since she had married Raff, not wanting him to be on his own now that she had moved out of the home they had shared in London since their parents died. She had even gone so far—horror of horrors!—as to introduce him to several women she thought might make him a suitable wife.

He *didn't* want a wife, suitable—whatever that might be!—or otherwise!

But he wanted *something*, he was willing to acknowledge that. Something. And he didn't know what it was—just knew he had an aching inside of him, an emptiness that couldn't be filled by Rhea-Jane and Raff, or their darling daughter Diana, and certainly not by some woman presented to him as suitable wife material!

These two boys, as they played together so innocently, somehow had, for all Jordan's wealth and comfortable lifestyle, so much more than he did. But at thirty-two he could hardly expect that same anticipation of the promise of the future that such youth was bound to have. Indeed, he wondered if he had ever had it.

The two boys were brushing the snow from themselves now, their faces aglow, grinning with the satisfaction of the battle.

The older boy glanced at a watch that seemed to be hidden between the cuff of his duffel coat and the snow-damp mitt; hopefully it was a waterproof one, or he would be in trouble when he got home!

'We had better get back.' He spoke in a voice that, although husky, didn't seem to have broken yet, but perhaps he was a little young for that.

The younger boy made a face. 'Oh, do we have to?' he protested.

His brother looked regretful. 'You know we do.'

'I suppose so.' The younger one sighed, not at all enthusiastic.

'Come on,' the older boy encouraged brightly. 'I'll race you back!'

The challenge had no sooner been offered than it was taken up, the smaller boy turning—luckily in the opposite direction to where Jordan still stood!—and running off towards the village.

Jordan watched as his brother deliberately gave him a good head start before giving chase.

Jordan was finally able to emerge from his hiding-place, well aware that in London his behaviour would have been looked upon with suspicion. Who would understand the explanation that he had been gazing upon a stolen childhood?

Was that really what he was looking for? Of course not, he chided himself. That time had gone and could never be given back to him.

As the two boys had gone by the time he looked in the direction they had run off to. Except for their footprints in the snow, the disturbed snow from their snowball fight, they might never have been here at all.

Except that seeing them had had an effect on Jordan that couldn't be dismissed as easily. That aching emptiness inside him was becoming so vast it was starting to control him rather than the other way around.

The last thing he felt like doing was going on with the business of visiting, and being charming to, the aged spinster Miss Grace Brown. She was sure to be a fluffy old dear who couldn't even begin to deal with a businessman of his calibre, and the idea of talking her into selling the 'ancient pile' that had probably been in her family for generations, so that he might make it into a leisure complex, somehow now left a nasty taste in his mouth. Most of the people who knew him—or thought they did—wouldn't recognise this emotion in him at all, would think he had gone soft. And maybe he had.

He gave one last wistful glance in the direction the two boys had taken, before turning on his heel and walking purposefully back towards his parked car, the mantle of Jordan Somerville-Smythe firmly back in place.

Or almost...

## CHAPTER ONE

MISS GRACE BROWN, when she came in answer to the jingling bell that could be heard in the depths of the house after he had pulled the bell-rope outside, was exactly as Jordan had imagined her to be from the letters she had sent to his solicitors in reply to their correspondence concerning selling her home: small and delicate, with fluffy white hair caught back in an untidy bun at her nape, sparkling—but faded in colour—blue eyes in a face that had once been beautiful, the pink twin-set accompanied by the customary string of pearls about her throat, her skirt the expected tweed, as her shoes were the expected brown brogues.

The house was as he had imagined too from the reports—huge, old, and dilapidated. But it did have extensive grounds, and a house could be renovated, made to be what you wanted it to be. As in a leisure complex...

At the moment this elderly lady ran it as a sort of boarding house, although she seemed to have only two permanent guests, with the occasional casual visitor during the summer months. There was hardly enough income there, his sources reported, to keep the place ticking over on a day-to-day basis. By the look of the threadbare carpet in the hallway behind Grace Brown, and the emulsioned rather than papered walls, that income didn't keep things 'ticking over' very well.

'Good afternoon.' She smiled up at him brightly, her movements birdlike, even her voice light and a little girlish. 'Come in.' She opened the door wider, turning to walk down the hallway where a light already glowed in the gloomy interior despite the efforts of the bright emulsion. 'We've been expecting you, of course.' She shot him another smile over her shoulder.

'You have?' Jordan frowned; David, his personal assistant, had already made the blunder of misplacing their main file on Charlton House and its inhabitants—if he had now also warned them of Jordan's arrival here, then Jordan had seriously misjudged him. Arriving here unannounced had been his only advantage without the benefit of that file!

'Do come in.' She turned at the end of the hallway to reveal a little reprovingly, 'You're letting in a draught!'

Suitably chastened, Jordan entered the house and quickly closed the door behind him. It wasn't much warmer inside than it had been out!

Miss Brown waited for him to reach her before turning into a sitting-room, a room that was shabbily welcoming, the worn sofa and four armchairs of differing patterned brocade, the carpet in here even more threadbare than the one in the hallway, in a pattern of faded pink and cream flowers.

There was too much furniture in the room, several tables, one with a chess-set on top of it, the pieces left about the board, as if the two players had been disturbed mid-game. And yet there was no one else in the room.

A tall old-fashioned standard-lamp stood beside the chair nearest the fireplace, alight, but really adding little to the illumination of the room. An old piano, its dark brown wood scourged with scratches, stood against one wall, the lid raised above the keys, a music sheet open on its stand, again giving the impression that someone had been playing it recently but been disturbed.

A fire gleamed in the darkened fireplace, logs crackling warmly.

It was a room totally unlike any Jordan had ever been in before, and yet just being here gave him a warm feeling inside, as if he had finally come home...

Miss Brown was looking up at him curiously. 'You're very late, you know.' She made it a statement rather than a reprimand, smiling sweetly.

Jordan was still dazed at the strange feeling that had enveloped him as soon as he entered the house, the cut-throat world he existed in in London fading into the background as if it had never been.

'I am?' he said uninterestedly.

'Very.' She frowned. 'Nick was sure you weren't coming,' she added sadly.

Jordan drew his attention from the yellow flames in the fireplace with effort, resisting, for the moment at least, the sudden urge he had to stretch out in one of the armchairs and fall asleep. 'Nick?' he prompted, fighting to control these feelings of lethargy that was such anathema to his usual character; he hadn't taken a holiday in years, let alone felt lethargic!

She nodded, giving him a coy smile. 'He boards here,' she explained trilly. 'But he's a little shy about meeting new people. He was playing the piano until you rang the doorbell. And he plays so well too,' she added wistfully.

Jordan instantly felt as if he had deprived this sweet little woman of a special treat, realising now that Nick must be one of the permanent boarders here. 'I'm sorry——'

'Don't be.' She dismissed the mood of melancholy that had swept over her as quickly as it had first appeared, smiling again now, her emotions erratic, to say the least, Jordan decided.

His solicitors hadn't mentioned that Miss Grace Brown, as well as owning Charlton House, was also a little strange!

'Nick will soon get used to you,' she told him confidently, squeezing his arm reassuringly.

Jordan gave a frown; he didn't think he was going to be here long enough for anyone to 'get used' to him.

Which was a pity...

Even Rhea-Jane, who, as sisters went, was one of the best, couldn't help but be surprised at the unexpected feelings of homecoming he felt in this house, wouldn't understand his feelings at all. He wasn't altogether sure *he* did!

He straightened his shoulders beneath the navy blue overcoat that was accepted wear among his contemporaries in town, but which, he realised, looked far too formal here. 'If we could get down to business——'

'Oh, you don't want to talk to me about that,' the tiny birdlike woman told him teasingly.

Jordan's frown deepened. No one had told him that Grace Brown had a business adviser. According to the last report he had, *she* had flatly refused to consider any offer for her home; in fact she hadn't even wanted to hear about it.

It seemed that someone had been a little remiss all round concerning Miss Grace Brown and Charlton House!

She picked up some letters from one of the coffee-tables. 'You'll need to talk to Grace about that,' she smiled. 'I have to take down the post that arrived today, so if she's in the kitchen I'll tell her you're here.'

Only one thing in that twittering speech really mattered to Jordan. '*You* aren't Grace Brown?' He hadn't spent the last ten minutes talking to a complete stranger, had he—a stranger, moreover, who was 'strange', in the nicest possible way, of course, but definitely a little odd, if harmless enough?

'Goodness, no!' She laughingly dismissed the very thought of that. 'Although it's nice of you to think so, Mr Gregory.'

Mr Gregory? Who the hell was——?

'I'm Jessica Amery.' She held out one tiny hand to be shaken. 'But everyone calls me Jessie.'

The other permanent boarder here, Jordan realised frustratedly, deliberately keeping the grip light, afraid he might crush her fragile bones in his much stronger hand. He shook his head. 'I think there must be——'

'You know,' she gave him a rather piercing look from beneath silvery brows, releasing her hand slowly, 'I always tend to judge a man by his handshake.'

Oh, dear, and his rather limp grasp hadn't found favour, he was sure.

But once again she had interrupted him when he had been about to correct her mistake concerning his own identity; he didn't know who this Mr Gregory was, but he certainly wasn't him. Although the mistake in identity at least explained a lot of her earlier remarks; they hadn't been meant for him at all, but for the absent Mr Gregory. The other man would probably find himself being addressed as Mr Somerville-Smythe when he did at last arrive, just to add to the confusion!

And no one deserved to be saddled with that name unless they had to be, Jordan thought with bitterness.

'Everyone calls me Jordan,' he invited dully, wondering how long before, or indeed if, he was going to be reconciled to the past.

'Jordan,' Jessie repeated brightly. 'We all wondered what the "J" stood for,' she nodded.

Whether from approval, he wasn't sure. But the mix-up in names seemed to be getting a little out of hand. 'I——'

'Ah, I think that must be Grace now.' Jessie tilted her head to one side as she listened to the slamming of the front door. 'I thought she was in the kitchen preparing dinner. That means the meal is going to be late.' She frowned. 'Unless we're having salad. But we wouldn't be having salad on a day like this. I wonder——'

'Jessie. Miss Amery,' Jordan cut in a little impatiently. Really, Jessie was charming, in small doses, and he was sure the subject of what she was being served for dinner was of interest to her; she didn't give the impression that her life was a hot-bed of new and wild experiences. But this habit she had of wandering from the point could be more than a little irritating, especially when because of it he had spent the last ten minutes believing he was talking to someone else entirely! 'I think perhaps I ought to meet Miss Brown,' he suggested pointedly.

'Grace?' Jessie blinked a little dazedly. 'Is she here?'

'She just came in—remember?' Jordan prompted as muffled voices could be heard in the hallway, making a move towards the door.

'So she did,' the elderly lady recalled happily. 'She will be so pleased you've arrived at last.'

And he would be glad when he could talk to someone who would understand the mistake there had been about his identity!

'Grace? Grace!' Jessie reached the door ahead of him, quick on her feet in spite of her years, stepping lightly out into the hallway. 'He's here! And we were all wrong—his name is Jordan,' she announced excitedly.

Quite what Grace Brown's initial reaction to this was Jordan had no idea, the other woman still being out in the hallway. He could only hope Miss Grace Brown wasn't as scatty as the irrepressible Jessie, or he was going to be explaining himself forever!

His eyes widened incredulously as it wasn't an elderly lady who entered the room but a young boy of about seven with a blaze of bright red hair, his gaze distinctly critical as he looked up at Jordan.

'Jordan!' he finally said disgustedly. 'I said you were a Jeremy. Jessie said it had to be John——'

'Because it's one of my favourite names,' the elderly lady explained dreamily.

'Nick chose James,' the young boy continued as if he hadn't been interrupted at all, probably used to the elderly lady's habit of deviating from the real point of the conversation, Jordan decided.

Jordan had no idea who this young boy was, but he had an appealingly impish face beneath that startling red hair, his eyes more grey than blue. 'And what did Grace—Miss Brown—think?' he prompted drily, prepared, for the moment, to humour the little boy. His friends in London would be astounded at his forbearance, he realised, but his time since he had arrived here had already been one of the strangest he had ever spent; why should it stop now?

'I refused to play guessing games with something as important as a person's name,' remarked a husky voice from the doorway.

Miss Grace Brown at last!

No, not Grace Brown but the elder brother of the two Jordan had been watching less than an hour ago...

The wellington boots had gone now, showing the denims tucked into thick black woollen socks. But the duffel coat was the same, and so was the red bobble-hat, the elfin features that so matched the younger boy's in the room the same, too, Jordan now realised.

A glance at the little boy revealed the red woollen hat stuffed into one of the pockets of his duffel coat, the dark mittens into the other.

Then *where* was Grace Brown? he wondered frustratedly. Even as he tried to look past the elder brother out into the hallway behind him, the boy lifted a hand and removed the red woollen hat. Jordan couldn't hold back his gasp as a riot of deep red curls fell down about the slender shoulders to surround the tiny features covered with that smattering of freckles.

Not a boy at all, but a young girl, a girl so startlingly lovely that she took Jordan's breath away!

'But if I had made a guess——' the girl came further into the room, dark grey eyes thoughtful '—I would have said—Joshua!' she announced with satisfaction.

Not just any young girl, it appeared, but *Miss Grace Brown*!

And not an elderly lady either, but a young woman of probably nineteen or twenty. He had *assumed* from the old-fashioned name, and the circumstances under which she lived, that Grace Brown was elderly. But he realised now that no one had actually said she was.

This young woman was ethereally lovely, long dark lashes surrounding the most beautiful smoky grey eyes he had ever seen, red hair so thick and luxuriantly lovely that Jordan had to clench his hands into fists at his sides to stop himself from reaching out and burying them in that fiery magnificence.

This simply wasn't like him. Oh, he had his relationships with women, beautiful women, but they had always been convenient arrangements for both of them, with very little actual emotion involved. He could never before remember an instantaneous response like this to any woman, let alone one who looked so delicately young.

He didn't know what was happening to him!

He didn't look like a Joshua, Grace had to admit ruefully. Not that she was sure *what* a Joshua would look like, but this tall, distinguished man with his expensively tailored clothing, short-styled dark hair and cobalt-blue eyes somehow wasn't a Joshua.

Because he was a Jordan. Although he looked more than capable of 'knocking down a few walls' if he chose to!

Grace looked at him consideringly. A stern man, she would guess by the harsh lines beside his nose and mouth. But forthright too, she would say, from the directness of that dark blue gaze. He had beautiful eyes, the darkest blue, and yet with that intense light behind them. She had seen a car that colour once, had commented on the beauty of its colour to Timothy; he had been absolutely disgusted with her for liking the *colour* of the car and not realising it was a Porsche! What she knew about cars, the expensive kind or any other, could be written on the back of a postage stamp.

Although as she and Timothy had walked up to the house a few minutes ago even she had recognised the sleek green model parked outside in the driveway as a Jaguar; even she knew what a Jaguar looked like. It was because Timothy had spotted the car that the two of them had come in the front door at all; they would usually have gone down the back stairs straight into the kitchen. But they had both been curious as to who their visitor was.

Jordan.

*Why* was he here?

There was something in the depths of his eyes, she realised compassionately, that same bewilderment she had known after the death first of her mother giving birth to Timothy, and then of her father eighteen months ago from a heart-attack. Jordan had known a similar loss; she could sense that.

He also looked a little dazed at the moment!

Jessie: darling, muddle-headed Jessie. Grace smiled fondly at the elderly lady; what had she been doing with the poor man while he waited for them to come home?

'What are we having for dinner, Grace?' Jessie looked at her anxiously.

Ah, so that was what they had been discussing. Or, at least, one of the things, Grace correctly read from Jordan's rueful expression. She knew herself how erratic Jessie's conversation could be, but she was a dear, none the less. And she did have a passion for her food. And why not, when her only child, a son, only ever came to see her with the intention of trying to talk her into going into a home? Food didn't hurt her. Grace smiled at the elderly lady affectionately. 'I put a casserole in the oven before I went to collect Tim from school,' she assured her.

Jessie's face instantly brightened. 'You're such a warm, considerate girl, Grace. There you are, Mr Gregory——'

'Jordan,' he put in abruptly.

Grace looked at him concernedly; he really was very tense. And extremely attractive, those dark blue eyes mesmerising, she had to admit. But also filled with that bewildered pain and disillusionment...

'Oh, thank you, Jordan.' Jessie clasped his hand warmly. 'And you must call me Jessie,' she invited with a coy smile. 'And how lovely for you, now that you've at last arrived, that you should get here in time for dinner. Grace is such a wonderful cook,' she added effusively.

'Chicken casserole is hardly cordon bleu, Jessie,' Grace said drily. 'I'm sure Mr—Jordan,' she amended at his sharp-eyed look, 'is used to much more exciting fare——'

'How long before dinner is ready, Grace?' Timothy cut in, his eyes bright.

She eyed her little brother suspiciously; he wasn't usually concerned with punctuality where meals were concerned. 'Half an hour or so...' she told him questioningly.

He turned excitedly to the tall man now standing beside the fireplace. 'Would you take me for a drive in your car before dinner?'

'Timothy!' she gasped incredulously, looking awkwardly across the room at Jordan.

Her brother looked slightly rebellious. 'But I've never been in a Jag, and——'

'Jaguar, Timothy,' she corrected quietly, still a little taken aback at this uncharacteristic show of bad manners; obviously the lure of the thought of a drive in a Jaguar superseded everything she had tried to teach him about politeness! 'And I'm sure Jordan would much rather go up to his room and unpack before dinner.' She turned to the man as he watched them so intently. 'The room has been aired, even though you are two days later than you expected to be in your original letter——'

'I——'

'But, of course, I realise you weren't a hundred per cent sure about the twenty-fifth as your day of arrival.' She smiled to take away any rebuke he might have read into her earlier words. 'I'm not that strict about arrival dates,' she said, and shook her head. 'And I don't exactly have people beating a path to the door this time of year!' Or the rest of the year really, although they did pick up the occasional summer visitor looking for solitude rather than luxurious accommodation;

the latter she certainly couldn't offer here! But Jordan was a 'winter visitor' in search of solitude.

Jordan looked at her wordlessly for several seconds, blue gaze piercing, flickering away with a vulnerability that was vaguely endearing. He seemed undecided. Which Grace guessed was an unfamiliar emotion to him. He had aroused her curiosity about him in spite of herself.

'Oh, please take me for a drive in your car!' Timothy was the one to break the silence, gazing imploringly up at Jordan. 'I've never been in a Jaguar before,' he added, eyes wide with anticipation, and Grace could already hear the tales he would tell his schoolfriends about the adventure in the morning.

Jordan was looking almost wistfully at Timothy now, Grace thought, her own frown thoughtful. He was an enigma, this man Jordan. And she felt an intense curiosity to know more about him.

'Did you enjoy your snowball fight earlier?' He was talking to Timothy now, his tone gentle.

Grace looked at him sharply, wondering how he could possibly know—she hadn't realised anyone had watched them earlier, but how else could this man know about the snowball fight if he hadn't actually seen them have it?

Timothy gave the grin of the victor. 'Grace isn't bad at snowballing, for a girl,' he shrugged.

'Timothy Brown, you only won at all because you played dirty and put one down my neck!' she rebuked good-naturedly.

Jordan watched her intently. 'You run this house alone, Miss Brown?'

'Grace,' she corrected as automatically as he had earlier, knowing that what he was really asking was where her parents were, that she should have the responsibility of Timothy plus the running of a big house like this one. From the intentness of his gaze she had a feeling he had intended disarming her with the unexpectedness of the question, knew herself matched with a sharp intelligence. 'I manage,' she dismissed, her gaze steady.

Jordan met that gaze. 'I'm sure you do,' he acknowledged quietly.

She straightened. 'And right now I had better take off the rest of these damp things and finish cooking dinner,' she said brightly, knowing that although the two of them knew little about each other they at least understood each other; Grace was here 'managing' this house because circumstances had dictated that she do so, and because they had she did it with all the love and care that she could. Jordan was here for reasons of his own, but those reasons owed just as much to circumstances as her own.

Timothy was still looking up at Jordan with hopefully expectant eyes. Grace knew that look only too well, had succumbed to the pleading there too many times herself not to know it. And she could see Jordan wasn't unmoved by the pleading over-big eyes either.

'If you would like to bring your things in from the car I'll show you up to your room...?' she politely prompted Jordan, removing her scarf.

He was looking at her again now, indecision in the dark blue depths of his eyes. She smiled at him, knowing instinctively that the vulnerability she sensed in him wasn't a part of himself he felt able to cope with.

Grace doubted he would be able to cope with her response to that either; he didn't look as if he very often had women he was barely acquainted with throw their arms around him because they felt an overwhelming need to comfort him in whatever pain it was he was suffering!

There was an answering flicker of warmth in the dark blue depths of his eyes, although he barely smiled in response to hers. She wondered what he would look like if he ever laughed. Younger, was her instant guess. He had an air about him of someone much older than the early thirties she guessed him to be. Too much responsibility at too young an age, she surmised, wondering if she had a similar air herself.

She didn't think so, because she wasn't unhappy. And this man obviously was. Very unhappy.

'I haven't brought much with me,' he finally answered in measured tones. 'But I'll bring it in after I've taken Tim for his drive,' he added decisively.

Any reply Grace might have made to this remark was drowned out by Timothy's whoop of delight and his cries for them to go right now, this very second. Just in case Jordan should change his mind, Grace guessed with affection.

Jordan stood across the room with Timothy's hand clinging determinedly to his much larger one, awkwardly so, as if the trust in him this young child showed came as a shock. 'Is that all right with you?' He looked at Grace enquiringly.

'Of course,' she nodded, smiling at her brother as he beamed his excitement up at her. 'Behave yourself,' she warned indulgently.

He replied in the affirmative, but in truth it was obvious he barely heard her remark, his thoughts already transfixed on driving in the back seat of a Jaguar. Compared to the old Mini Grace drove him about in he would feel like royalty, the leather interior of the car parked outside being plush to say the least.

She watched them walk to the door together, the tall dark-haired man, and the small red-haired boy who was the centre of her world.

She had known from the day her father died so suddenly and left Timothy in her sole care that she would always do everything she could to ensure that her brother's world would be as secure as she could make it for him. As she stood and watched Jordan and Timothy walk out to the car side by side she had a vague feeling of disquiet, as if *her* world would never be quite the same again from this moment on...

## CHAPTER TWO

WHAT the hell was he *doing*?

He should have told them exactly who he was the moment he realised the mistake there had been over identity. But something had held him back from doing that. Jordan deliberately pushed the image of dark grey eyes surrounded by long dark lashes to the back of his mind.

He was here, in Grace Brown's home—a Grace Brown who had turned out to be far from the elderly spinster he had expected to meet—under a false identity, and false pretences.

He looked about the room he had been given for his stay—or rather, J. Gregory had been given! It was as worn and faded as the rest of the house, but it was clean and comfortable, and somehow homely and welcoming.

There was another flowered carpet on the floor, green this time, cream-coloured paper on the walls, and Jordan hadn't seen a candlewick bed-spread like the one on the double bed that took up most of the room for years, the convenience of duvets not seeming to have entered this old-fashioned household.

The bathroom was down the hallway, something he definitely wasn't used to, and yet he felt at home here already. Rhea and Raff were going to think he had taken leave of his senses, but he intended staying on here.

He would have to telephone them, of course, otherwise they were likely to send out a search-party after a couple of days. And, as he was here as a 'Mr Gregory', the last thing he wanted was for them to do that.

Mr J. Gregory...

The other man had obviously changed his mind about coming here after all, and hadn't bothered to let Grace Brown know that. At least, Jordan hoped that was what had happened. He was going to look worse than ridiculous if the real Mr Gregory should turn up after all. Especially as he would then have to tell them who he really was.

Oh, hell! He should leave here now, he knew he should. And yet somehow he couldn't do it, felt at peace for the first time in a very long time. Over two years, in fact.

Two years... Since he had discovered the man whom he had always believed to be his father wasn't his father after all.

It had been the merest chance that his sister Rhea had met Raff Quinlan in the first place. Fate, Rhea called it.

And the secrets that had emerged after that meeting had shattered Jordan's world forever.

Rhea was married to Raff now, and they had a beautiful daughter Diana, with Rhea's red hair and Raff's serious charm, but for the last two years Jordan had been avoiding facing the confusion and pain he felt about even his own identity. He wasn't really Jordan Somerville-Smythe, had no right to that name, and yet, if he wasn't Jordan Somerville-Smythe, who was he?

He wasn't sure any more. The Lake District, this house, seemed a strange place to begin to find the answer to that, and yet this was the first time he had felt truly relaxed in years. He couldn't leave now even if he wanted to.

Besides, he excused his own actions, his curiosity had been well and truly aroused now. The boy, Tim, had talked incessantly when Jordan had taken him for the promised drive in his car, but he hadn't seemed to find the fact that he lived in this huge house with his sister, Jessie Amery, and the elusive Nick—the other man had still been absent when Jordan had returned with Tim a short time ago—interesting enough to go into in great detail.

It was a very strange household for a young woman of the nineteen or twenty Jordan had guessed Grace to be. A girl of those tender years should be out enjoying herself with other people her age, but Grace didn't give the impression she in the least resented the responsibilities she had.

In fact, she had a calmness and serenity that Jordan envied...

* * *

What a strange mixture of contradictions her new boarder was, Grace mused as she set the dinner out on the big tray ready to take upstairs to the dining-room—where hopefully Timothy would have laid the table for their meal by now.

Jordan looked a stern, uncompromising man, as if he wouldn't suffer fools gladly, and yet he had given in to the whim of a child good-naturedly enough. Timothy hadn't yet been able to stop his bubbling excitement over being driven about in a Jaguar, his face aglow still with the pleasure of it.

When she had shown Jordan into his room a short time ago she had been quite able to see its clean shabbiness through his eyes, knew from the very look of him that this couldn't be the class of place he was used to staying in.

And yet she also knew, instinctively, that he didn't want to leave.

She only hoped his presence here wasn't going to be too disruptive to the rest of the household, wondered, curiously, what he and Nick were going to make of each other.

Jessie was already seated at the dining-room table when Grace entered with the laden tray, and Grace knew it wasn't that the elderly lady was particularly greedy, or even that she would eat a lot of the meal anyway—her appetite was birdlike—it was just that mealtimes were the most sociable times of the day for Jessie, who spent a lot of her time alone. Nick kept to his room a lot, Timothy was at school during the day, and Grace had her part-time job at the library to go to every morning during the week and had work to catch up on when she was at home. Breakfast and dinner were really the only times all of them were together.

She smiled at Jessie. 'Ready at la——' She broke off with a start as Jordan stepped out of the shadow of the bay-window across the room, her smile returning as she realised who it was.

He still wore the trousers to the suit he had been wearing earlier, and the cream shirt, but he had pulled on an Aran sweater over the latter, emphasising the fitness of his body, and darkening his skin.

From the small overnight bag he had finally brought in with him Grace had a feeling the Aran jumper was the only other clothing he had brought with him, giving the impression he hadn't intended staying long. The thought made her frown.

'Is something wrong?'

She looked up to find Jordan watching her intently, doing her best to shake off the sudden heaviness that seemed to have descended over her mood. It was ridiculous, she didn't even know this man, so why should the thought of his leaving have any effect on her?

Because he was another of her lame ducks, her father would have pointed out affectionately. As a child she had always been bringing home birds and animals that had been abandoned or injured, taking care of them until they could fend for themselves.

It had been a trait her father had believed she had carried on into adulthood, pointing out Jessie as a prime example of her compassion. And maybe she was, Jessie's son Peter making no secret of where he thought she should live, but Jordan hardly fitted into the same category. Although perhaps he did in a different way; she didn't think she was wrong about the emotional pain she glimpsed in his eyes at unguarded moments.

'No, nothing,' she answered him brightly, straightening. 'I'm glad you seem to be finding your way about the house so easily.' She had a feeling there was very little that this man wasn't completely in control of in his life!

He shrugged, as if to say he had found no difficulty with the problem. As, indeed, he probably hadn't, Grace acknowledged ruefully.

She frowned as she set the food dishes down the centre of the table so that they might each help themselves to what they wanted of the casserole and vegetables. 'Timothy seems to have missed laying a place——'

'Nick won't be coming down to dinner,' Jessie told her disappointedly—Nick being a favourite with her, she had tidied her hair and powdered her cheeks before coming down for the meal.

Grace couldn't say she was surprised at Nick's decision, had half guessed what would happen when he had made himself scarce on Jordan's arrival.

She put one of the warmed plates back on the tray, starting to take the lids off the steaming bowls of food. 'Timothy?' she called as she began, absently, to spoon food on to the plate she had put back on the tray.

'I'm here, Grace.' He came bouncing into the room with his usual energy.

'Hands washed?' She arched dark brows teasingly.

'Yep,' he grinned.

She glanced up with a conspiratorial smile for the other adults in the room, noticing as she did so that Jordan was watching her as she put the chicken casserole and accompanying vegetables on the plate. 'For Nick,' she explained awkwardly, instantly wondering at this need she felt to explain herself to this man. 'He—often eats alone,' she added dismissively. 'Although I don't make a habit of providing food in the rooms,' she was quick to add, not wanting there to be two of them she ran up and down the stairs after. Nick was different.

Jordan nodded non-committally. 'Then I should take it up while it's hot.'

For some reason she felt irritated as she carried the tray up the stairs to Nick's room. It hadn't been so much what Jordan had said as the way he had said it. A man accustomed to giving orders and expecting them to be obeyed unquestioningly.

As she had just done!

Jordan was feeling more and more curious about the man Nick. Timothy had mentioned the other man a couple of times when they had gone for their drive before dinner—nothing specific, but it was significant enough, it seemed to Jordan, that the other man should have been mentioned at all.

And now Grace was running up the stairs with the other man's meal on a tray because he had decided he 'wasn't coming down to dinner'.

It was the idea of Grace having to do such menial tasks that Jordan found he didn't like. Which was ridiculous; *he* was probably the reason the elderly man had disappeared into his bedroom in the first place!

He gave Grace a rueful smile when she came back into the room to have her own dinner, although even as he did so he realised she couldn't possibly know the stupidity of his thoughts. The smile felt unfamiliar, and he realised it was the first relaxed smile he had given anyone for months. By the widening of Grace's calm grey eyes that was an easily recognisable fact!

'Could I use your telephone after the meal?' He decided to change the subject altogether, knowing he would have to telephone Rhea and Raff tonight or they would worry he hadn't arrived safely. He had only brought an overnight case with him—a fact he was sure Grace had noticed earlier!—and so the other couple would be expecting him back some time tomorrow at the latest. He would have to let them know of his change of plan, of his intention of taking a holiday in the Lake District.

'Of course,' Grace confirmed instantly. 'Timothy, don't do that with your potato, dear,' she turned to scold gently.

Jordan watched her firm gentleness with the small boy, realising it was an occupation he could become fond of.

He must be getting senile!

Maybe he needed this holiday more than he had realised. He certainly was in a reflective mood today, for him.

But the food was good, even if the conversation did consist mainly of Timothy's questioning as to his opinion on one fast car after another. Never having owned any of the exclusive models the little boy mentioned, his opinion was an unlearned one, much to Timothy's obvious disgust. He could see by the end of the meal that he had fallen a couple of notches in the little boy's estimation.

Strangely, that mattered to him very much...

His experience with children was limited to his niece Diana, but, as she was only fifteen months old, and the admiration he felt for her was more than returned, it wasn't a very good example.

Timothy, for all that he was only seven years old—another snippet of information he had given Jordan on that short drive out!—was an intelligent and discerning little boy. And, for reasons Jordan couldn't even begin to explain to himself, he wanted the two of them to get on together.

Although if he stayed on at Charlton House long, enjoying Grace's delicious cooking, he was going to put on weight!

Even at the leisure complex which Raff had made of his home, and which he and Rhea ran together, as a family they tended to eat in the hotel restaurant for convenience, and so it was months since Jordan had enjoyed the luxury of a home-cooked meal. Grace's chicken casserole had reminded him of just how good it could be.

'The telephone is in the small room, next to the sitting-room, that I use as an office,' Grace informed him as she stood up to clear away after the meal.

Jordan stood up too. 'I'll help you do this first——'

She was shaking her head even as he began to gather up the plates, firmly taking them from him. 'You're a guest here, Mr—Jordan,' she amended at his fierce look. 'This is what you pay your rent for,' she added dismissively.

And a very small amount it was too, he had learnt earlier. Jordan found it incredible to believe Grace could make any money at all from the small payment she asked for overnight accommodation and meals.

A house like this must have ten or twelve bedrooms already, and would benefit greatly by extension—could be worth a small gold-mine if it were renovated properly and run on a more businesslike basis.

His wandering thoughts had brought him back to the reason he had come to Charlton House at all. He and Raff, business partners in the luxury complex Raff had made of Quinlan House, had been searching around for another suitable house with grounds to make into a similar venture. His own personal assistant, given the task of seeking out such a property, had come up with Charlton House in the Lake District. Unfortunately, their advances to Grace Brown about selling the house to Quinlan Leisure, the name of the company Jordan and Raff ran the business under, had been rejected with a haste that had seemed pretty final. Not to be put off, Jordan had continued to correspond with Miss Grace Brown through his solicitors. She had remained adamant in her decision not to sell, which was when Jordan had decided to come up here himself to talk to her.

Taking on a false identity, which was sure to be misconstrued if discovered, seemed to have put an end to any negotiations he might have pursued in that direction himself. But for the moment he didn't care, felt more at peace with himself than he had for a long time. There was just Raff and

Rhea's minds to put at rest and then he could forget about business completely for a while. Who knew? He might even start to enjoy life again. Now that would be a novelty!

'If you're sure...' he accepted politely, much more interested in going in search of the 'office', he had to admit.

It wasn't so much an office as a private sitting-room, had the charm and neatness of Grace Brown stamped all over it. Not that the furniture or the décor in here were any more luxurious than in the room next door, because if anything the floral-covered sofa and armchair in here looked older than the furniture in the adjoining room. But they were clean, completely neat and tidy, as was the sideboard bearing several photographs, and the small dining-table Grace seemed to use as her desk, from the look of the neat piles of correspondence upon its surface. Jordan wouldn't be at all surprised if the half-dozen or so letters sent through his solicitor didn't sit among this number.

Sitting neatly in the middle of the table was the sought-after telephone. But it was to the sideboard bearing the photographs that Jordan went. There were several photographs of Tim, instantly recognisable, from babyhood up, and, next to these, formal photographs of a man with hair as bright a red as his two offspring—for this surely had to be Grace's father—and he was laughing down into the face of the woman who stood at his side, a woman with Grace's face and yet somehow different: her mother and father, Jordan knew without a doubt.

On the other side of these was a display of ones of Grace Brown from babyhood through to adolescence and on up to the present day. In at least two of these—it was exactly two, Jordan knew without hesitation!—a tall, blond-haired man stood at her side. Tall and blond, handsome in a rakish way, several years older than Jordan himself, vaguely familiar, as if Jordan should recognise him, and yet he didn't.

What was he doing in the photographs with Grace? Could he be her boyfriend? Jordan frowned at this possibility.

'Did you manage to find the telephone?'

He turned with a guilty start at the husky sound of Grace's voice, although she didn't look accusing, just curious.

'The pictures of Timothy caught my attention,' he excused with a shrug—although it must be obvious to Grace that he hadn't been standing anywhere near the photographs of Timothy when she entered the room! 'He's a lovely child.'

'Yes,' she acknowledged indulgently, moving further into the room to pick up one of the earlier photographs of her brother. 'He was a good baby too,' she reminisced, remembering the fun she and her father had had with the contented baby

Timothy had been; it had been an outlet they had both needed after the death of her mother.

Jordan looked at her as she stood bent over the photographs, lost in memories he couldn't even begin to guess at, let alone share, her face given a warm glow from the light given off by the small lamp that stood on the sideboard.

She looked very young and vulnerable at that moment, no more than a child herself, certainly not capable of carrying all the responsibilities she seemed to have. Jordan wanted to take her in his arms and relieve her of all those responsibilities, wanted to smooth that frown from between her eyes, wanted to kiss the soft peach of those slightly parted lips—what the hell...?

Grace looked up, misunderstanding the scowl on his face, putting the photograph down with a thud. 'I'll leave you to make your call,' she excused, turning to leave.

Jordan was too dazed by his unexpected response to her seconds ago to try and stop her!

Oh, he wasn't as cold and removed from human need as his sister seemed to think he was, had been attracted to women, desired them, made love to them. But that attraction had always been to *women*, moreover women who knew exactly what sort of relationship he required of them, the relationship always terminating amicably, with perhaps an expensive gift of jewellery on his part to soften the blow of parting. These affairs had been games, with both players knowing the rules.

Grace Brown wasn't a player.

She wasn't even a woman, merely a vulnerable young girl. But a few minutes ago he had wanted her with a fierceness he could never remember experiencing before! His hand shook slightly as he reached out to pick up the receiver, needing contact with his normal life.

He should really leave here now—that would be the best thing to do before he became any more embroiled in Grace Brown's life. Before he couldn't control that desire he had had to take her in his arms and kiss her until they were both breathless.

Rhea answered the call on the private line at Quinlan House, her voice warm with recognition once he had said hello, the contentment she had found as Raff's wife evident even over the telephone. 'How did you get on?' she prompted interestedly.

'Fine,' Jordan evaded.

'And Miss Brown, is she——?'

'We'll talk about it when I get home,' he cut in curtly.

'OK,' his sister accepted easily, used to his abrupt ways.

'The thing is…' he continued. No, Jordan, *no*, he anxiously instructed himself. Tell Rhea you'll be back tomorrow, as originally planned, that you'll be back in time for lunch, dinner at the latest. 'I've decided not to come straight back,' he heard himself add lightly. 'I thought I might take a short holiday up here.'

He should leave *now*. Not tomorrow. Not in a few days' time. But *now*. He *knew* he should leave.

'We've been telling you for months to take a holiday,' Rhea said with warm approval. 'But isn't the weather a little cold up at the Lakes this time of year?'

'Possibly,' he accepted non-committally. 'But I need the break more than the warm weather.' But not *here*, he was desperately telling himself inside his head. Not anywhere near Grace Brown!

'Yes, but——'

'Rhea,' he cut in tersely, 'unlike you when you decided to flit off and not tell anyone—least of all me—where you were going, I *am* over twenty-one! And I'm taking a short holiday, so I'm not coming home just yet.' He quietly replaced the receiver as he heard her initial gasp of surprise turn into a dozen questions.

And that wasn't in the least surprising.

The time Rhea had disappeared from their home had been when she had first met Raff. And fallen in love with him. And Jordan had just repeated almost word for word what Rhea had said to him then during the one brief telephone call she had made to him to reassure him she was at least well and in no danger.

Now why had he done that?

## CHAPTER THREE

WHO was Jordan telephoning? Grace wondered. A wife, possibly. She very much doubted that he was telephoning another man, unless it was for business purposes, and it was well past business hours. Although Jordan had an air about him of being able to command attention and respect no matter what time of the day or night it was.

And yet the guess that it was a woman he was calling persisted. Had he had an argument with his wife—was that why he had chosen to stay on here when everything about him pointed to his being used to much more luxurious accommodation when he was away from home?

But somehow he didn't *look* married. And there was that bewildered pain in his eyes.

No, perhaps not a wife, but definitely a woman. Grace didn't know why she believed that, she just did. What sort of woman would a man like Jordan be interested in? she wondered. Gloriously beautiful, she would guess, wondrously sophisticated, a woman who knew all the rules.

A woman, in fact, who bore absolutely no resemblance to herself.

Now what on earth had made her think a thing like that...?

'Grace, why are you standing all alone in the hallway?' Timothy looked up at her. 'And why do you have that funny look on your face?' He frowned at her expression.

It took the innocence of a child to make her realise how ridiculously she was behaving! She gave Timothy a rueful smile, putting her arm companionably about his shoulders. 'I was miles away,' she excused. 'I suppose I had better finish clearing away,' she added briskly, having only intended to come up here briefly to make sure Jordan had found the telephone. Although why she should doubt it she didn't know; he seemed more than capable!

Timothy was watching her with a frown. 'You don't mind Mr Gregory being here, do you?'

'Do you?' she delayed, her thoughts still in conflict concerning Jordan. It was a very uncomfortable feeling.

Her brother gave a predictable grin. 'No, I think he's great.'

She raised dark brows ruefully. 'Jordan? Or his Jaguar?' she teased.

His grin didn't falter. 'Both!' His answer was unabashed. 'The car is great,' he announced the obvious. 'And Jordan talked to me while we were driving around.'

'Did he?' she encouraged softly, turning back in the direction of the dining-room; she really would have to finish clearing away—it was getting late.

The dining-room was empty now, although Jessie had piled all the used crockery up and put it at one end of the dining-table. Timothy helped Grace with loading it on to a tray without even seeming aware that he did so; he was so used to helping out with the running of the house, much more so than other little boys his age, that he did it automatically now.

He nodded now in answer to her question, his hair gleaming redder than usual in the lamplight. 'He lives in London a lot of the time,' he revealed, eager to share his new friend. 'He has a married sister. And a baby niece. And——'

'Timothy, this list of revelations sounds more like the answers to rather personal questions to me than Jordan actually sitting having a conversation with you,' Grace cut in disapprovingly, knowing her guess was correct by the unattractive way his cheeks became flushed, his freckles more prominent. 'You know I've told you not to intrude into the privacy of the people who stay here,' she scolded disappointedly.

'Jordan didn't mind,' Timothy defended a little indignantly.

Possibly not—she had noticed a certain gentleness on Jordan's part when dealing with the young boy. But even so... She wanted to know more about Jordan herself, was intensely curious about him, but she certainly had no intention of asking Timothy what else Jordan hadn't 'minded' revealing about himself!

'Well, I don't want you to do it again,' she told her brother firmly.

'He wanted to know about us, too,' Timothy continued to defend stubbornly.

Her hand was arrested in the act of putting the salt and pepper pot on the tray with the other things, although she recovered from this revelation quickly, keeping her expression deliberately bland now. 'And just what did you tell him?' she prompted, almost dreading the answer, sure that Timothy, in his youth, had been indiscreet.

He shrugged unconcernedly. 'That I live here alone with you because Mummy and Daddy died. That you're twenty, and I'm seven. That——'

'Our life histories in a few short words, in fact!' Grace frowned her dismay. 'We don't have anything to hide, Timothy,' she told him gently, 'but you really mustn't go about revealing our personal business to a complete stranger in that——'

'He isn't a stranger, he's Jordan,' Timothy announced happily, as if that made everything perfectly all right.

There wasn't a lot Grace could say to an argument like that. And yet she didn't want Timothy confiding in Jordan. Of all people...

Jordan woke slowly, for a moment unsure what had woken him, no radio-alarm clock at his bedside blasting out the seven o'clock news as it usually did to rouse him. And then he realised that was because there *was* no radio-alarm clock on the cabinet beside his bed. In fact, there was no cabinet either!

Instead, a cup of tea, still steamingly hot, he noticed as he focused on it, sat on the table beside his bed. A bed that, although comfortable, was a little soft for his normal taste. A feather mattress, in fact. He hadn't known such things still existed. But obviously they did here. At Charlton House.

Grace Brown's home.

And someone had been kind enough to bring him up early morning tea. Now he knew what had woken him. And it wasn't such early morning either; a glance at the plain but expensive watch on his wrist had told him it was after nine o'clock. He couldn't remember the last time he had slept this late. Maybe he could live with the softness of the feather mattress after all.

The tea was still refreshingly hot when he sat up to drink it, and someone seemed to have noticed too, probably when he had a late-night cup of tea with them the previous evening, that he didn't take sugar in his drinks.

Grace...

It was sightly unnerving, for a man who rarely, if ever, let down his guard, to realise that a young woman who had already shaken his perfectly controlled equilibrium had probably come into his bedroom a short time ago and seen him at his most vulnerable—sleeping like the proverbial baby!

It was disconcerting, to say the least.

But one of the things he had noticed with some surprise when he had retired to bed the previous evening was that there were no locks on the bedroom doors. It was fine, as far as he was concerned, to treat guests like part of the family, but no locks on the bedroom doors seemed to be taking things a little too far, Jordan felt.

Not that he hadn't been perfectly well covered when Grace had come into his room with the tea; far from a restless sleeper, the bedclothes were barely disturbed by his presence beneath them. And, because he had been very conscious of the unlocked bedroom door, he had chosen to sleep in his briefs rather than completely naked as he would normally have done.

No, it wasn't that that disturbed him; he just somehow felt—emotionally exposed.

Well, it was done now, beyond his control, and so he might as well enjoy the rest of his tea, then get a wash and a shave before going downstairs in search of coffee and toast.

The thought of sitting in the cosiness of the well-scrubbed kitchen downstairs, possibly chatting to Grace as she moved effortlessly about the room, filling the space with her warm gentleness and—maybe he wouldn't bother with breakfast after all!

He needed more clothes if he was to stay on here, would drive down to Windermere and pick up a few things as soon as he was ready. He could get some coffee and toast there.

'Good morning, Jordan.' Amazingly, Grace was in the hallway when he came downstairs fifteen minutes later, apparently dusting, from the cloth in her slender hand. And she looked just as warm and beautiful this morning, in the fluffy pink jumper and fitted black skirt, as she had yesterday.

Jordan had convinced himself while he showered and shaved that he had exaggerated all that beautiful tranquillity Grace Brown seemed to carry around with her like a cloak. But he only had to look at her again to know that he hadn't!

This morning Grace looked even more beautiful, more serenely lovely than he remembered, her young face glowing healthily, from where she had recently been outside, Jordan would guess, probably taking Timothy to school.

Every time Jordan looked at her he felt as if the air had been knocked out of his lungs. And it was an experience completely beyond his control.

'Breakfast?' she suggested brightly, not seeming in the least offended that he hadn't responded to her greeting.

It hadn't been that he hadn't wanted to, only that for the moment his voice seemed to have deserted him. Only!

Maybe he was starting a cold; it would certainly explain some of the symptoms he seemed to have—voice loss, and a slightly disorientated feeling that usually went along with a fever.

He refused to even contemplate any other explanation for those feelings!

Grace had already turned in the direction of the stairs that led down to the kitchen, seeming unaware of Jordan's inner conflict. 'I hope you like tea first thing in the morning?' She talked quietly, filling in for his obvious silence. 'I thought you would rather just be left to sleep until you woke up, but Jessie insisted on bringing a drink up to your room while I took Timothy to school.' She turned briefly to give him an apologetic smile.

*Jessie*? *Jessie* had been the one to enter his bedroom with the cup of tea. So much for his earlier disquiet!

He felt rather foolish now, didn't think the elderly, vague lady would have been in the least interested in what he looked like in bed!

And why should he have assumed Grace would be any more interested? Apart from giving him those long, searching looks occasionally, she had shown little interest in him. Which was understandable, he supposed; he was twelve years older than her, after all.

'The tea was very welcome,' he found his voice at last. 'And I was very grateful she brought it up when she did,' he added lightly, more harshly than perhaps he meant to, but the feeling of foolishness was still very much with him. 'I never sleep late.' Now he was being pompous, he realised with an inward groan; he *had* slept late this morning. He had to get himself back in control of this situation!

But to refuse breakfast now, when Grace had obviously been waiting to cook it for him, everything out ready on the work-top, the wooden table in the centre of the large room set with one place, wouldn't just have been rude, but churlish too.

He didn't usually bother with a full breakfast, but, as bacon began to sizzle appetisingly in the pan, coffee to percolate, and bread to toast, the sudden hunger he felt told him he would have no trouble eating the cooked breakfast today.

As he had known she would, Grace chatted lightly as she worked, about the area and her neighbours, and Jordan found himself just enjoying watching her as she moved about the room, her hands long and delicate, and yet obviously capable, her movements economically efficient, her fiery red hair framing the elfin face dominated by large grey eyes, a relaxed curve to the shell-pink of her lips.

Jordan could never remember just enjoying sitting looking at a woman before. He could never remember having the time before!

Although he had a feeling, dangerously so, that just sitting looking at Grace Brown could become a compulsive pastime for him...

Did she have a smut on the end of her nose? A cobweb in her hair from where she had been dusting earlier? Had only remembered to put one earring in—something she regularly did? Why *was* Jordan watching her over the top of his coffee-mug in that way? Grace wondered self-consciously.

He looked less strained this morning, some of the bewilderment starting to fade from his eyes. The Aran sweater was casual, although she noticed the dark blue trousers were still the ones from the suit he had been wearing the day before. But the small overnight case he had finally brought in last night couldn't have held much more than the sweater, a change of underwear, and some toilet things.

She put the laden plate down on the table in front of him, aware that any responses he *had* made to her inconsequential chatter—and there hadn't been many!—had been monosyllabic; Jordan obviously wasn't a morning person. 'I'll leave you to enjoy your meal in peace,' she excused lightly.

'You don't have to do that,' he surprised her by saying—and then looked slightly surprised by the protest himself! He turned away. 'I don't want to drive you out of your own kitchen,' he muttered. 'I'm sure I've inconvenienced you enough for one day by coming down so late.'

There was something so endearing about this man. Grace couldn't help wondering when anyone had last held him in their arms and told him he was loved. She could be completely wrong, of course, but she had a feeling it was a very long time. Although Timothy had said he had a sister, so he must have a family who loved him somewhere.

'It's what I'm here for,' she assured him lightly.

He frowned, as if he didn't particularly care for the idea, his next remark seeming to confirm the impression. 'This is a very odd life for someone of your age.'

'Someone my age with a seven-year-old brother to bring up,' she added pointedly. 'I'm sure Timothy told you yesterday a little of our life here together,' she said challengingly; he had to know that she was aware he had been questioning the young boy.

Dark blue eyes became shuttered. 'He said you also work part-time in the local library?'

She nodded, not at all surprised he should know this. 'Ten till one, Monday to Friday. In fact,' she looked at her wristwatch, 'I should be leaving for there now.'

'I'll drive you,' Jordan instantly offered.

'You haven't finished your breakfast,' she pointed out gently.

He looked down at the food on his plate as if he had forgotten it was there. 'No—of course not. I—I'll see you later, then.' He turned away, determinedly keeping his head downbent.

Grace watched him for several seconds longer, before giving a slight shrug and leaving the room. She really did have to finish off and get ready for work. She had made a point, since getting the job two years ago when Timothy started school, of always being punctual and reliable. As only a part-time worker her position at the library was more precarious than the full-time staff's, but, with the responsibility of Timothy to consider, and that of her boarders, she couldn't do any more hours than she did, and the more indispensable she made herself when she was there, the more chance she had, she hoped, of not losing her job if the need for fewer staff arose.

But she had better check with Nick before she left to see if there was anything he wanted while she was out; he had left his rooms even less than usual since Jordan's arrival yesterday.

Nick rented the rooms on the third floor at the top of the house; in fact they were the attic rooms, but they were the ones he preferred. By tacit agreement Grace only went in there once a week to clean, and even then she didn't tidy up the rooms; Nick thrived best on disorder, he claimed.

Although Nick usually joined them downstairs for his meals, he did have a kitchen of his own, and more often than not he would get himself toast and coffee for breakfast.

But he didn't look as if he had been long out of bed this morning when he answered the door to her knock, still wearing his old blue towelling robe, his hair in disarray.

He opened the door wider for her to enter. 'You're later than usual,' he observed tersely, sipping coffee from the mug in his hand.

Grace reached up and kissed him lightly on the cheek. 'Good morning to you too, Nick,' she teased lightly.

He looked unabashed by the gentle rebuke, shrugging as he closed the door before strolling across the room. 'I wasn't complaining,' he dismissed. 'Only observing. Besides, I haven't looked out of the window this morning yet, so I have no idea whether it's a "good" one or not!'

She pulled back the curtains in answer to that, smiling a little as Nick winced at the daylight now streaming into the room. 'It snowed a little more in the night, but everywhere looks beautiful,' she told him happily.

Nick threw himself down into one of the armchairs, making no effort to look out of the window himself. 'I find this enthusiasm you have for snow strange, to say the least,' he scowled.

Grace smiled down at him fondly. 'You just don't like fresh air of any kind!'

'There is that,' he drawled. 'How is the new lodger settling in?'

He spoke lightly enough, and yet Grace knew him well enough to realise he was disturbed at having someone new staying here, otherwise he wouldn't have mentioned the other man at all!

'Fine,' she dismissed. 'Do you want anything from town today?' She changed the subject, well aware that Nick would get out of meeting Jordan at all if he could possibly manage it.

Nick eyed her morosely. 'Tim tells me this Jordan has a fantastic car, that he comes from London, that he——'

'You really shouldn't encourage him to gossip.' Grace sighed her impatience. 'And you haven't answered my question,' she prompted a little more sharply than she would normally have done. But she was very aware that there was something she wasn't telling Nick, and it made her feel slightly defensive. Nick had become such a fixture in her life, had been here for so long, that she tended to confide in him. And yet telling him about Jordan was different...

'Actually,' Nick sprang to his feet with more energy than he usually displayed, 'I would like to come in with you this morning; there are one or two things I need to get for myself.'

She raised dark brows. 'Then you had better hurry up and get ready; I'm going to be late for work otherwise.'

'Time-watching,' he taunted before going into the adjoining bedroom to dress.

Grace didn't stay in his room waiting for him, going back downstairs. The kitchen showed no evidence of Jordan, or the breakfast he had eaten, even the pots she had used for cooking washed and put away. She somehow didn't think this was the way Jordan usually began his day!

Jessie would have gone back up to her room now, resting until Grace came back at lunchtime. The elderly lady didn't sleep well at night, so was always in need of a nap during the day. Jordan would have gone out by now, and Nick would be going with her; it appealed to her sense of order that everyone was organised for the morning.

A last check of her hair, a fresh application of lipstick, and Nick still wasn't downstairs, she realised frustratedly.

'I'm sorry, are you waiting for me after all?'

She turned to smile at Jordan as he came down the stairs, realising her mistake—that he must have been up in his room collecting his overcoat.

Her breath caught in her throat as he returned her smile, those cobalt-blue eyes warm and sensual. He had an instant command of respect, this man, but it wasn't only that about him that disturbed her, made her legs feel slightly weak...

'Grace?'

She was staring! Like a silly teenager, she was staring at him and had completely forgotten to answer his original question!

She smiled brightly. Too brightly? Oh, this was so silly, she was behaving like a gauche schoolgirl! 'I have my own car,' she thanked him. 'I'm just waiting for Nick to join me.'

'Oh, yes?' Dark blue eyes narrowed. 'I haven't met your other guest yet.'

Nick was hardly a 'guest'; none of them were, Grace thought ruefully. They were all wounded people who had found somewhere to rest and lick their wounds while their emotions healed, she realised with a start. Yes, even this man in front of her...

She shrugged dismissively. 'Nick is something of a—loner.'

'Shy, you mean,' Jordan nodded understandingly.

That wasn't what she meant at all. Nick could be scornful, sarcastic, downright rude if he thought his privacy was being invaded; but it owed nothing to shyness!

'Something like that,' Grace avoided drily, inwardly wondering what these two men would make of each other. They were both such private people, it was difficult to even hazard a guess. Maybe her newest 'guest' would cause more of an upset to the household than she had bargained for, but, the truth of the matter was, she hadn't even considered Nick's feelings yesterday when she'd first met Jordan!

'Don't let us delay you,' she advised Jordan lightly as he lingered in the hallway. 'Nick has absolutely no sense of time.' And if he didn't soon hurry up she was going to have to go without him!

Jordan gave a curt inclination of his head, as if he resented what he felt was a dismissal. 'I'll see you this evening, then.'

Grace looked at his rigidly held back as he walked down the hallway towards the front door, his reaction to what she had meant as a casual remark somehow making the conversation feel unfinished, inconclusive.

'Jordan!' she suddenly called out to him. He turned slowly, dark brows raised questioningly.

And now she didn't know what she was going to say, had just somehow felt as if their conversation was incomplete. But of course it wasn't; she was being over-sensitive, and now she had to find something to say to fill the awkward silence. 'Um—we have dinner at six o'clock,' she invented quickly, instantly disappointed in the weakness of her apparent excuse for delaying him. 'Is that too early for you?' She inwardly cringed at her own inadequacy. Really, she could have come up with something better than that!

His dark brow settled into a frown. 'Six o'clock is fine. Did I give you the impression it wasn't?' He looked puzzled.

'Er—no,' she replied truthfully. 'I was just—checking.'

Jordan shrugged dismissively. 'I certainly don't expect you to alter your routine for me.'

'That wasn't exactly what I was suggesting,' Grace told him ruefully, knowing that Jessie for one would be the first to complain if they had dinner any later, and Timothy wouldn't be long after her! 'Despite what I said last night, if you wanted something on a tray in your room a little later in the evening, I'm sure it could be arranged.'

He frowned again. 'No, I don't think so, thank you.'

Delicate colour darkened her cheeks. 'It was just a thought,' she mumbled.

'And a kind one,' he nodded. 'But I actually enjoyed the family meal last night.'

He sounded as if he weren't sure which of them should be the most surprised by this admission!

An enigma, Grace decided again as she let him leave unhindered this time. She was sure, in his normal way of life, that Jordan was a man who preferred his own company. But apparently not now. Not here.

'Penny for them,' Nick invited derisively as he came down the stairs, dressed casually as usual, his hair looking as if he might have run a comb through it. But that wasn't a certainty; he might just have smoothed it back with his hand—Nick never seemed to particularly care how he looked.

She gave him a bright, dismissive smile, picking up her coat and bag. 'I don't have the time just now to satisfy your curiosity.'

Nick easily matched his longer strides to her hurried ones. 'All this rushing about all the time, clock-watching——'

'Not now, Nick,' she warned levelly, hurrying out to her car. 'Some of us have to "clock-watch", as you call it,' she added pointedly. 'Will you just get in the car?' she ordered frustratedly over the bonnet of her Mini, as he seemed in no hurry now to stop admiring how pretty the jungle of a garden looked buried under a few inches of snow, and actually get inside the car!

'No respect for their elders, that's the trouble with some people,' he grumbled mockingly as he finally folded his length inside the vehicle.

Grace gave him a brief glance as she got in beside him. 'Older doesn't necessarily mean better.' She turned the key in the ignition. 'Respect has to be earned, not just expected as one's due.' She put the car into reverse.

'Mind the tree,' Nick warned without even attempting to look backwards.

She braked instantly, although she knew she had actually been nowhere near any of the trees edging the driveway. It had been an instinctive reaction; Nick would never let her forget the time, just after she had passed her driving test, when she had put the car into reverse instead of first gear and ended up badly damaging the Mini on the tree she had hit.

'It's just as well I love you,' she finally muttered as she drove down the driveway.

His only answer was to turn and grin at her knowingly. He was irresistible when he smiled like that, Grace decided, and she found herself grinning back at him, her bad humour forgotten.

She certainly didn't notice the green Jaguar parked on the side of the road facing in the opposite direction to the one she was driving...

So that was the elusive Nick, Jordan realised as he watched the car accelerate away. The rakishly attractive man with Grace in the photograph that stood in her small private office.

The blond hair was even longer now, and from the harsh angles of the attractive face the man was also thinner than in the photograph. But it was still the same man, Jordan was sure of it. And in the flesh he looked even more familiar.

Who was he?

More important still, what was he to Grace? Why was he staying in her home?

The two of them had looked so comfortable together, laughing over some shared joke as the Mini emerged out on to the road, not even seeming to notice him as he sat looking through a road-map trying to decide which way he should have turned to Windermere. He had passed through the small lakeside town on the way here, and yet from the look of the map he had turned the wrong way completely from the house.

What rankled the most? he questioned himself. Was it the fact that his usual sense of direction seemed to have deserted him, or was it the fact that Grace had been so engrossed with the other man she hadn't even noticed his car parked at the side of the road, let alone Jordan himself?

He must be cracking up, if he could be bothered about something so trivial, he decided. He certainly wasn't acting in character.

He barely knew Grace Brown, had only met her for the first time yesterday, and, even if he did reluctantly find himself attracted to her, he was hoping for a little too much that other men wouldn't find her equally as attractive, that she didn't have a boyfriend already.

But actually staying in her own home? Albeit in his own room. At least, Jordan assumed that was the arrangement! And the man Nick looked far from being a 'boy', was at least six or seven years older than Jordan's thirty-two.

But it was really none of his business, was it, who Grace Brown chose to go out with? Or anything else, for that matter.

Self-lecture over, he very firmly turned on the ignition, putting all thoughts of Grace Brown from his mind, concentrating on the purchases he needed to make while in Windermere.

He even fooled himself into thinking he didn't notice the fact that he deliberately drove slower than usual so that he shouldn't catch up with the Mini on the winding roads...

# CHAPTER FOUR

'JORDAN GREGORY, Nick Parrish,' Grace introduced the two men at dinner that evening.

But, having persuaded Nick to join them, having done so under duress after she had told him she had no intention of permanently providing his meals upstairs on a tray just because he wanted to hide out from the new guest—a direct challenge that even Nick couldn't ignore—she wasn't altogether sure how he was going to behave now he was here.

One thing she was sure of, however—the two men were more than a match for each other!

They faced each other now across the dining-table, one so fair, the other so dark, equally powerfully built, although they were dressed totally differently, despite the fact they were both dressed casually. Nick wore his customary denims and an over-big dark green sweatshirt, and Jordan wore dark tailored trousers with a formal shirt unbuttoned at the throat beneath a navy blue V-necked jumper.

Clothes the latter had bought only today, Grace felt sure.

The two men shook hands, eyeing each other like adversaries.

Grace could understand Nick's behaving in that way; he viewed all new people with suspicion. But she didn't know why Jordan should feel so defensive. Jessie, bless her, was completely oblivious to any tension in the room, intent upon her food, and Timothy was still puffed up with his own self-importance at being able to go to school and claim his friend Jordan had a Jaguar and that he had taken him out for a drive in it! It was a gross exaggeration, considering his real relationship to Jordan, but it was what Grace had herself heard him claim as he had hurtled into the school playground this morning.

He might even be plotting right now how to get Jordan to take him out in the car again. Even worse, he may be working himself up to asking Jordan if he would take some of his schoolfriends plus himself out for a drive! Grace wouldn't put that past him, from the look of the little half-smile on his lips. She had better have a chat with this particular young man at bedtime.

But right now it seemed she was the one who would have to act as a buffer between the two men sitting so obviously silent at the table. At least, it was obvious to her!

She turned to Jordan. 'Did you have a nice day?' Hardly scintillating conversation, but it would do as a start. He shrugged dismissively, his narrowed gaze still fixed on Nick, the latter meeting that gaze challengingly.

Grace could cheerfully have hit Nick; he drew attention to himself just by his rude behaviour!

'I just picked up a few essentials in Windermere,' Jordan decided to answer her question.

Like a change of clothes, Grace guessed. In fact, probably several of them. She couldn't help wondering what had happened to change his mind about the length of his stay; he had so obviously originally intended it to be of short duration.

'This is a strange place for a man like you to choose to stay,' Nick drawled almost accusingly.

Dark blue eyes glazed over coldly, and Grace was able in those few seconds to see just how formidable Jordan could be when he chose to be. And yet he had been so kind with Timothy, infinitely gentle and considerate with her...

'"A man like me"?' he repeated in a voice that was dangerously soft.

Nick looked him over consideringly. 'You're hardly the type for a brief winter break in the Lakes,' he finally scorned.

'I'm not?' Jordan met his gaze steadily.

Neither of them was making any attempt to eat the beef pie she had made for the meal, which was a pity because, even if she said it herself, it was one of her better efforts at cooking.

'No.' Nick rested his chin on his hand as his elbow rested on the table-top. 'What *are* you doing here?'

Grace gasped out loud at the audacity of this question; Nick really was the absolute end!

Jordan looked unruffled. 'Taking "a brief winter break in the Lakes",' he bit out evenly. 'What's your excuse?'

Grace choked as a piece of food lodged in her throat, coughing frantically, her eyes watering. Neither man made any attempt to come to her aid, and so she gulped down her water gratefully, looking anxiously at Nick once she had regained a little of her composure, alarmed by his narrowed eyes and the tightness of his mouth.

'Here.' Jordan held out his own glass of water for her, an amused glitter in his eyes as he met her gaze.

He was enjoying Nick's challenge, she realised! He couldn't know quite the time-bomb he was walking into, but then, he didn't know Nick very well either. Yet. Grace had a feeling that was going to change very soon.

'Thank you.' She took the water more to be polite than anything else, although her coughing fit did at least seem to have diverted both men's attention, as Nick turned to her too.

'Food go down the wrong way?' he taunted, obviously wishing he had never given in to her persuasions to come down here for his dinner in the first place. She shot him a reproachful glance; he could be hard, embittered, but he wasn't usually cruel.

He turned back to Jordan, his mouth tight. 'I don't need an "excuse",' he bit out harshly. 'I happen to live here!'

Jordan gave an acknowledging inclination of his head. 'And, for the moment, so do I.'

Stand-off—Grace hoped! Things could get very awkward indeed around here if these two men should decide to lock horns and continue to fight every time they saw each other; mealtimes especially could become very uncomfortable for them all.

She was aware that Nick was the main antagonist, that Jordan was actually only, at the moment, responding to the other man's aggression. But Nick's mood at the moment was such that he couldn't be reasoned with.

'So you do,' Nick said steadily. 'How long do you intend staying?'

Grace sensed Jordan's restrained glance in her direction, knowing Nick's rudeness was inexcusable, but also knowing that Jordan felt restricted, because of the company they were in, in his answers.

And as both men were guests in her home she felt responsible for what was happening, despite the fact that she knew both of them were perfectly capable of defending themselves, both verbally and physically.

'That, surely, is up to Jordan,' she attempted to gently rebuke Nick.

Challenging brown eyes met her eyes. 'Not necessarily,' Nick ground out.

Her cheeks became flushed. She allowed Nick a certain amount of familiarity in the running of the household, as she did Jessie too, knowing the two of them regarded Charlton House as their home and not just a boarding-house. But, even so, Nick was taking his position here a little too far.

She stood up to clear the plates, not caring that neither man had eaten anything; they had had their chance! 'And me,' she snapped. 'And, as far as I'm concerned, Jordan can stay here for as long as he wants to!'

She was usually very slow to anger, was more irritated than actually angry now, feeling the whole conversation to be unnecessary and hurtful.

'I haven't finished yet,' Jessie protested in a wounded voice as Grace would have automatically removed her plate too. Poor Jessie was only halfway through her meal, Grace realised. Really, these two men had her so unnerved that she didn't know what she was doing any more!

'Sorry, Jessie,' she said ruefully, replacing the plate, frowning her displeasure with Nick for creating this situation.

He stood up abruptly. 'I think I'll go up to my rooms,' he stated shortly.

Grace looked at him concernedly, knowing from the desolation in his eyes that he needed to get away from them all.

He hesitated at the door, looking back at Grace. 'You'll—come up later?'

She smiled gently, her irritation with him instantly gone. 'Yes.'

He nodded, leaving without another glance or word for anyone else in the room.

Timothy and Jessie knew better than to question Nick's moods, used to them by now, and Grace did her best to pretend she didn't notice Jordan's questioning looks as she moved quietly about the room.

She couldn't even begin to explain Nick's behaviour to the other man, was too close to it all herself to even attempt it.

The man was a bore, Jordan decided impatiently, *whoever* he was; he was still on edge from his conversation with the other man a good hour after the meal had finished and he sat in the comfort of the sitting-room with Jessie and Timothy, the latter supposedly studying the spellings he had been given for homework ready for a test later in the week.

Nick Parrish hadn't liked him before he even met him, that much was obvious to Jordan, although what he was supposed to have done to upset the other man he had no idea. Unless Nick

Parrish just didn't like the idea of a young man in the house, with his own interest in Grace.

Jordan felt more convinced than he had this morning that there was a special affection between the two; they had a way of communicating without the need of speech, an easy familiarity that came with emotional closeness for a long period of time.

Which rather put Jordan's own attraction to Grace in doubt. And he *was* attracted to her, to the point where he had actually thought of little else all day.

He had just enjoyed watching the movements of her hands and the tilting of her head during dinner, loved the slender delicacy of hands and face. The fantasies he had had of those hands caressing the nakedness of his body were just so incredible that he broke out in a cold sweat every time he thought of them!

She had disappeared into the kitchen again to clear away after the meal, refusing his offer of help, gently reminding him that, although she had appreciated his tidying away this morning after his breakfast, he was in fact a guest here, and so not expected to do it.

That had been an hour ago, and she still hadn't joined them in the sitting-room. He stood up restlessly, Jessie looking up from the knitting she was haphazardly doing; Jordan had already guessed, from what she had done so far, that it was a Balaclava for an elephant!

'I think I'll just take a stroll,' he excused lamely.

Jessie frowned. 'Outside? But it's very cold out there now, dear.'

'Er—no, I wasn't thinking of going outside,' he admitted ruefully.

The elderly lady nodded, smiling sweetly. 'Grace will be in her little sitting-room now,' she told him as if it was the most natural thing in the world to expect him to be looking for Grace.

Jordan gave her a sharp look, but there was such an expression of childish innocence on her face that he couldn't possibly read any hidden meaning into her words. 'Thank you,' he nodded abruptly, looking up to find Timothy grinning at him too; he scowled as he left the room with more haste than he would have wished.

Was his interest in Grace so obvious that even the slightly vague Jessie and a child could see it? It was ridiculous, made him feel utterly foolish, like a gauche schoolboy himself.

And yet he was drawn to that small sitting-room like a magnet, found himself knocking lightly on the door, entering after Grace had called out softly for him to do so. His breath caught in his throat as he looked across the room at her.

The lamp on the table was the only illumination, giving her hair the glow of burnished copper as it fell loosely down to the dark grey jumper she wore. Her skin had a peachy glow in the half-light too, her eyes a luminous grey.

And those eyes were gazing back at him curiously now as he stood tongue-tied just inside the doorway. He was thirty-two years old, for goodness' sake, not a raw teenager!

He closed the door firmly behind him, crossing the room to stand beside the big table she used as her desk. 'Bearing in mind what Nick said earlier——' he cleared his throat, his voice gruff '—I thought *you* might be wondering how long I intended staying on.' That hadn't been what he meant to say at all, he groaned inwardly, wishing he hadn't said it now as her face clouded over concernedly; the last thing he wanted to do was cause this woman any distress, for whatever reason.

She put down the pen she had been working with. 'I really should apologise for Nick's behaviour towards you earlier——'

'Why should you?' Jordan cut in lightly. 'He certainly doesn't intend to!'

Grace gave an answering rueful smile. 'No,' she acknowledged with a sigh. 'Nick very rarely apologises for anything.'

Jordan perched on the side of the table. 'I had already guessed as much,' he shrugged. 'I won't ask what his problem is, because I wouldn't ask you to break a confidence. Don't give the situation another thought,' he dismissed. 'Parrish and I are both big enough to take care of ourselves. At least,' he grimaced, 'we should be!' He stood up again, finding her closeness unsettling, moving restlessly about the room.

'Jordan...?'

Looking at her was his undoing, into those gentle grey eyes that seemed to see so much, to see the pain deep inside of him, holding his gaze now with questioning compassion as she stood up to cross the room to his side.

'Jordan, what's wrong?' she prompted softly.

His mouth twisted. 'Is it that obvious that something is?'

'I could lie and say no,' she said softly. 'But it *would* be a lie. At least, as far as I'm concerned.'

And this young lady rarely lied, he would guess. And if his disturbed emotional state was so obvious it was no wonder Jessie and Timothy had guessed he was, unknowing at the time, going off in search of Grace; everyone else in this household seemed to go to her when they were troubled or in pain—it had seemed the most natural thing in the world to Jessie and Timothy that he should do so too.

But that was a very good reason why he shouldn't burden her with his problems. Who did *she* go to when she was troubled? Parrish seemed the obvious answer to that question, and Jordan found he didn't like the idea of that at all.

'Come and sit down and talk to me.' Grace misread his sudden frown for anguish, her hand on his arm as they moved to sit on the sofa together.

Talk to her, she said, and yet he had never actually tried to put any of this into words before, not finding it easy to talk on a personal level to anyone at the best of times.

But Grace, with her warm grey eyes and gentle smile, was somehow different... He drew in a ragged breath. 'Two years ago, by the merest chance, I discovered that the man whom I had always believed to be my father wasn't my father at all!' It all came tumbling out in a rush, his voice edged with the pain of the revelation.

'Oh, Jordan——' tears welled up compassionately in Grace's eyes, her hand reaching out to clasp his '—what a shock for you!' That didn't even begin to describe how he had felt on learning the truth of his birth! 'But Timothy says you have a sister.' Grace frowned at the recollection. 'Is she... too?'

'No.' He gave a strained smile at Grace's awkwardness with the question, not least, he would guess, because Timothy must have gossiped that piece of information to her. 'Rhea is definitely legitimate. Although, ironically, she now bears the surname that should be mine,' he grimaced. 'You see, two years ago, she married my half-brother.'

It was no great wonder that Grace looked stunned; he had been numbed with shock himself for months after learning the truth!

It was an incredible story, and if Rhea hadn't met Raff Quinlan then Jordan would probably have lived the rest of his life never knowing that his father had, in fact, been Donald Quinlan and not James Somerville-Smythe.

Rhea had, quite literally, almost been run down by Raff one night, the latter insisting on taking her back to his home once it had been professionally established that she definitely hadn't sustained any injuries. Jordan and Rhea had been at odds with each other at the time, Rhea trying to convince the trustees of their father's will that she was responsible enough to take charge of her own inheritance when she reached twenty-one in a couple of months' time.

The long and the short of it was that, after starting out as antagonists, Rhea and Raff had fallen in love with each other. Jordan had liked the other man instantly, approving the match, finding himself very quickly introduced to the rest of the Quinlan family once Rhea and Raff had decided they were getting married. It had been a momentous meeting for all of them, Raff's aunt so stunned to realise who Rhea was, and consequently Jordan himself, that she had revealed the truth of his birth.

Years before, Jordan's mother, Diana, had been Raff's nanny. Raff's parents had been separated at the time, intending to divorce, and Diana and Donald had fallen in love, intending to marry themselves once Donald's divorce from

Helen was final. And then Raff's mother had been seriously injured in an accident, left paralysed, confined to a wheelchair, and Donald had been left with the intolerable choice of caring for the woman who was the mother of his son and actually still his wife, if only in name, or divorcing her regardless and marrying Diana, the woman he really loved.

It had been an impossible situation for all of them, and Diana had eventually been the one to make the decision, leaving Quinlan House without telling Donald she was going. Only Donald's sister had known Diana carried his child, that she chose to go rather than force him to make a decision that he could blame her and the child for, for the rest of his life.

Extraordinarily, Diana had met James Somerville-Smythe, a man already middle-aged, unable, or so he believed, to father a child of his own. And so Diana's predicament had seemed ideal to him. Diana, knowing she could never be with Donald, had decided to do the best that she could for her unborn child—had married the wealthy businessman, and Jordan had been brought up as James's son. Miraculously, eight years later, Diana and James had a child of their own, but Rhea's birth had robbed Diana of her own life, a fact James never quite forgave Rhea for. It was ironic, really; James had been determined that Jordan, who was no longer his legitimate heir, should inherit and run his business empire, while most of the time ignoring Rhea's very existence.

So, who was he—Jordan Somerville-Smythe or Jordan Quinlan? At the moment he just didn't know.

And Grace believed he was Jordan *Gregory*, he realised with a groan. And he couldn't tell her any of this, he also realised—not without revealing who he really was and promptly being asked to leave! It wasn't even possible to tell her Raff's surname; he was listed as the other director, along with Jordan Somerville-Smythe, of the company that wanted to buy this house!

He straightened. 'Forget I said any of this,' he dismissed lightly. 'You have enough worries of your own without listening to my problems too.'

'Oh, but——'

'You shouldn't be such a good listener,' he chided teasingly, tapping her playfully on the tip of her nose, realising, even as he did it, that the action must seem condescending.

She looked up at him with reproachful eyes, and he knew he had hurt her feelings. But he was hurting himself more, if she could only but know it; he would like nothing more than to pour his heart out to this hauntingly lovely young woman. Her lips were soft and pink, slightly parted, and he moved towards her as if drawn to a magnet.

* * *

Grace knew he was going to kiss her seconds before his mouth claimed hers, parting her lips slightly even as she tilted her head towards his.

His lips were firm as they touched hers, moving gently, rhythmically, his arms enfolding her almost tenderly against the hardness of his body. Warmth spread through her body, making her tremble; her arms moved up about his neck as she increased the pressure of his mouth on hers, the trembling of her body becoming a tangible thing as one of his hands moved down her back, exploring the gentle contours there before moving lower and fitting the perfect curve of her body into his.

Gently he outlined the soft tremor of her lips with his tongue, seeking entrance, but not demanding it, groaning low in his throat as her lips parted in response.

He was gentle and yet strong, teaching her of a passion that, although it burned beneath the surface, he could control for both of them. But as his mouth hardened, his arms tightened about her, it was a passion he didn't seem to want to end any more than she did.

His hands moved over her restlessly, barely touching her breasts, and yet she quivered beneath the caress, feeling a leaping of her senses. Jordan raised his head with a shuddering groan, looking down into her dazed, passion-filled face. It wasn't that she had never been kissed before, Grace thought, only that she had never responded in quite this way before! What was it about this man that was so different? This man, of all people!

His smile was strained as he smoothed her hair back from her flushed cheeks. 'You shouldn't be so tempting to kiss, either,' he spoke gruffly, moving abruptly away from her. 'I think I had better go for that walk outside in the cold after all!'

Grace watched him go, that feeling she had had yesterday, of her life having changed irrevocably with this man's arrival here, even more forceful...

## CHAPTER FIVE

'I KNOW, I know.' Nick held up his hands defensively as he opened his door to Grace's knock a short time later. 'I behaved disgracefully to the new guest,' he admitted without any sign of apology for having done so.

She had forgotten all about that because of what had happened later, couldn't even remember what had been said during dinner between the two men, had come up here to the sanctuary of Nick's rooms for a completely different reason!

But now that he mentioned it...

'Yes, you did behave disgracefully,' she agreed disapprovingly, strolling past him into the lounge, not surprised to see it was even more untidy than it had been earlier in the day. 'And without provocation, I might add.' She turned to him, frowning her displeasure.

Nick gave a grimace, closing the door. 'The man is a walking provocation! You might at least have warned me——'

'Of what?' Her frown deepened.

His look was scornful. 'Grace, the man doesn't belong here——'

'Neither do you,' she pointed out firmly. 'Your place is in London.'

Nick's mouth tightened. 'I choose to stay here,' he bit out.

'So, for the moment, does Jordan,' she reasoned with a shrug.

'Why?' His eyes were narrowed to dark brown slits. 'He's obviously wealthy, certainly isn't lacking in self-confidence,' Nick scorned, 'so what is he doing hiding out here?'

'Nick——'

'The man is up to something, Grace.' He paced the room. 'I can feel it!'

'What you can *feel* is your own prejudice!' she told him impatiently. 'Jordan has just as much right to stay here, if he wishes, as you do——'

'So you told me earlier,' he recalled bitterly.

'Nick,' she sighed, 'I'm sure you're right, and he does have his own reasons for choosing to come *here*, of all places,' she added placatingly as he looked unconvinced, knowing better than anyone why Jordan was likely to be here. 'But shouldn't we respect the privacy of those reasons?' she encouraged softly.

'I don't like him——'

'Well, I do!' She could feel the heat spreading up her cheeks as Nick looked at her searchingly for her vehemence, shaking her head wearily. 'The conversation is irrelevant anyway, Nick, because I have already agreed he can stay on here. And I have no intention of going back on that decision,' she added firmly as he would have interrupted.

'Even if his presence here proves disruptive to the general peace and harmony of the household?' Nick challenged harshly.

Jordan had already proved to be very disruptive to her own peace and harmony! Grace had never felt so disturbed and unsettled, filled with a nervous tension that was completely alien to her nature. But the thought of his leaving now—oh, God, what was happening to her?

'I'm sure you're exaggerating the effect of his being here, Nick, because of your own dislike of him,' she sighed.

'I know the type——'

'Jordan isn't a *type*!' she snapped, and then sighed frustratedly as Nick's gaze narrowed on her suspiciously. 'Look, would you mind if I don't stay up here this evening? I'm really too tired.'

Tired was the last thing she actually felt, but she knew if she stayed up here long enough Nick would keep on and on at her until he discovered just how much she *didn't* dislike Jordan. And if he did that she would never hear the end of it!

'Not at all,' he snapped coldly, his displeasure obvious. 'I'm not in the mood tonight anyway.'

He was really very angry with her, she could tell that, and the last thing she wanted was to fall out with Nick; they had been together too long, shared too much pain and suffering. But the time she had spent in Jordan's arms earlier had thrown her into complete confusion, and she could see there was going to be no sympathy from Nick tonight in helping her understand that confusion.

Maybe Timothy's young innocence would offer more comfort . . .

She came to an abrupt halt in the doorway of her little brother's bedroom as she saw he wasn't alone, that seated on the side of his bed, reading him one of the adventure stories he liked so much, was Jordan!

Jordan had his back towards her as she came quietly into the room, and so he didn't see her, but Timothy did, and she raised a silencing finger to her lips so that he shouldn't alert Jordan to her presence and thus have his story interrupted.

She stood silently at the back of the bedroom, listening to the deep tenor of Jordan's voice rather than the story itself, watching him in profile, the normally harsh lines of his face softened to indulgence as he read to the rapt Timothy. Grace could easily understand her brother's fascination; Jordan told the story well, using all the differing voices to make it more interesting.

'I think perhaps you had better try to go to sleep now,' Jordan told the little boy ruefully when he came to the end of the story five minutes later.

'I think perhaps he had better try to go to sleep, too,' Grace remarked teasingly from behind him.

Jordan spun around guiltily, standing up, the book still in his hand. 'I was passing Tim's bedroom earlier, and——'

'You don't have to make excuses to me,' she laughingly replied as she moved towards them both. 'I know only too well how enticing this young man can be.' She ruffled Timothy's hair affectionately as he grinned up at her.

'I haven't intruded on something you usually do with Tim, have I?' Jordan looked deeply troubled at the thought.

And Grace could guess why, in part, from the little he had confided in her earlier. She knew there was a lot he hadn't told her, but it had been enough for her to realise how difficult he would find it to be accepted as part of any family now that he was very aware of the childhood he had lost with his own brother, and would hate to feel he was intruding now upon the relationship between Grace and her young brother.

'Not in the least,' she easily—and truthfully—dismissed that idea. 'If I have time I read Tim a story, but more often than not it just doesn't happen. I'm sure he's grateful you came along when you did. Besides,' she added teasingly, as he still didn't look convinced, 'you read so much better than I do!'

Jordan relaxed slightly, although he looked a little embarrassed that she had overheard him telling the story. 'I had plenty of practice with my sister Rhea,' he said, shrugging off that explanation.

He couldn't have been that old himself when his sister was old enough to enjoy having stories read to her; so where had his parents been?

There was so much she wanted to know about this man still, but until he chose to tell her—if he chose to tell her!—she couldn't force the issue. She was sure, having come to know him as little as she did, that he had already told her more about himself than he would have most people on so short an acquaintance. On any acquaintance! He was a solitary man, she felt sure of it.

'Sleep, young man.' She ruffled Timothy's hair again, didn't think he would appreciate her bending down for the hug and kiss he usually gave her, not in front of this man he was rapidly becoming fond of—not very manly, Timothy would probably think.

Grace gave him an understanding smile, waiting while he thanked Jordan for the story, and closing the door softly behind the two of them on their way out. She suddenly felt very self-conscious now they were alone in the hallway.

'He may protest a little, but he'll be asleep in minutes,' she told Jordan with certainty.

He looked down at her with dark eyes. 'Have you looked after him very long yourself?' His voice was gently enquiring.

'My mother died of complications at his birth,' she confirmed, her voice lowered too, so that Timothy shouldn't hear.

'My God!' He swallowed hard. 'So did mine. At Rhea's birth, I mean,' he explained a little agitatedly.

What a terrible thing for them to have in common. How terribly, terribly sad for all of them...

Grace put her hand on Jordan's arm. 'That must have been awful for you, given the other—circumstances,' she added awkwardly.

'Oh, I didn't know about any of that then.' He shook his head, giving a harsh, mirthless laugh. 'Thank God!'

But it gave them a bond.

She broke his gaze with effort, feeling herself being drawn further and further into whatever spell was being cast over the two of them. Not this man, she tried to warn herself. She couldn't become involved with this man, not emotionally or any other way.

'I'd better go down and pack Tim's lunch for tomorrow.' She turned away.

'Er——'

She turned back with a frown at the uncertainty in his voice; it was so unlike him that she couldn't help but give him her full attention.

Jordan looked a little embarrassed, another emotion that was alien to him, Grace was sure. 'I—would it be all right if I drove Tim to school in the morning? I—half promised him that I would. If you had no objections.' He grimaced.

Grace frowned up at him for several seconds while she took in exactly what he was asking, and then her lips began to twitch, and finally she couldn't stop the laughter. 'You've been had, Jordan,' she chuckled. 'You do realise that?' She shook her head ruefully. 'Today Tim went to school and boasted to all his friends about "being in a Jag"; tomorrow he intends to actually turn up in it!'

Jordan relaxed, grinning too. 'I guessed it was something like that,' he nodded ruefully.

'But you want to do it anyway?' she realised softly.

He looked a little anxious at the sudden disappearance of her humour. 'Only if you agree that I can. I wouldn't want to——'

'Jordan, Tim has too little contact with men as it is,' she cut in gently. 'I certainly wouldn't want to stop your driving him to school if that's what you want to do. Nick does his best, but—well, he has his own ghosts to deal with,' she dismissed abruptly. 'He does what he can,' she insisted firmly.

The uncertainty had disappeared from Jordan's face at the mention of the other man's name, and now he looked more like the distantly forbidding stranger she had first met yesterday. What was it about Nick that antagonised him so much?

Nick could be a little unorthodox in his way, she had to admit, but his heart was in the right place; he just didn't always know how to express what he was feeling.

Although neither he nor Jordan seemed to have had any problem in that direction earlier!

Damn Nick Parrish! Jordan inwardly cursed the other man. Why was the other man living here at all? What was he to Grace?

It was a sure fact that Parrish didn't belong in this gentle atmosphere any more than he did. Now that he had spoken to the other man he recognised the type only too well. There were dozens just like him in London—brash to the point of rudeness, cynical after years of mixing with a crowd where anything went, literally. Jordan despised the type, had never had time for any of them when he spent most of his time in town, so perhaps that was the reason Parrish had seemed so familiar the first time he had seen him.

And, whatever his reasons for being here, Jordan didn't like the thought of the other man being anywhere near Grace.

But he realised, despite the fact that Grace hadn't repulsed his kiss earlier, that he had no right to tell her how he felt about Nick. He felt hopeful at her response to him, knew she would never have let him kiss her, let alone responded to him the way she had, if she were involved with Parrish. So what was the relationship?

Timothy would know...

He despised himself now, for even thinking of stooping to such a level!

But the temptation was there, none the less...

'Let me make you a coffee while you pack Tim's lunch,' he found himself offering, whether as an apology for even having such underhand thoughts, or because he just didn't want to say goodnight to this beautiful woman just yet, he wasn't sure. A little of both, he suspected.

'I should say no.' Grace gave a regretful smile. 'After all, you are the guest here. But, to be truthful,' she added conspiratorially, 'the thought of someone making me a cup of coffee is a luxury that makes me feel thoroughly spoiled!' Her eyes glowed with the unexpected pleasure of it.

How easily pleased this young woman was, Jordan thought, once again held captive by her beauty, following her down the stairs, slightly regretful at leaving the intimacy of the dimly lit hallway, although the cosy comfort of the well-scrubbed kitchen more than made up for any disappointment he might feel.

As he made the coffee and Grace moved easily about the room preparing the lunch-box, he realised they might almost be any young couple enjoying the easy intimacy of a quiet evening together.

Incredible! He had never before had such disturbing thoughts. Disturbing to his enjoyed solitude, that was.

But did he actually enjoy that solitude any more, or was it just a comfortable cloak he draped about himself whenever he felt the need? Had seeing Rhea and Raff together the last couple of years made him hunger for the intimacy they had, the intimacy of a loving relationship?

God, *that* wasn't the 'something' he had been aching for—was it?

Because when he was with Grace that ache wasn't there any more...

## CHAPTER SIX

'OH, TIMOTHY, we can't,' Grace protested wearily. 'It's far too early.'

'It's the first of December,' he pointed out hopefully, grey eyes raised in silent pleading.

They couldn't possibly put their Christmas decorations up yet; it was far too——

She had looked up and seen the same silent pleading in cobalt-blue eyes, Jordan having picked Timothy up from school a short time ago, the three of them now enjoying a warming drink together in the kitchen.

Over the last few days Jordan had been very helpful where Timothy was concerned, and as the two of them got on so well Grace could hardly object to the amount of time they spent together. She was a little concerned, however, about how Timothy was going to feel when it came time for Jordan to leave...

Although she had to admit she had started to put off that thought herself, Jordan having become so much a part of the household over the last four days.

That look of pleading, part of a conspiracy between the two, she was sure, over the Christmas decorations, was her undoing!

'We'll be the only people in the area with decorations and lights up,' she grumbled unconvincingly, already trying to remember where she had packed the decorations away when they had taken them down the previous year. After weeks and weeks of having the house cluttered up with them—or so it had seemed at the time!—she had just been glad to get them down out of the way. Besides, last Christmas had been their first since—— It hadn't been a happy time, although they had all tried, for Timothy's sake. To a child a week could seem a long time, and it had been six months since their father died—aeons to a small child. This year would be better, Grace was sure.

Would Jordan still be here at Christmas? It was over three weeks away; he had certainly given no indication that he would be staying as long as that. Although he had been out and bought another new jumper and a pair of trousers yesterday...

'That means she's given in—that we can!' Timothy was jumping up and down excitedly now, his eyes glowing. 'Can we do it now, Grace?' he urged eagerly. 'Can we? Oh, please——'

'After dinner, when we can all join in,' she cut in firmly, acknowledging that she had 'given in'. 'Christmas decorations are for the whole family.' She blushed slightly as dark blue eyes met her gaze steadily.

Timothy looked disappointed, but he quickly brightened again. 'Well, then, can Jordan and I get the things out ready?'

Jordan and I. Almost as if the two of them were on a level. And perhaps to Timothy they were, Grace realised ruefully.

'Homework first if you're going to spend the evening putting up decorations——'

'Oh, Grace, no!' her younger brother complained disgruntedly.

'Grace is right, Tim,' Jordan put in softly. 'This way you can enjoy the evening.'

Grace watched the emotions flickering across Timothy's face as the excitement of looking for the Christmas decorations and yet the desire to also please his new hero warred within him. The latter finally won as Timothy picked up his schoolbag before slowly going up to his room to do the homework.

The silence he left behind him was one of slight awkwardness.

'I shouldn't have interfered.' Jordan was finally the one to speak, grimacing as he did so.

'Of course you should,' Grace dismissed in some surprise. 'I don't mean interfered——' she felt warmth in her cheeks '—because I don't consider that was what you did. Timothy respects you, listens to you.'

Jordan was slightly pale, the new jumper he had bought and was wearing the same dark cobalt-blue of his eyes. His hair curled slightly over its polo-neck, looking very dark. 'I'm intruding,' he muttered harshly.

She acted on impulse, moving to where he still sat at the kitchen table to bend down and lightly kiss him on the cheek. '*You* are far too sensitive,' she teased him lightly. 'I'm really not the type of woman to get in a possessive froth because someone else chooses to help discipline Timothy. I just want him to grow up respecting his elders. And I believe he already does that,' she shrugged.

A nerve pulsed in Jordan's cheek where she had just kissed him. 'I've been accused of being *in*sensitive.'

She made a face. 'Only by people who don't really know you, I'm sure.'

His mouth twisted. 'They seem to think they do!'

'Well, we know better. Timothy and I,' she explained at his questioning look.

He stood up slowly, suddenly very close. 'You don't really know me at all,' he told her huskily.

'What I do know, I like. And I trust Timothy's judgement,' she added firmly, aware of the faint noises of the other people in the house, and yet feeling very much alone down here with Jordan, almost as if they were in a world apart from everyone else.

Jordan shook his head. 'He could be wrong about me too.'

Grace met his gaze unblinkingly. 'I don't think so.' She spoke huskily as he moved even nearer.

'Don't say I didn't try to warn you,' he groaned, his arms going about her waist as he stepped in close to her body.

There was so much strength in his wide shoulders, tapered waist and powerful thighs, his legs long and muscular beneath dark trousers, and yet he didn't try to use any of it on her.

He didn't have to! She swayed towards him, her eyes closed.

'Grace...?'

She blinked up at him, just wanting him to kiss her as he had before.

'Don't say I didn't warn you!' he repeated forcefully, his head lowering to hers.

There was no tentative exploration this time, lips possessing, bodies welded together, hers somehow fitting perfectly along the lean length of Jordan's, her arms up about his neck as her fingers became entangled in the dark thickness of his hair.

She was even starting to love the smell of him, a clean, muscular smell with the faint tang of aftershave that was only Jordan!

Their lips moved together hungrily, warm breath scalding her cheeks as Jordan trailed kisses down her throat to the pulse that beat at its hollow base. Pleasure coursed through her body as a fiery tongue caressed that hollow, sending shivers of sensation down her spine and arms to her very fingertips.

She gasped as his hand moved to cup her breast, but her gasp quickly turned to a groan as a single caress sought the hardened tip, the heat in her body becoming a blaze now, her fingers in his hair roughly pulling him to her as his lips returned to hers.

But suddenly she was no longer in his arms but standing alone, her hand reaching out to grasp the table in case she should sway and fall, staring at him in numbed surprise at his sudden desertion of her. Was this what he had been warning her about? What had happened to make him——?

'Well, well, isn't this cosy?' drawled an all-too-familiar voice from behind her.

Grace spun round almost guiltily to look at Nick, whose blond brows were raised tauntingly in his cynical face, then turned slowly back to look at Jordan as he stood so tautly across the room, knowing he must have heard the approach of Nick's footsteps down the stairs and moved away so suddenly to save her embarrassment with the other man.

Thank God he had; Nick would have demanded an explanation if he had actually found them in each other's arms! And even she wasn't sure what was happening between herself and Jordan, certainly couldn't explain the attraction to Nick.

He was looking at the two of them slightly suspiciously anyway, as if he half guessed what had taken place in this room minutes ago.

Which wasn't altogether surprising; Jordan's usually immaculate hair was still ruffled by her fingers, and she was sure she hadn't escaped unscathed herself, her hair in more disarray than usual, her lips feeling swollen from the kisses they had shared. She knew Nick wouldn't miss such obvious signs of intimacy. Which was unfortunate, because in his unnecessary guise as protector to her he was sure to be even more brittle and sarcastic with Jordan than he usually was.

She looked at Jordan pleadingly, willing him not to react. But it would be too much to hope that he wouldn't; the two men were too much alike!

'We were just discussing Christmas decorations,' she spoke in a voice she knew was far too loud!

Nick adopted a challenging pose as he leaned back against one of the kitchen units, his arms folded across the chest of the thick shirt he wore tucked into worn denims. 'Oh, yes?'

Her mouth firmed at the taunt in his voice. 'Timothy wants to put them up this evening.'

'And?'

She felt the colour enter her cheeks. 'And so we're putting them up this evening,' she admitted ruefully.

'I thought we might be,' Nick drawled derisively.

'Timothy is just excited about the prospect of Christmas,' Jordan put in defensively.

Brown eyes flashed angrily at the rebuke. 'I haven't forgotten what it's like to be a child at Christmas, Gregory,' Nick growled.

Jordan stiffened, glancing at Grace, as if he half expected—— No, he couldn't think she would have confided any of the things he had told her about his private life to Nick!

'Nick believes I over-indulge Timothy,' she hastened to explain Nick's attitude.

'Timothy is a well-balanced little boy,' Jordan instantly defended. 'Certainly not spoiled.'

Oh, dear, she had introduced yet another volatile subject between these two men. Was there one that wasn't?

'I——'

'To get back to the subject of the decorations,' she firmly cut into what she knew was going to be Nick's angry reply. 'We'll need them to be brought down from one of the bedrooms.'

'I'll get them, I know where they are—after all, I helped put them away last year,' Nick answered her, but he was looking at Jordan with narrowed eyes. 'It seems a pity that you'll be helping to put up the Christmas decorations but won't actually be here then,' he added challengingly.

The next remark was predictable in the face of Nick's deliberate baiting of the other man!

'I have no plans to leave before that time,' was Jordan's instant come-back.

Anger flared in Nick's eyes, and, although it had been slow in coming, Grace thought he might finally be beginning to realise he had met a man who was more than a match for him. He made no answering comment anyway, leaving abruptly to go in search of the decorations!

Arrogant bastard!

Jordan watched the other man leave the room with narrowed eyes, wishing his personal assistant would hurry up and find that file on Charlton House and its occupants, wanting to know more about Nick Parrish, feeling out of his depth with him without that detailed information. He should have read the damned thing more thoroughly when it was originally on his desk!

And now, it seemed, he had been antagonised into committing himself to staying on here for Christmas. Three and a half weeks away...

The situation with Grace was getting beyond his control already; God knew what would happen after another month in the same house as her!

And Rhea and Raff would be expecting him back at Quinlan House for Christmas; in fact they were counting on it—they always spent Christmas together.

Besides, he couldn't continue to ignore his business commitments indefinitely. Much as the temptation was to do just that.

That realisation stopped him in his tracks. He had never felt that way about his work before; it had always come first with him...

'Jordan?'

He turned to Grace, forcing a reassuring smile as she looked at him anxiously. Whatever his problems, this enchantingly lovely woman, both inside and out, was not one of them. His growing feelings for her were, but Grace herself was not...

'Miles away,' he excused, quite truthfully as it happened; Hampshire, and Rhea and Raff, *were* miles away. It might be better if they weren't. 'Do you think I could——?'

'Ah, here the two of you are.' Jessie smiled at the pair of them glowingly as she entered the kitchen. 'Jordan, there's a telephone call for you.'

He could feel himself growing pale. 'For me?' he echoed hollowly. It couldn't be. No one knew—Rhea...?

It had been too much to hope that his little sister would meekly accept his decision to take a break here without trying to make further contact with him; he should have known her better than that, Jordan realised.

But she could have ruined everything for him, blundering in the way she had!

That realisation made him aware of just how emotionally involved with Grace he was becoming, of how reluctant he was to have the gentle trust in her eyes when she looked at him turn to disgust and suspicion. As it surely must, even if the reasons for his assuming the identity of J. Gregory were completely innocent, his original reasons for coming to Charlton House all but forgotten—certainly they had been dismissed. Grace, and the other people who lived in this exceptional house, should be left to enjoy living here in peace and harmony.

Although, in the circumstances, Grace was hardly likely to believe he felt that way, would hate his subterfuge, being so lacking in it herself.

'Oh, yes,' Jessie confirmed lightly. 'It's a young lady,' she added coyly.

Definitely Rhea, because there was no other 'young lady' in his life. Damn! How was he going to explain any of this to Grace?

'Jordan?' Grace prompted now in a puzzled voice as he still made no effort to go upstairs and take his call.

'Oh, yes,' he acknowledged with a feeling of dread; Jessie was sure to blurt out the truth of his identity—even though she perhaps didn't realise the enormity of it!—while he was upstairs talking to Rhea! And Grace would know exactly what she thought of it—and him! 'I—shouldn't be long,' he added lamely, reluctant to leave the two women alone, but knowing he had no choice.

He would have time enough to attempt to defend his actions to Grace after he had spoken to Rhea, he realised dully.

Nick Parrish was clattering back down the stairs as Jordan approached them, and so he stood and waited for the other man to get to the bottom.

'Quite right,' he drawled mockingly. 'It's bad luck to cross on the stairs.'

Bad luck; Jordan felt as if his world was about to fall apart before he was completely sure what he was looking for!

'Changed your mind about the decorations?' the other man taunted, easily carrying the box of them, and assuming Jordan was going to his room.

They faced each other at the bottom of the stairs, obvious adversaries.

'I rarely change my mind once it's made up,' Jordan told the other man harshly. 'And I knew from the minute I met you that I wasn't going to like you; nothing that has happened since that time has changed that opinion!' With this parting shot he moved unhurriedly up the stairs.

He knew he had been provoked, after their earlier conversation, into declaring war on Nick, and yet the man seemed to take delight in being deliberately insulting. The same instant dislike Jordan had felt for him, he would say.

But he had much more important things to think about than Nick Parrish just now!

He picked up the telephone receiver from where it lay on the table-top in Grace's office-cum-sitting-room. 'Rhea?' he rasped without preamble, absolutely furious at the trouble she had undoubtedly caused for him here with her unwanted telephone call.

'Mr Gregory, I presume?' she returned drily, not at all deterred by his anger.

'What—how——?' He knew he was gabbling, but for once, he admitted, Rhea had caught him off guard.

His sister laughed softly. 'I've just had a rather garbled conversation with your Miss Brown——'

'Grace?' That startled him out of his confusion. Grace had been down in the kitchen with him when the call had come through; he could still remember the imprint of her body pressed up against his so that not even a wisp of air separated them...so how could she possibly have——? Jessie! Somehow Rhea had made the same mistaken assumption he had when he'd first arrived here. 'Oh, yes?' he prompted lightly; there might be hope for him yet, Rhea had mockingly called him 'Mr Gregory', after all!

'She sounds very sweet, Jordan,' Rhea acknowledged. 'But a little odd too.'

'She is very sweet,' he confirmed warily.

'Always the gentleman, Jordan,' Rhea teased. 'But, among all the confusion of our cross-purpose conversation, I managed to ascertain that the man I wanted to talk to was the new boarder, a Mr Gregory. Gregory?'

'It's a long story, Rhea,' he sighed, wishing he weren't having this conversation at all.

'I'm in no hurry,' she mocked.

'But I am!' He sat on the side of the desk. 'I'll explain everything when I get back.'

'And just when is that going to be?' she put in quickly.

'I'm not sure,' he dismissed easily. 'Do you happen to know if David has found the Charlton House file yet?'

'That's one of the reasons I telephoned there; none of us was absolutely sure where you were staying, and so David has no idea where to send the file. Or if you're still interested,' Rhea added curiously.

'I'm still interested,' he told her firmly. 'And now you know David can send the file here.'

'To Mr Gregory,' she guessed drily.

'To Mr Gregory,' he confirmed tautly. '"One of the reasons you telephoned"?' he prompted abruptly.

She laughed softly at his astuteness. 'I also wanted to know how you were,' she admitted ruefully.

'And exactly where I was,' he guessed shrewdly. 'Well, now you know!'

'So I do,' Rhea teased unconcernedly. 'Feel any more inclined to tell me what you're up to?'

'No.'

She laughed softly. 'I thought not,' she drawled. 'Well, as long as you're sure you're all right...?'

'I'm a big boy now, Rhea,' he sighed, 'so stop worrying about me.'

'I can't do that, Jordan.' She was suddenly serious. 'I happen to love you.'

They weren't a sentimental family, their affection for each other just an accepted thing between them, and so his sister's declaration was all the more touching because of that.

'I love you too,' he told her gruffly. 'But don't telephone me here again!' he added hardly.

Rhea chuckled in delight at his instant switch back into character. 'No, sir. I must say, you sound happy enough,' she said curiously. 'The change is obviously as good as a rest in your case.'

'Rhea, you're starting to waffle yourself now,' he told her with his usual brutal honesty. 'Go away and pester your husband, or feed the baby, or something!'

'Raff is busy at the moment playing "mine host", and Diana is already in bed for the night,' his sister dismissed lightly.

'There's always "or something",' Jordan reminded her callously. 'Goodnight, Rhea.'

'Goodnight, Jordan,' she came back unconcernedly. 'Take care.'

All he could think of once he had replaced the receiver was that his real identity hadn't been revealed after all!

* * *

Grace didn't think she would ever tire of watching Timothy's face as the decorations went up, giving the rooms and hallways a glittering festivity, albeit a tarnished adornment that she knew the adults, at least, would be long tired of before Twelfth Night, when they officially had to all come down again!

But for the moment the faded rooms were taking on a light and colour that was mesmerisingly beautiful, and all of them seemed to be infected with the Christmas spirit.

Even Nick—who had decided to join them at the last minute—and Jordan seemed to have dropped hostilities for this special time! Although there had been one small dispute over where a particular shining star should be suspended from...

Timothy had ended that disagreement before it could actually become a proper one by putting it over the fireplace, so that none of them should forget that Christmas was actually about Jesus being born. Grace had ruefully recognised her own words being thrown back at them! But she was pleased to learn that Timothy had actually listened to her and understood what she had been trying to say to him.

She watched Jordan now as he stood on one of the step-ladders draping holly behind a mirror. Would he be with them for Christmas this year? He had said 'yes' earlier, although she realised that that had been after much provocation. She couldn't honestly see him staying on here that long.

'You're supposed to kiss each other,' Timothy giggled beside her.

Grace looked down at him a little dazedly, shaken by his remark after her thoughts had so recently been on Jordan; Timothy couldn't possibly know anything about the kisses they had shared both this morning and tonight, and yet what else could he——?

'Up here, Grace!' Jessie called teasingly, and Grace looked up to find the other woman on the other pair of step-ladders with a piece of mistletoe she was intending to attach to the ceiling with the aid of a drawing-pin.

As Grace was innocently standing next to Nick when the challenge was made, it was clear what the mischievous pair's intention was!

Jordan had turned to look at them all now, eyes narrowed, waiting to see what her next move would be. Grace hesitated because of that, but Nick felt no such qualms, sweeping her up into his arms to hug and kiss her.

'Your turn now, Jordan,' Timothy dared, his eyes aglow.

Jordan shook his head, coming down the ladder. 'I don't think that's the way it works, Tim,' he said ruefully.

'You have to get the girl you want to kiss actually next to you underneath the mistletoe,' Nick explained to the little boy, his arm still about Grace's shoulders.

'Well? Tim frowned pointedly at Jordan, as the latter didn't move.

'I don't think——' Jordan broke off, his gaze fixed somewhere behind Grace and Nick. 'Jessie, I think perhaps you ought to come down from there,' he advised in a calm voice, moving towards the elderly lady as he did so.

'Yes, I think you—oh!'

Before any of them could reach Jessie she had misplaced her foot on the next step, missing it completely as she tumbled down on to the carpeted floor with a telling thump.

## CHAPTER SEVEN

GRACE hated hospitals, had done so ever since her mother had died, and then her father followed her eighteen months ago. For some people they could be a place of hope, of life reborn, but they had only ever held unhappiness for Grace and her family, and she hated being here now.

They were examining Jessie, the elderly lady clutching on to Grace's hand, the pain in her ankle the obvious cause of the trouble. Grace knew that boded ill. It hadn't been a very big fall, a couple of feet at most, but Jessie was old, her bones brittle, and Grace very much suspected she might have broken her ankle. It would be awful if she had.

Jordan had taken control of the situation after Jessie's fall, insisting she wasn't moved, instructing Nick to go and call an ambulance once he had seen just how much pain Jessie was in—too much really for her to just be bruised. Nick ordinarily wasn't a man who liked being given orders by anyone, but even he recognised the seriousness of the situation and went without demur to use the telephone.

Tim had been the one who worried Grace the most, ashen-faced, standing back across the room from them all.

Grace would have liked to go to him, to reassure him, but Jessie was crying softly, obviously in shock as well as pain, and holding Grace's hand so tightly she felt as if the bones were crushed.

And Jessie had continued to hold her hand, had refused to let go even once the ambulance had arrived and the men with the vehicle had managed to get her outside on a stretcher and inside the ambulance.

There was no question but that Grace would accompany the elderly lady to the hospital, and yet she was still concerned about Tim, so she was grateful to Nick when he opted to stay behind with the little boy, while Jordan went with the two women in the ambulance.

Grace was grateful for his reassuring presence, for the way he had taken charge at the hospital, sitting outside in the waiting-room now.

Jessie wept anew when the doctor confirmed her ankle was broken and that they would have to admit her, and her bony fingers grasped Grace's hand as if she was frightened to let go in case she should never see Grace again.

Grace wanted to say something to comfort her, to reassure her, and yet the words stuck in her throat, words she had used twice in her life already—and they had proved to be lies. Neither

her mother nor father had ever left hospital again.

And then, miraculously, Jordan was there, talking softly to Jessie, comforting her in the way Grace couldn't, promising that they would stay with her while she was taken to the ward, that they wouldn't leave her until she was asleep—the doctor murmured that they were seeing about giving the elderly lady something to kill the pain and help her sleep right now—and that they would be back again in the morning; Jessie wouldn't even realise they had been away!

Grace felt ashamed that she wasn't able to give Jessie the support she needed, although for the moment, with Jordan's strength to draw from, it seemed to be enough for Jessie to have her hand to cling to while Jordan talked to her.

'She'll be fine,' Jordan reassured her in the taxi on the way back home.

But would she, *would she*? Jessie was as much a part of Grace's family as Timothy and Nick were, had become like an honorary grandmother to herself and Timothy. Charlton House was going to seem very empty without Jessie's happy presence.

'I should have made her get down from the ladder as soon as I saw her there,' Grace berated herself. 'I hadn't even realised she was up the ladder until——'

'Grace, self-condemnation, from any of us, isn't going to help anyone——' Jordan's hand stilled the nervous movements of hers '—least of all Jessie.'

Tears welled up in her eyes. 'I love her so much, I don't think I could bear it if——'

'Now that is just ridiculous,' he cut in briskly, unconcerned by the presence of the man driving the taxi as he slipped his arm about Grace's shoulders, nestling her snugly against him. 'Jessie is very healthy for her age——'

'But that's just it,' she choked, the tears starting to fall. 'Jessie is seventy-three, and——'

'As strong as an ox, despite her obvious look of frailty,' Jordan insisted firmly. 'She eats well, and is well looked after, and I see no reason why she shouldn't make a complete recovery from this.'

Grace looked at him searchingly in the dim lighting given off by the streetlamps before they reached the open countryside on the approach to the house. 'You aren't just saying that?'

His mouth twisted. 'Have I given you any reason to suppose I ever "just say" anything?' he said self-derisively.

Grace gave a tearful smile. 'No.'

'And I'm not about to start now,' he assured her decisively. 'Jessie needs *you* to be strong and positive now, so I recommend you get a good night's rest so that you feel able to cope with tomorrow.'

'Recommend?' she teased, feeling as if a weight was being lifted from her shoulders, but not daring to question why she trusted Jordan enough to accept it as being so when he told her everything was going to work out fine; she might be too disturbed by the answer she might find!

'Order, then,' he acknowledged ruefully. 'But my sister tells me I'm far too fond of giving orders.' He grimaced. 'And expecting them to be obeyed!'

'She sounds nice,' Grace said interestedly.

'I like her—but then, I daren't do otherwise!' He chuckled softly.

'Tell me more about her,' she encouraged, sure there wasn't a woman alive whom Jordan was genuinely in awe of. 'She sounds a lot like you.'

He started to talk about Rhea, of her madcap teenage years, the sense of fun she still had, although it was tempered slightly now by the responsibilities of marriage, her daughter, and by the way she helped her husband run their business on a day-to-day level.

Grace could hardly tell Jordan she would like to meet his sister—that sounded a little too familiar in the circumstances—and yet Rhea was only a couple of years older than herself, and she sounded good fun. She *would* like to meet her.

She knew Jordan was talking now for the sake of distracting her, but she liked listening to him, enjoyed the sound of his voice, as she rested her head drowsily against his shoulder, loving that male smell of him.

By the time they reached the house she did feel in control again, with the conviction that, with their help, Jessie would get well again. She had to, they all needed her!

There was only a light on in the hallway downstairs when they let themselves in, and Grace guessed that both Nick and Tim would have gone to bed by now; it was very late, after all.

'I'll make you some coffee or a hot chocolate to help you——'

'I'll do that,' Nick interrupted Jordan's offer as he came noisily down the stairs. 'I think you had better go up to Tim, Grace,' he sighed. 'I've tried to reassure the little chap, but he seems convinced Jessie is going to die, and refused to even think about going to sleep until you got back from the hospital.'

'Oh, God.' Grace paled. 'I knew he was upset, but—I'll go up to him.'

'He's in my rooms,' Nick told her heavily.

'I'll go up with you,' Jordan instantly offered.

Grace turned to him, knowing it wasn't an offer at all, that Jordan intended coming upstairs with her whether she wanted him to or not.

But she wanted him to.

Jordan just wanted to hold her, to tell her everything was going to be all right, but he had known as he had held her in the taxi earlier that Grace didn't very often give in to her own feelings of emotional need, that she had carried the responsibilities of this house and her family for too long to be able to do that easily.

She was too young for all this, too young and lovely, and he wanted to protect her from any more distress.

He was shaken by the fierceness of his own emotions. He knew he cared for Grace, but was he actually falling in love with her?

The possibility of that shook him more than anything else ever had in his life—even the trauma he had experienced two years ago. What did he know about love, especially for a unique woman like Grace?

He followed her now as she went up to the top of the house, where Nick Parrish's rooms seemed to be; Tim was sitting up on the sofa in the sitting-room there, albeit covered with a blanket. The grey eyes so like Grace's were wide with fear, his face deathly white, and he stared silently at Grace as she entered the room, seeming afraid to speak.

Grace went straight to him, and sat on the edge of the sofa. 'She's all right, Tim,' she soothed calmly, her own earlier panic put firmly to one side as she concentrated on the distressed child. 'Her ankle is broken—but she's strong,' she added firmly as Tim gave a dismayed gasp, using Jordan's words as her own in an effort to comfort him. 'I'll take you in to see her tomorrow.'

He shook his head. 'I don't want to go.'

'Tim!' she gasped her dismay, turning to Jordan again for help.

'Tim, for Jessie's sake I think you should go in and see her.' Jordan stepped forward out of the shadows. 'She needs you,' he added as Tim would have protested again. 'How do you think you would feel if the positions were reversed and Jessie refused to come and see you in hospital?' he reasoned gently.

He could see the child was beginning to waver at this, obviously not liking that thought at all. 'Jessie is going to be very lonely in hospital until they allow her to come home again.' Jordan pressed home his point while he felt he had some chance of success.

'Yes, we have to be very strong for her,' Grace said, taking up his line of argument as she saw it was having some effect on Tim. 'Jessie can't do it all alone,' she added softly.

Tim still looked indecisive, although some of the colour had returned to his cheeks. 'I'm not getting the tree or decorating it until Jessie comes home,' he finally said stubbornly, but it was at least an indication that he now accepted the elderly lady *would* come back.

Jordan hoped, more than anything, that he wasn't wrong about that! Old and slightly scatty as Jessie was, this family loved and needed her, he could see that. Jessie couldn't know just how fortunate she was...

But his attention returned to Grace and Tim as the little boy began to look anxious again.

'Peter won't come and take Jessie away now, will he?' Tim frowned up at Grace.

Her eyes widened, and Jordan could see the suggestion was a shock to her. 'I hadn't thought of that...' she gasped.

'But will he?' Timothy persisted worriedly.

'Of course not,' Grace dismissed with a certainty Jordan could see she was far from feeling, by the sudden shadows in her eyes. 'Jessie belongs here with us,' she added determinedly—although the shadows still remained.

Who the hell was Peter? Why should he want to take Jessie away from here? What *right* did he have to do so?

Hell, he hated being this much in the dark about anything. If that file on Charlton House didn't turn up in the post on Saturday morning, at the latest, he was going to give David his notice!

There was still the puzzle of Nick Parrish to bother him. This room obviously bore the stamp of the other man's personality, an indication of how at home he was here. The kitchen area could be seen through an open doorway to the left, but there were two other doors firmly closed to prying eyes—and Jordan readily admitted his *were* prying. His growing feelings for Grace made it vitally important that he know just how important Nick Parrish was to Grace herself.

What lay behind those two closed doors? A bedroom behind one, of course, but the other one? As far as Jordan could tell the other man rarely left the house, certainly hadn't gone out to work on any of the days Jordan had been there. So what did he do with himself all day?

Saturday morning at the latest, or David was sacked!

It was no good to keep telling himself he should have taken more notice of the Charlton House file himself in the first place instead of just treating it like another business proposal. He hadn't, and he knew that part of the reason for that was his growing dissatisfaction with his life, business as well as personal. And so to all intents and purposes he had arrived here completely unprepared, floundering about in the dark, too proud to ask David or Rhea to read out the relevant details over the telephone to him; God knew what Rhea would make of that if he did!

But he would find out about Nick Parrish; it was becoming vitally important to his peace of mind that he did so!

'Hot chocolate all round,' the man in question announced lightly as he came into the room bearing a tray containing four mugs.

Timothy blossomed in the reassuring presence of the three adults, brightening considerably as they all sat and drank their chocolate. This was obviously a treat for him, and one, now that he was less upset, he took full advantage of.

'Bed,' Grace finally told him firmly as he did his best to keep his eyes open.

His eyes instantly widened in an effort not to look tired. 'I'm not going to be ready for bed for ages yet——'

'You're going to bed now, young man,' he was told firmly by his sister. 'I'll take you to your room now, and then I have to make a telephone call. Peter,' she murmured softly to Nick as he looked at her frowningly for the lateness of the call, while Timothy was busy collecting up his things now that it seemed he wasn't about to get away with staying up any later.

The other man's frown didn't lighten at this brief explanation. 'Jordan and I can put Tim to bed,' Nick told her firmly. 'You go and make your call.'

Grace stood up, laying a gentle hand against Timothy's cheek. 'That all right with you?'

'Oh, yes,' he grinned at her as Nick picked him up and threw him over his shoulder.

Considering the other man's previous antagonism, Jordan couldn't help but admit to feeling surprised at his inclusion of him now, but he followed the man and boy unquestioningly down to Timothy's bedroom.

Nick had managed to get Timothy into his pyjamas earlier, but Tim had obviously stubbornly held out against anything else. The other man put the giggling little boy down in the bed now before turning to Jordan. 'Tim tells me you read a mean bedtime story.'

'Oh, yes, Jordan——' Timothy clapped his hands together in approval of this suggestion '—please!'

Jordan was still taken aback by the other man's sudden friendliness, he had to admit. From resenting him without even giving him a chance, the other man now seemed to have accepted him. Nick Parrish was an enigma!

'A short one,' Nick told Timothy now. 'You have school in the morning.'

Jordan gave a rueful shrug. 'I think he's going to have to give school a miss tomorrow.'

'Hurray!' Timothy squealed excitedly.

Nick gave Jordan a conspiratorial smile. 'I think you could be right,' he nodded.

Jordan didn't have any more time to ponder Nick's change of attitude, although he wasn't surprised to see, for all the boy's claims to the contrary, that Tim fell asleep after only three pages of the wanted story. He quietly closed the book, looking down at the youthfully vulnerable face, so like Grace's; he just wanted to hug the little boy.

'Endearing little devil, isn't he?'

Jordan looked up with a start, having briefly forgotten Nick Parrish was still in the bedroom with them. He stood up abruptly. 'Yes—yes, he is,' he nodded curtly.

The two men eyed each other awkwardly once outside the bedroom.

'Look,' Nick finally began slowly, 'I think I might have been a little—unwelcoming, when you first arrived here.' His voice was gruff. 'I—but you were there tonight, for Jessie, and for Grace, when they needed you, and so—well——' he struggled to find the right words '—welcome to Charlton House!' He held his hand out to shake Jordan's.

Jordan returned the gesture a little dazedly; this was the last thing he had been expecting.

Great; now he had been put in a position where he felt a certain responsibility of friendship towards the other man. That was the last thing he needed, feeling as he did himself about Grace!

Nick grimaced. 'I can tell you now that there's going to be trouble from Peter Amery. Jessie's son,' he explained at Jordan's questioning look. 'We had better go down and see how Grace got on with her call to him,' he sighed, obviously expecting the outcome to be a bad one.

Jessie's *son*! And he sounded as if he was going to be a complication. But no more so, surely, than the sudden friendliness of the man Jordan considered to be his rival where Grace was concerned!

Grace sat behind her desk in the little sitting-room, heard the two men come down the stairs together, and their approach to the sitting-room now. She blinked up at them a little dazedly, having received another blow she hadn't even considered earlier.

She had told Peter, Jessie's son, the situation, and was sure from his reaction to the news that he was going to use this situation to try to force the issue of having Jessie put into a home.

Most sons would have just been concerned that their mother was all right, the relief of that superseding everything else. But not Peter Amery—he would use this situation to his advantage if he could; Grace had no doubt of that.

In fact, he had just implied as much, had told her he would be going to see his mother in the morning, and that he would assess the situation then. Grace knew exactly what he meant by 'assess the situation'!

She had had a long-running battle with Peter Amery about his mother. He wanted Jessie put into a home, where he wouldn't have to give her another thought if he didn't want to. Jessie wanted to maintain her independence for as long as she could, to stay here at Charlton House, where she felt so much at home, with the people she loved; Grace knew that.

The accident, with Peter Amery's implication that there had been a lack of caring for Jessie's welfare for it to have happened at all, could jeopardise all that. And possibly now he would have the power to insist upon it.

Grace stood up abruptly. 'I think battle over Jessie is about to commence,' she choked, the tears finally beginning to fall in earnest.

And she didn't realise, for some time afterwards, that it was to the reassurance of Jordan's arms that she moved...

## CHAPTER EIGHT

GRACE stared at the woman who stood on the doorstep, completely tongue-tied for once in her life, having answered the ringing of the doorbell in all innocence a couple of minutes ago.

Was this Charlton House? the young woman had frowned. When Grace had confirmed it was, she had then asked if she might see Jordan!

His wife?

The woman was certainly lovely enough, deep-red hair almost down to her waist, although the burnished waves were secured back at the moment in a single plait down the length of her spine, her face small and pointed, dominated by dark blue eyes.

Jordan's wife? Grace wondered again. Who else would come all the way up here, hundreds of miles away from his home, to look for him?

Jordan's wife, Grace realised with a sinking heart; it had to be.

When, last night, he had kissed *her* with passion and need. Not just earlier in the kitchen, but later on in her bedroom too.

She had felt so tired and defeated after her call to Peter Amery and then her fit of weeping, had raised no objections when between them Nick and

Jordan had decided she needed to get to bed and have some sleep.

She had been too weary to even notice the new-found truce that seemed to exist between the two men, had only realised that this morning when Nick joined them downstairs in the kitchen for breakfast and the two men had actually shared *The Times* newspaper that had been delivered, Jordan taking the business section, Nick the other part!

But last night she had been too tired to notice any of that, going along meekly with Jordan when he insisted on accompanying her to her bedroom—she should have realised then that something had happened to change things between the two men; Nick wouldn't normally have let any man go to her bedroom with her. Not without a fight!

Grace had been surprised at how exhausted she had felt once she got to her bedroom—almost too weary to bother to get undressed.

Jordan had been the one to remove her clothes, item by item, with infinite gentleness, until he had slipped her silky nightgown over her head, and turned back the bedclothes before tucking her comfortably beneath them.

Grace had been the one to reach up and entwine her arms about his neck, pulling him down to her, groaning low in her throat as his lips gently claimed hers.

But gentleness wasn't what either of them wanted, and desire had quickly raged out of control; Grace's nightgown was soon discarded again, and Jordan's lips trailed moistly down her body to capture one turgid peak, caressing the hardened nub with the heat of his tongue.

She had wanted him so badly at that moment, arching up against him, seeking further contact, needing——

'I can't make love to you now!' Jordan had pulled back, breathing heavily, a slight flush to the hardness of his cheeks. 'Not now, Grace,' he groaned. 'It isn't that I don't want to——' he looked pained at the bewilderment in her face '—but when I make love to you I want it to be with no shadows hanging over us. Grace, do you understand?'

She had understood, but it hadn't stopped her longing for him; her body had ached for hours after he had left her, only the fact that he had said 'when' and not 'if' he made love to her stopping her from going to his bedroom.

And now, the very next afternoon, his wife had turned up here looking for him!

She looked nice too, her eyes warm, her smile friendly, her expression completely unsuspecting, full of bright enquiry. And Grace was the one left feeling guilty—when she had responded out of complete innocence!

'Is Jordan here?' The woman's smile began to falter. 'I do have the right house, don't I?'

'Oh, you have the right house,' Grace confirmed huskily, much to the other woman's obvious relief. 'Jordan just isn't here.'

'He hasn't left, has he?' she groaned. 'I haven't driven all this way for nothing?'

'Oh, no, he's still here. At least, he's still staying here,' Grace confirmed stiltedly. 'He just isn't here at the moment. He—he's taken my brother to the cinema,' she explained lamely.

Timothy had been far too tired to go to school this morning, and so, after going in to see Jessie in hospital earlier, Jordan had offered to take Timothy out for tea and then on to the early showing of a film that was all the rage with the youngsters at the moment, and which Grace hadn't yet found the time to take him to. As it was Saturday tomorrow, she wasn't too worried if he was a little later to bed tonight, and to be completely honest she had been glad to have him diverted in this way, still being deeply worried about the consequences of Peter Amery, who hadn't yet found the decency to go to see his mother, let alone come here to cause trouble!

The woman standing in front of her looked a little taken aback at this information. 'Jordan has gone to the cinema . . .?' If Grace had said he had taken a trip to the moon the woman couldn't have looked more astounded!

'Yes, he—— Look, you had better come in,' Grace invited awkwardly; they really couldn't continue this conversation standing on the doorstep—for one thing there was still snow on the ground, and it was freezing cold outside! Besides, Jordan wouldn't be back for at least another hour or so yet.

'I would love to,' the woman grinned gratefully. 'I'll just go and get the baby from the car.'

Baby? Baby! My God, Jordan wasn't just married, he—— Baby...?

The woman grimaced. 'She fell asleep in the back of the car ages ago, so I'll probably have her awake most of the evening now. I won't be a minute.' She turned and hurried off.

She... Suddenly Grace knew exactly who this woman was. A little belatedly she went over to the car to help carry the baby-bag that had appeared on the snow-covered gravel, while the woman bent inside the back of the car to unlock the baby's car seat.

Grace looked at her with new eyes, seeing the firmness of the jaw, the dark blue eyes. Admittedly there was little else to tell of her real identity, but even so Grace felt more than a little foolish for her earlier assumption.

As the woman straightened with the baby in her arms Grace couldn't help smiling at the impishly lovely face surrounded by curls as red as her mother's—as red as Grace's own. Jordan seemed to have a weakness for redheads!

'This must be Diana,' she murmured admiringly, touching one starfish hand, finding herself the focus of dark grey eyes. 'And you're Rhea,

Jordan's sister,' she said more confidently. 'You must have thought me very rude just now,' she apologised ruefully as they walked over to the house, the light and warmth inside looking very welcoming.

The other woman looked at her with new eyes. 'Jordan told you about us?'

'He—mentioned you,' Grace nodded truthfully.

Rhea was still looking at her with curiosity, although the baby's attention had now wandered to her new surroundings. 'I hope you don't think me awfully rude,' she finally said regretfully, 'but I'm afraid he's told us absolutely nothing about you!'

She couldn't help but laugh at the other woman's candour. 'There's no reason why he should have done,' she dismissed lightly. 'I'm Grace Brown.' She transferred the baby-bag to her other arm, holding out her hand in greeting.

For a moment Rhea looked even more stunned than she had when Grace had told her of Jordan's whereabouts, but she recovered quickly, returning the gesture warmly. 'Perhaps I understand Jordan's omission now,' she said enigmatically.

'Sorry?' Grace frowned her puzzlement.

'It isn't important.' Jordan's sister shook her head, her attention returning to the baby in her arms as Diana struggled to be put down. 'Do you mind?'

'Not in the least,' Grace invited instantly, enchanted with the little girl as she began to toddle about curiously.

And so it was that when Jordan and Timothy returned to the house a short time later they found Grace and Rhea chatting comfortably in the sitting-room, Diana playing happily at their feet with some old toys of Timothy's that Grace had managed to find hidden away in a cupboard.

Jordan looked totally stunned at seeing the three of them together!

The three most important females in his life were all redheads!

It had never occurred to him before, probably because for a lot of the time he had known Grace he had been fighting the feelings he had for her, but, as he looked at Grace and Rhea sitting together so naturally, baby Diana playing at their feet, he knew that these three females possessed most of his heart.

He was shaken by the realisation, too confused to speak.

Rhea, misunderstanding his silence as anger with her for being here at all, jumped to her feet to come over and hug him warmly. 'I decided to bring those papers you wanted myself,' she explained brightly.

'So I see,' he returned drily, his gaze mocking in its rebuke.

She met that gaze for several seconds, and then she couldn't sustain it any longer, so turned away. 'Look, Diana.' She bent to scoop the baby up into her arms. 'Look who's here,' she encouraged softly as the little girl looked slightly rebellious at being interrupted with her new toys.

Eyes as dark a grey as her father's were turned on Jordan, and he felt his heart melt—Diana was Rhea's ultimate weapon when she thought she might be in danger of seriously incurring his displeasure; she knew he couldn't resist the darling in her arms.

'Uncjordan!' Diana recognised him instantly—she should do, really; there had hardly been a day in her young life when she hadn't seen him—if only for a short time!—and she held out her arms to be taken for their usual cuddle.

The way she had of making 'Uncjordan' one word was endearing in itself, and, after handing Grace the mail Timothy had got out of the box at the end of the driveway, Jordan gently gathered the baby into his arms, nuzzling softly against her throat until she gave a delighted chuckle.

'I was just asking Grace if I might use the telephone to call Raff,' Rhea announced briskly—as if daring Jordan to challenge her.

Grace put the letters and cards away in the pocket of the pinafore dress she wore over a pale green jumper. 'Of course you can,' she said instantly. 'I'll just show you where the telephone is.'

'I take it you don't intend driving back to Hampshire this evening?' Jordan softly taunted his sister before she could leave the room.

Rhea gave him a reproving look. 'Grace has kindly offered us a room here for the night, and as I brought Diana's travel-cot with me it works out perfectly.'

'How clever of you,' he drawled, not fooled by his sister's innocent expression for a moment, knowing she was here because she was curious about his sudden need to spend time alone.

She gave him a bright, unconcerned smile, his double meaning not lost on her, but completely unimportant to her way of thinking. 'Yes, wasn't it?'

Jordan was shaking his head ruefully as he sat down with Diana on his knee, Timothy watching him with widely curious eyes.

The two of them had spent an enjoyable time visiting Jessie, who seemed a lot better today, and then going on to the cinema. Neither of them had envisaged their evening ending like this, Jordan felt sure!

'Come and say hello,' he encouraged gently at the little boy's apprehensive look at the tiny human being in Jordan's arms who looked so fragile she might break; babies were obviously out of Timothy's usual experience.

Timothy touched Diana's hand tentatively until she took the initiative, reaching out with one of her hands and grabbing a handful of his hair. 'Ouch!' he complained.

Jordan chuckled as he easily released the little boy. 'Not as fragile as she looks, hm?' he teased, putting Diana back down among the toys, and watching indulgently as Timothy sat down on the floor too and began to play with her.

They might have been brother and sister, identical redheads bent over the toys. The children Jordan might have had, could still have. That brought him up with a jolt; he had never even considered having children of his own before, not as an actual reality, more as a vague idea for the future.

What did he have to offer any woman? He was a man who couldn't even claim the name that rightfully belonged to him!

'She's so tiny, Jordan.' Timothy looked up at him with the same enchanted look in his eyes that Jordan knew he had too whenever he was with the bewitchingly innocent baby.

'You were that size too once, Tim,' Grace teased as she came back into the room. 'Although you never had those curls!'

'I should hope not,' Timothy replied disgustedly. 'I was a boy!'

Grace looked at Jordan with a conspiratorial smile that said Timothy was 'still a boy', but Jordan knew that the smile he gave her in return lacked warmth; these two were capturing his heart, and Rhea, for all that she basically meant well, had just complicated things for him by coming here.

He looked up at his sister as she came back into the room. 'How was Raff?' he drawled.

Her eyes gleamed mischievously. 'Intrigued,' she mocked.

These two weren't going to let him off lightly about the way he had omitted to correct the impression they had all had of Grace Brown's being a much older woman. Heaven help him when he saw Raff again!

'Not pining away for you?' Jordan returned drily.

'Oh, that too,' Rhea dismissed lightly. 'But he would like *you* to give him a call, when you have the time, of course.'

He would just bet the other man would! Since he and Rhea had married, Raff had picked up some of her impish sense of humour.

'When I have the time,' Jordan confirmed with a vague nod of his head. Raff could damn well wait for an explanation; it was enough that he had allowed Rhea to come here to torment him. Although he had to admit that it probably hadn't been a question of allowing his sister to do anything; Rhea was a law unto herself. And he had been missing Diana...

'I've told you before, Jordan——' Rhea's gaze was deceptively innocent '—you must make the time for the things you really want to do.'

His mouth tightened at her implication. 'And I've told you——'

'Grace was telling me about poor Mrs Amery before you arrived back,' Rhea cut in with a frown, intent on avoiding an argument if possible. 'How was she when you saw her earlier?'

'She was very smiley, Grace,' Timothy put in excitedly. 'Not at all like I expected her to be.'

'As I expected her to be,' Grace corrected automatically, looking at Jordan for his opinion on Jessie's condition.

He nodded confirmation. 'The sister of the ward seemed very pleased with her.' He didn't mention that he had arranged a private ward for the elderly lady; he could explain about that when——

'And she has a lovely room, Grace,' Timothy enthused. 'With her own television, and flowers, and everything.'

'Out of the mouths of babes and innocents,' Jordan inwardly winced. He had felt it would be better for Jessie to be in a room on her own, to arrange for her to have the best treatment available.

He had told himself he would have done the same for anyone he cared about, but he also knew that part of the reason he had acted so promptly was because he knew how important Jessie was to Grace.

He couldn't bear to see that look of pain and bewilderment on Grace's face again. He had intended telling her what he had done when he could find a quiet moment to explain. There were a lot of things he needed to explain to her, but that would have done as a start!

Grace was frowning, obviously remembering that Jessie had been on a main ward with other patients when she'd seen her this morning, but Rhea looked at him knowingly; she wasn't easily fooled, this sister of his!

Which was probably another reason why she was so delighted at having caught him out where 'Grace Brown' was concerned!

Grace turned to look at him worriedly. 'She isn't worse, is she?' She forgot all caution in front of Tim in her anxiety.

'Not in the least,' Jordan instantly assured her, cursing himself for not realising she might jump to that conclusion. 'She—ah, I think I hear Nick now,' he said with some relief as he heard the front door slam, the other man having been to see Jessie this evening. 'I'm sure he will confirm that Jessie is doing well.'

'Nick?' Rhea queried in a whisper as Grace hurried out to meet the other man.

'Oh, shut up,' Jordan rasped disgruntedly. 'Isn't it time you put Diana to bed?' he scowled.

His sister grinned, unabashed. 'Are you joking? I'm enjoying myself far too much to risk missing anything!'

'You——'

'She's absolutely lovely, Jordan,' she confided softly. 'I'm not in the least surprised you wanted to stay on here and get to know her better.'

He gave a weary sigh. 'Rhea, it isn't what you think——'

'Isn't it?' she teased indulgently.

'No!' He gave a weary sigh at her knowing look. 'I happen to feel comfortable here——'

'I know,' she nodded.

'And—you do?' he frowned.

'Hm,' Rhea nodded. 'I told you, I think Grace is charming.'

'I wasn't talking about Grace,' Jordan bit out impatiently.

'You aren't trying to tell me you would still be here if she had been the elderly lady you first thought?' Rhea derided knowingly.

'I——'

'Good heavens, who is *he*?' she exclaimed admiringly, gazing over at the doorway.

Jordan didn't need to turn to know who 'he' was; Nick Parrish seemed to have this effect on the female population. But Nick looked slightly subdued for him, and Grace wasn't with him, which alarmed Jordan.

'Grace had to go to her office for something,' Nick excused abruptly. 'She'll be with us in a moment.'

That didn't reassure Jordan at all, but he took the opportunity to introduce Nick and Rhea.

When Grace came back into the room a couple of minutes later she was very pale. Something was very wrong. 'Timothy, why don't you go up and help Rhea to set up Diana's cot?' Jordan suggested lightly.

He sensed Rhea giving him a puzzled frown, but he gave her a barely perceptible shake of his head, still smiling encouragingly at Timothy.

'Yes, why don't you do that, Timothy?' Grace stiltedly joined in the suggestion.

'Sounds good to me.' Rhea bent down and scooped up her daughter, reaching up to kiss Jordan warmly on the cheek. 'Problems?' she murmured worriedly before stepping back.

'I think so,' he confirmed gruffly as he bent down to kiss Diana.

'Come on, Tim,' she turned to briskly instruct. 'I need a strong young man to help me carry up the cot and our overnight bag.'

Tim was still preening at the description when they reached the door.

'The room next to yours, Tim,' Grace told him abruptly.

Jordan could see Grace physically wilt once Rhea had departed with the two children, their light banter audible from the hallway, receding as they went up the stairs.

'What's happened?' he instantly demanded to know, his nerves stretched tautly.

Grace sank down into an armchair, looking as ill as she had the night before.

'Peter Amery was there tonight,' Nick informed him quietly, although his worried gaze was also fixed on Grace. 'In fact, he's on his way here now.'

'For what purpose?' Jordan rasped.

Nick shrugged. 'It's as we thought; he wants Jessie to go into a home once she's well enough.'

And Grace was obviously breaking her heart at the thought of it. As well she might! So much for his empty assurances last night.

'Why on earth would he want to do a thing like that?' Jordan prompted harshly.

The other man sighed. 'Why the hell do you think?'

'I don't——Money?' he realised incredulously. 'But Jessie doesn't have any money—does she?'

'A few thousand,' Nick sighed. 'Some people's greed level isn't very high,' he scorned. 'Jessie was left some money by her husband when he died, and of course it will go to the son eventually, when she dies. But in the meantime——'

'Putting Jessie into a home would give him some control of that money now,' Jordan realised disgustedly.

'Exactly,' the other man confirmed with distaste. 'Peter Amery is one of the dregs of life. We've been battling against his machinations ever since Jessie moved in here.'

Jordan decided to ignore the 'we' and the air of intimacy the claim gave the other man in Grace's life; now was *not* the time to feel jealous and possessive! He shook his head now. 'I don't understand how any man could do something this callous——'

Grace turned to him with dull eyes. 'Don't you?' she prompted harshly.

The accusation in her voice was like a slap in the face; Jordan hadn't believed she could possibly be as cold as this, to anyone. But she was upset, under strain, and everyone acted differently under those conditions...

'Don't you, Jordan?' she challenged again, harder this time. 'Would you mind explaining to me why you had Jessie moved to a private room?'

That sounded like another accusation. But why? What was so wrong with making the elderly lady's stay in hospital more comfortable? Admittedly he should probably have talked it over with Grace first; but he had thought there would be time for that this evening.

But Grace wasn't giving him chance to do that; all the anger she felt towards Peter Amery seeming to be directed at him at the moment. He didn't understand.

Obviously Nick didn't either, looking completely baffled by the whole conversation. 'I don't think we should start arguing among ourselves just now, Grace,' he began. 'We need to show a united front when Amery gets here.'

'We?' she echoed tautly, standing up. 'You make us sound like the Three Musketeers—but we're far from being that. Aren't we, Jordan?' she challenged with shining eyes.

He hardly recognised her like this, so angry, so—so embittered.

'I didn't think that it mattered——' she shook her head '—that it was unimportant, that when you were ready you would talk to us. But I realise how wrong I was to trust you.'

A nerve pulsed in his cheek. 'Grace——'

'It won't make any difference, Jordan,' she warned him harshly. 'Jessie may be ill, and Peter Amery out to make trouble because of that, but nothing you do or say will make me change my mind!'

'Grace, what the hell——?' Nick looked as stunned as Jordan felt.

She turned to him. 'Of course, you still don't know, do you?' she sighed. 'But, you see, Nick, Jordan isn't quite what he seems.'

Jordan felt himself tense, as if for the blow he knew was about to fall. And when it did it was just as devastating as he had guessed, from the change in Grace, that it would be!

'He's Jordan Somerville-Smythe, Nick,' she revealed flatly.

Nick frowned. 'Not Gregory?'

'No,' Grace confirmed dully. 'Jordan Somerville-Smythe is the man who had lawyers enquiring several months ago as to whether or not I would sell this house to his company. I said no at the time, as you know, Nick,' she added with a scathing glance at Jordan. 'But it appears *Mr Somerville-Smythe* wasn't satisfied with my answer,' she said disgustedly.

It was that disgust that told Jordan all was lost for him with Grace. Had Rhea unwittingly said something to give him away? Had he given himself away?

Whatever, Grace knew the truth now, and it was all over for him with her. . .

## CHAPTER NINE

GRACE was trembling from the effort of trying to remain at least halfway calm; she felt totally betrayed. She had trusted this man, even though every instinct had cried out for her not to, and today, tonight, she realised what a fool she had been.

The worst of it was, she knew she was falling in love with him.

'How long have you known?'

Jordan looked as if she had physically hit him, his face pale, his eyes dark.

Grace couldn't have felt any more physically ill inside if she *had* hit him. She swallowed hard. 'I've always known you weren't "Mr Gregory".'

'You have?' He looked totally stunned. 'Then why didn't you say something?' He frowned his confusion at her behaviour.

And maybe it was confusing, but, when he had arrived here, with that lost and bewildered look in his eyes, accepting the name Gregory when Jessie had unwittingly made the mistake, she had believed it was because he needed time alone, where no one would connect 'Mr Gregory' with who he really was. What Jessie, and none of the others, had realised at the time was that Grace already knew *Jason* Gregory wouldn't be coming, that he had telephoned her and cancelled his stay, and that she hadn't the heart to tell any of them because they were having such fun guessing his name. It had seemed harmless enough fun at the time.

When Jordan had turned up the way he had the other man's cancellation had seemed heaven-sent. What Grace hadn't realised was that his reasons for adopting that assumed name so readily were purely mercenary!

'I didn't think there was anything *to* say,' she bit out. 'I had no idea who you really were.'

'Only that he wasn't this man Gregory,' Nick put in incredulously. 'My God, Grace, you could have been harbouring a criminal or something! You——' He broke off as the doorbell rang loudly. 'That will be Amery now,' he scowled. 'What the hell do we do now?'

She looked across the room coldly at Jordan. 'I don't think there's any need for you to stay.'

A nerve pulsed at his jaw. 'You're asking me to leave?'

The house was going to seem very empty once he had gone, although she knew it would have to come to that. Just not yet.

'Only the sitting-room,' she explained dully, the doorbell ringing again, seeming more insistent this time.

'I'll go and answer that,' Nick muttered, but he paused at the door to look back at Jordan.

'But our conversation is far from over,' he warned grimly. 'I want explanations. From both of you.' He looked at Grace pointedly.

He was entitled to feel that way, she knew. She should have at least told him the truth from the first, but, having met Jordan and formed an opinion of him, she had thought—she had thought wrong! Jordan was a businessman first and foremost. She had been a fool to ever believe he could be starting to care for her.

The silence was awful once they were left alone together, but what needed to be said between them couldn't possibly be covered in the short time it would take Nick to let Peter Amery into the house.

And so the silence dragged on.

Jordan was the one who finally moved restlessly. 'Grace, what have I done to make you doubt me in this way?' He took a step towards her, stopping when she would have moved away. 'A name is only that, Grace,' he added persuasively. 'And I'm not even sure what mine is any more——'

'It's Somerville-Smythe,' she told him firmly. 'The same Somerville-Smythe who is a partner in the company that offered me an exorbitant amount of money for this house——'

'You were offered the market value,' he defended, his hands out imploringly. 'There was no subterfuge, Grace, no deceit intended.'

She shook her head, her eyes dull with pain. 'You must want this house very badly to try to use Jessie's accident against us——'

'What?' he gasped disbelievingly. 'Grace, I don't know what you're talking about,' he rasped. 'And I'm not sure you do either!'

She wasn't a hundred per cent sure what was going on herself; she only knew alarm bells had started to ring in her head as soon as she had realised Jordan had moved Jessie to a private room. She had already felt uneasy inside herself—the names Jordan and Raff weren't all that common, and they sounded familiar to her when she heard them together like that.

And so she had gone to her sitting-room a short time ago to check the heading on those letters she had received from Quinlan Leisure all those months ago. Sure enough, the two partners in the company were Jordan Somerville-Smythe and Rafferty Quinlan. She still didn't know quite how Jordan intended to persuade her into selling this house, but she did know that was why he was here now.

'Grace——'

'Here we are.' Nick made a point of announcing his arrival into the room with Peter Amery. 'Come in, Peter,' he invited softly. 'We don't bite,' he added lightly, but there was a warning edge to his voice that the other man would do well to take note of.

Grace knew Peter Amery well, despite the fact that he rarely came to see his mother here; on the few occasions she had met him he had made enough of a personality impact for him not to be easily dismissed from the mind.

Tall and thin, with thinning blond hair, his face was sharp and angular whereas Jessie's was sweet and soft, his eyes a pale blue that made Grace think of cold, heartless seas.

Grace had been wary of him from the first, knew that he had tried to put Jessie into a home straight after her husband died, but that Jessie had resisted and moved in here. Peter Amery had been trying to get her to move out again ever since, even though he could see she was happy here.

'Grace, I think the time has surely come——'

'Just a moment, Peter,' she interrupted quietly, turning pointedly to Jordan.

His gaze clashed with hers, searching, probing. 'I'm not leaving,' he finally bit out.

She stiffened at his arrogance, her hands clenched at her sides, feeling as if her whole world was falling apart at this moment. Why, oh, why, had she trusted this man? She drew in a steadying breath. 'If you won't leave, then I will!' she told him tautly.

Peter Amery gasped his amazement at the statement. 'Now look here, Grace——'

'No, *you* look here, Peter,' she cut in fiercely, more forceful in that moment than she had ever been in her life before. 'Your mother is in hospital, and is likely to be so for some time. Any conversation we have about where she is to go when she is discharged can surely wait. Quite frankly, I find your whole attitude distasteful!' She was breathing hard in her agitation, her eyes glowing deeply grey.

'But—I don't—now look——' Peter Amery floundered about incoherently.

'You heard Grace, Peter,' Nick told him happily. 'And I happen to agree with her,' he added hardly, his eyes glacial.

Grace could feel her control starting to slip, not least because Jordan stood so silently across the room, not saying a word, seemingly having made his point by not leaving as she had wanted him to.

She had to get out of here!

'You can talk about it all you like, Peter,' she snapped. 'With whom you like,' she added pointedly, her head back. 'But at the end of the day it will be Jessie's decision, still, whether she wants to come back here or go elsewhere. She has a home here with us for as long as she wants one, and I intend to make sure she knows that,' Grace told him challengingly before walking out of the room, her head held high.

It was just her luck to find Rhea Quinlan out in the hallway.

'Hey.' Rhea reached out to steady her as the two of them would have collided, the smile fading from her lips as she saw the paleness of Grace's cheeks. 'What's happened?' she prompted in a concerned voice.

Like her brother, Rhea had a way of getting straight to the point of things, and, much as Grace had come to like the other woman, she *was* Jordan's sister, Rafferty Quinlan's wife, and as such her presence here had to be suspect too. A family conspiracy!

'I should ask your brother,' Grace advised flatly, looking around for Timothy.

'He's upstairs talking to Diana while she plays in her cot.' Rhea easily guessed the reason for this extra anxiety. 'I could hear the raised voices upstairs and thought it best to leave the two of them up there.'

'Thank you,' Grace accepted stiffly. 'I'll go and get him to bed now.'

'Grace...?'

She turned briefly, sorry for the puzzled hurt on the other woman's face at her distant behaviour after their earlier friendliness together. But there was little she could do to change that.

'It's late,' she answered abruptly, determinedly not looking at Rhea again before turning away and going up the stairs.

There was a stunned silence after Grace left the sitting-room the way she did; whatever Peter Amery had been expecting from the meeting, it certainly hadn't been to have his opinion dismissed as irrelevant by the virago Grace had become!

Jordan was very aware that it was because of him that Grace had attacked the other man so vehemently. He also knew that, ultimately, she wouldn't thank him for it. And from the way she had left now he knew she wasn't even willing to discuss the discord between the two of them. Maybe she would listen to Rhea; the two women had seemed to like each other.

In the meantime there was Peter Amery to deal with; Jordan had not been fooled for a moment by the other man's stunned silence, knowing from experience that the sort of bully Peter Amery was—the sort who badgered and harassed women—could often be the worst kind, never knowing when to keep their mouth shut.

He was right!

'Well, Nick,' Peter Amery bristled indignantly. 'I really feel that Grace has overstepped the line this time——'

'Do you, indeed?' Nick interrupted softly—too softly, if the other man was astute enough to realise it, although Jordan very much doubted that he would be. 'Personally,' Nick's voice was deceptively smooth now, 'I think we should have told you where to go years ago!'

A ruddy hue suffused Peter Amery's cheeks, and he looked as if he was about to choke on his indignation. 'I—you—I——'

'Quite honestly, we've only continued to give you the time of day because we didn't want to upset Jessie,' Nick told him contemptuously. 'We didn't want her to realise what an obnoxious little creep you really are!'

'How dare you——?'

'I dare because we're her family now,' Nick said, poking the other man in the shoulder. 'We love her. And we'll take care of her. And if you try to take her away from here, by whatever means, you'll have me to deal with.'

Nick was telling the other man exactly what Jordan would have liked to but didn't feel he had the right to do. Even less so after the way Grace had dismissed him. And so he had no choice but to let Nick do all the talking now. The other man was having little trouble in that direction anyway!

'Understood?' Nick challenged the gasping Peter Amery.

The other man glared at him. 'You haven't heard the last of me——'

'Oh, I think we have,' he was told in a dangerously soft voice.

'I am still my mother's next of kin——'

'What you are is a slimy little toad,' Nick ground out. 'Jessie certainly isn't dead, and she is certainly still in control of all her faculties too, so who *you* are really isn't important, to any of us.'

The other man was all bluster now, his gaze shifting from Nick to the silent Jordan and then back again, Jordan's brooding silence seeming to bother him almost as much as anything Nick had said to him, his cheeks going very pale now.

'We'll see,' he challenged weakly, going to the door. 'As Grace pointed out earlier, my mother isn't out of hospital yet!'

'Little bastard!' Nick growled fiercely once the other man had slammed out the front door.

Jordan agreed with the sentiment wholeheartedly, having found Peter Amery totally objectionable. How sweet little Jessie had ever produced such a son was beyond him.

'Now what the hell have you been doing to upset Grace?'

Jordan turned back to Nick. 'You heard—my name isn't Gregory,' he shrugged.

'And?'

He shrugged again. 'And it's Somerville-Smythe.'

'And?' Nick watched him with narrowed eyes.

'How should I know?' Jordan came back exasperatedly, feeling totally impotent about the whole situation. 'She believes I'm trying to trick her into selling the house to me, I suppose,' he acknowledged impatiently.

'And are you?' Nick prompted.

'No!'

Nick frowned. 'Then why does Grace think that you—oh, never mind.' He shook his head. 'I've never seen her quite that upset before,' he said worriedly.

That didn't comfort Jordan in the least!

'Of course she's under a lot of strain, with Jessie's accident, and that damned Amery,' Nick frowned, deep in thought. 'She could just be overreacting to the whole situation. Although I don't understand what you're doing here, of all places, under an assumed identity as well.' He looked at Jordan with narrowed eyes.

'It's a long story,' Jordan sighed.

'One I'll be glad to listen to, when I have more time,' Nick told him warningly. 'Right now I'm more concerned with Grace, and how I can best help her. I've neglected my responsibilities where she's concerned, been so wrapped up in myself for so long I've let her carry everything alone.' It seemed to be something he had just realised, and it troubled him deeply.

All Jordan could think of was that he had been wrong, that there was something between Grace and Nick after all. And after the way she had looked at him earlier, half disgust, half pain, whatever she might have been starting to feel for him had been totally destroyed in those few brief minutes.

He made his excuses to the other man, Nick nodding dismissively, not even seeming to notice Jordan going, lost in his own thoughts. And from the expression of self-loathing on his face they were far from pleasant.

Jordan's eyes widened as he came out into the hallway and saw Rhea sitting on the stairs, her chin resting in her hand. He grimaced at her raised brows. 'You heard?'

'Some of it,' Rhea sighed, straightening. 'But none of what made Grace rush out of the room the way she did.'

Jordan winced. 'You saw her?'

His sister nodded. 'She's gone up to put Timothy to bed. Jordan——'

'Don't ask.' He ran a weary hand over his eyes, feeling utterly defeated.

'But——'

'Could we please get out of this hallway, Rhea?' he cut in tautly. 'Before I make an absolute idiot of myself!' He had never felt more like crying in his life!

James, as a father, had very quickly taught him that it wasn't manly to cry, and as a child he had rarely done so, as a man never. Maybe he had just never cared about anything or anyone before as strongly as he cared about Grace...? The thought of having to leave here, of possibly never seeing her again, was tearing him apart.

But, when it came to it, he would have little choice.

Rhea looked mortified at the pale anguish on his face. 'Let's go up and say goodnight to Diana,' she suggested gently. 'I doubt if she's gone to sleep yet.' She put her arm companionably through the crook of his as they went up the stairs together.

But even Diana, the baby he adored, offered him little comfort that night.

Grace couldn't believe she had acted the way she had, and still trembled at the thought of her cold anger.

And what if she was wrong? What if she had misjudged Jordan's motives after all? She couldn't wipe out the memory of how stunned he had looked by her attack, his utter bewilderment at her accusations. Oh, God, what if she *had* got it wrong?

All she could think of, once she discovered who he really was, was that he had to be deceiving them for a reason. But what if her first belief had been the right one—that he was just a man whose emotions were battered, who needed to rest here until he felt able to face the world again?

Did the fact that he was Jordan *Somerville-Smythe* really change that? She had known from the beginning that his name wasn't really Gregory, so what difference did his real name really make?

It was *Somerville-Smythe*!

It *had* to be more than just coincidence that he had chosen to come here, of all places.

He had made himself so popular with Timothy and Jessie, even Nick had seemed to accept him at last. The thought that he might just have been quietly and steadily undermining the security of their life here, for his own gain, even going as far as to make love to her until she was utterly confused by her feelings for him, was an unpleasant—as well as humiliating!—and unpalatable one, but it was all she had been able to think of once she had finally put two and two together and come up with the necessary four.

'Grace...?'

She looked down at Timothy, realising he must have been watching her for some time as she was lost in thought. She had put him to bed, talked to him for a while after reading him a story, and then fallen silent, making no effort to leave. He must wonder what was wrong with her!

She gave a rueful smile, standing up to tuck him in. 'I was miles away.'

He nodded, accepting her excuse, his gaze flickering towards the door. 'Jordan hasn't been up to see me tonight,' he finally commented.

She had been right to have her initial worry that Timothy could become too fond of Jordan, and yet at the time she had also hoped—oh, God, how stupidly romantic had been her own hopes!

She had to talk to Jordan, find out once and for all if she was right about him.

'He's probably busy tonight as his sister has arrived,' she soothed Timothy. 'After all, he hasn't seen her for a while.'

'Diana is lovely, isn't she?' Timothy said sleepily, without a trace of rancour for Jordan's obvious affection for the baby.

'Lovely,' Grace echoed, sure that Timothy was going to be asleep almost as soon as she left the room. Which was probably as well; if Jordan had decided to leave immediately she didn't want Timothy upset this evening—in the morning would do!

But at least if Jordan had decided to leave she would have the answer to those little niggling doubts.

The sitting-room was empty when she got downstairs and went looking for him—so were Nick's rooms when she had trudged back up to the top of the house, which only left Rhea Quinlan's room to be investigated; the three of them surely hadn't sneaked off without a word?

She knew they hadn't when she could hear the soft murmur of voices from inside the room, and was about to knock on the door when it was suddenly wrenched open and Jordan walked straight into her, the impact knocking the papers out of his hand so that they scattered all over the carpet at their feet.

Jordan just stood and stared at her for several seconds, as if he didn't know what to say, wasn't even sure of her mood after their earlier conversation. Grace couldn't blame him for that; she felt strangely tongue-tied herself.

She loved this man!

She loved him, and she couldn't quite believe he would deliberately deceive her for his own personal gain, had to at least hear that from his own lips if it was true.

'Jordan, I have to talk to you,' she told him shakily, automatically bending down to collect up the scattered papers and put them back into the file that had also fallen. 'I——' She broke off, staring down in horrified fascination at the sheet of paper she held in her hand, the names typed there seeming to leap up off the page.

'Grace, I can explain——'

Her furious glare silenced him, and she picked up several more of the loose typed sheets, only needing a glance at them to know that this file was on Charlton House, and its inhabitants, on the changes that would need to be made to transform it into a leisure complex.

'Correction——' she swallowed hard '—we don't need to talk at all, about anything; *this* says it all!' She thrust the papers into his hands before turning sharply and almost running away from him this time, tears scalding her cheeks.

It was only much later, when Jordan read the file through completely himself, feeling utterly helpless at its damning evidence in Grace's eyes, that he finally discovered exactly what Nick meant in her life...

## CHAPTER TEN

HER uncle.

Nick Parrish was the brother of Grace's dead mother.

It was a simple enough explanation for the other man's presence here, for his slightly possessive air when it came to Grace and Timothy, but it was quite honestly one Jordan would never have thought of if it hadn't been written down in black and white in front of him. In the file that had damned him forever in Grace's eyes.

He had stayed in Rhea's room after Diana had fallen asleep because he had needed to talk to someone who at least understood him, to try to explain to her exactly how he felt about Grace, to try to explain too why he had taken the opportunity, when it was presented to him, to be someone other than himself for a while—that he needed time to find out which was the real him!

And Rhea had understood, although she didn't accept that it was all over between himself and Grace; after all, she argued, hadn't she practised a similar deceit on Raff two years ago? And although he had been upset initially, look at the two of them now!

He lay back against his pillows now as sleep still eluded him—Grace hadn't returned like the virago she had been earlier to insist that he pack his bags and leave immediately, and until she did he was staying put. But he was sure that he and Grace couldn't have the same happy ending Rhea and Raff had found. Some things just couldn't be forgiven, and Grace now believed he had been plotting and planning to coerce her into selling Charlton House to him if it couldn't be achieved any other way; he was sure that was what she thought, and why she had reacted the way she had.

'Go and tell her the truth,' Rhea had urged after Grace had left them so abruptly.

What was the truth? That he loved her? Oh, he did. That he wanted her? More than anything else in this world. That he wanted to marry her? He ached to make her his wife, to know she would be with him always.

And she wasn't going to believe any of that, believing what *she* did about him, would probably think it was just another ploy to get his hands on this house.

Oh, God, he had never felt so utterly *helpless*!

'Grace?'

She looked curiously at the man standing on the doorstep.

Tall and dark, with assessing grey eyes, he was one of the most handsome men Grace had ever seen. But she had never seen him before; she would have remembered him if she had. He wasn't the sort of man one could easily forget!

He wore denims and a thick corduroy shirt beneath a leather jacket, but it was obvious that he would have been just as comfortable in a business suit seated behind an imposing desk surrounded by an army of secretaries.

The handsome face was so hard it looked as if it might have been carved from granite, his chin firm and square, a certain arrogance of bearing in his eyes, and yet the smile he directed at her was warm enough.

Grace *knew* she had never met him before, and yet he knew her name.

Unless he had come from Peter Amery, she realised with a sinking heart. It would be too much to hope Jessie's son would just give up and leave them all alone. But was only eight-thirty; surely lawyers didn't make house-calls this time of morning, especially on a Saturday?

Well, whoever he was, she couldn't just stand here staring at him for the rest of the morning; otherwise he was going to think Peter Amery was perfectly justified in believing her incapable of caring for his mother!

'I—'

'Darling!' A glowing Rhea came hurtling down the length of the hallway to launch herself into the waiting arms of the man standing on the doorstep. 'Oh, darling, I know it's only been overnight, but I've missed you so much!' she groaned before pressing her lips against his.

Raff Quinlan...

No doubt about it, Rhea wasn't likely to be kissing any other man this passionately!

Grace looked at him objectively—what she could still see of him. The dark hair was like Jordan's, if worn a little longer, and the eyes, she remembered, had been more grey than blue, and his face was just as hard and angled as Jordan's, although their facial characteristics bore little resemblance to each other. However she had no doubt that, if one stood the two tall, dark-haired men next to each other, the family connection could quite easily be made, much more so than between Jordan and Rhea.

How strange Jordan must have felt the first time he looked at this man and knew he was his brother—— She mustn't start feeling sorry for Jordan. Or, indeed, for the man standing before her. As well as being half-brothers, they were business partners, and Raff Quinlan had just as much interest in buying Charlton House as Jordan did!

'I've missed you too, love,' Raff murmured gruffly to his wife. 'But I think we may be embarrassing Grace.' His arm was still around Rhea's shoulders as he looked across at Grace apologetically. 'I hope I can call you Grace?' he added warmly. 'I've heard so much about you I feel I know you already.'

Did all the men in this family have a natural charm? Grace thought crossly, finding herself unable to resist placing her hand in the one he held out to her.

'And I'm Raff,' he introduced unnecessarily. 'Seeing as no one else seems to be interested in explaining who I am.' He looked down at his wife mockingly.

'I had already guessed that,' Grace returned drily.

Dark brows rose. 'You were right about the voice, Rhea,' he told her softly, but not so softly it wasn't intended to be overheard. 'It is sexy!' He chuckled softly as Grace instantly began to blush and Rhea punched him playfully on the arm.

'I'm sorry about this, Grace,' Rhea grimaced as she and Raff moved further into the hallway. 'I've tried to teach him some manners in the last two years, but, as you can see, I haven't been too successful.'

Never mind about that, Grace inwardly protested dazedly. She was starting to feel as if this family had already taken over her home; they were starting to outnumber her own family!

'Where is our darling daughter?' Raff's voice softened indulgently.

'Down in the kitchen.' Rhea shot Grace an apologetic glance. 'Jordan is feeding her her breakfast. I hope you don't mind, Grace.' She turned to put her arm through the crook of

Grace's, making it impossible for Grace to avoid going down to the kitchen with them. 'I didn't know where you were. And Diana was hungry. And then I heard the doorbell ring. And——'

'My love, you're waffling,' her husband derided.

She glared at him. 'You would be waffling too—babbling, in fact!—if you knew the mess Jordan has made of every—— I'm sorry, Grace,' she sighed as she obviously felt the other woman stiffen beside her. 'But, for an intelligent man, Jordan *has* made a mess of everything! I telephoned Raff late last night—I apologise for not asking permission first, but I don't think you were in a mood to see any of us again at the time!—in the hope that he might be able to come up here and help sort some of this out!'

'And you told me it was because you missed me,' Raff teased in a wounded voice.

'It was! I was! But——'

'You've had a wasted journey, Mr Quinlan,' Grace began stiffly.

'I think you had better call me Raff,' he told her gravely.

'*I* think, for our short acquaintance, that Mr Quinlan will do just fine,' she returned tautly.

'You're right,' Raff told his wife with a sigh. 'Jordan has made a mess of things!'

The man in question was seated at the kitchen table, Diana on his knee, as he fed her from the bowl of porridge.

And, judging by the adept way he managed to balance the child on his knee while supporting her with one arm and feeding her with the other hand, it was far from the first time he had done so.

Grace felt a terrible ache in her chest just at the sight of the red-haired baby in his arms. Diana was obviously fast tiring of the porridge, and starting to squirm in Jordan's arms. 'All gone,' she told him hopefully.

'It is not "all gone", young lady,' he returned indulgently. 'And your Mummy will shoot me if I don't——'

'Daddy!' The baby had finally spotted her father as he stood across the room watching them, reaching out her arms for him.

Raff laughed softly, moving forward to sweep his tiny daughter up into his arms. 'I've missed you too, poppet,' he told her gruffly.

It was like looking at a different Raff Quinlan, watching him with his baby, all the hard lines of his face softened, his eyes no longer cold but a warm grey.

'Raff...?' Jordan stood up slowly as he took in the other man's unexpected presence here, frowning darkly, before turning accusing eyes on Rhea.

'It seemed like the best thing to do,' she shrugged awkwardly.

Jordan's mouth twisted. 'Your belief that Raff can right all the wrongs of the world is very touching, Rhea,' he derided hardly, 'but it hardly applies in this situation.' He looked briefly at Grace as she stood so stiffly across the room.

She straightened. 'I think I'll go up and——'

'Oh, don't leave, Grace,' Raff Quinlan requested warmly. 'The sooner this situation is sorted out, the better it will be for everyone.'

'Raff——'

'Jordan,' he returned drily, his gaze steady on the other man. 'I seem to remember another situation very like this one two years ago.'

Jordan sighed. 'This is hardly likely to have the same outcome.'

The other man shrugged. 'That all depends on whether or not you want it to.'

Dark blue eyes flashed with anger. 'Don't be so damned stupid!'

'Right,' Raff grinned, satisfied with the answer, aggressively as it had been given. 'I've brought a contract with me, Grace—one I think you should see before——'

'I've already told Jordan, and now I'll tell you, I'm not interested in anything you have to offer me,' Grace cut in furiously. How dared they come into her home and try to do this to her? How *dared* they?

'I think you'll be interested in this,' Raff drawled unabashedly.

'Raff, what the hell do you think you're doing?' Jordan looked dazedly at the other man. 'You aren't helping at all!'

'But I will,' the other man assured him confidently. 'I will.' He put Diana into her mother's waiting arms, and reached into the breast pocket of his leather jacket to pull out a single sheet of paper, slowly unfolding it before handing it to Jordan. 'Read that, brother mine, before you accuse me of making matters worse,' he drawled, turning to Grace as Jordan began to frown over the single sheet of paper. 'Rhea tells me you know of our complicated family history?' he prompted conversationally.

Grace knew he was trying to put her at her ease, but her attention was all on Jordan as he slowly read the contract in his hand. 'Yes,' she confirmed vaguely.

'Jordan wondered for a while if he should be called Uncle-Uncle Jordan,' Raff continued drily. 'But——what do you think?' He turned interestedly to Jordan as he finally looked up at them.

Jordan shook his head. 'I think I should have thought of it!' he said self-disgustedly.

'Too close to it, old son,' Raff sympathised. 'You'll see I've already signed it.' He took a pen from his breast pocket too now, holding it out to Jordan.

Jordan took it, putting his own signature to the contract.

Grace watched the exchange with puzzled eyes, her heart leaping with dismay when Jordan handed the sheet of paper to her; hadn't he hurt her enough already? She read the contract. And then read it again.

Because she just couldn't believe what was written there.

'I love you, Grace,' Jordan told her quietly. 'I want to marry you.'

As she looked up at him the tears began to fall.

'I think it's time we left them to it, darling,' Raff told Rhea softly. 'Jordan at least left me to propose to you in private; we should do the same for him and Grace.'

Grace was hardly aware of the other couple leaving and taking the baby with them. The contract she held in her hand, signed by both partners of Quinlan Leisure, stated that the said company had no intention now, or in the future, of making any attempt to purchase Charlton House from its owner Grace Brown!

It had to be the most reverse contract ever written, and yet it released the chains that had been strangling her heart ever since she had realised who Jordan really was.

'Did you mean it?' her voice was huskily soft.

'Of course I mean it, Grace; the contract is binding——'

'Not that bit.' She let the contract flutter to the floor, no longer important. 'The part about loving me and wanting to marry me.'

'Oh, God, yes,' he groaned. 'It's what I want—would like, more than anything else in the world!'

He looked as if the admission filled him with elation, that aching emptiness in his eyes a thing of the past.

Grace laughed softly, a slight catch in her throat. 'Being humble doesn't suit you, my love.' She caressed the hardness of his cheek.

He swallowed hard. '"Your love,"' he repeated. 'Am I?'

'Oh, yes.' Grace's eyes glowed. 'From the very beginning, I think. That was probably how I was so easily able to convince myself that it didn't matter that you weren't Mr Gregory, that whoever you were you weren't out to hurt anyone, that you were in pain yourself.'

Jordan shook his head. 'I still don't know what made me even start that subterfuge.'

'Don't you?' she smiled gently.

'Maybe I do,' he accepted ruefully. 'Grace, tell me again that you love me.'

'I haven't told you at all yet.' Her smile was a little shaky now. 'But I do love you, Jordan, so very much.'

'Enough to marry me?'

'Oh, yes, more than enough to marry you,' she glowed.

'And to live here with me for the rest of your life?'

Grace frowned at him, not sure what he meant. 'Your business——'

'Goes where I go,' he dismissed easily. 'And I want us to live where you'll be happy.'

She swallowed hard, more moved than he could possibly realise; Jordan was willing to change his whole life for her. What could she offer him in return?

'Grace. Oh, love——' he enfolded her into his arms as he saw the uncertainty in her face '—everything I could possibly want is here; you, Timothy, Jessie, even Nick. My God, Grace——' he gave a self-derisive laugh '—if you knew the bad moments I've had over your *uncle* Nick! I had no idea he was your uncle!' he explained at her questioning look.

'No idea—he——?'

'No one had bothered to explain the relationship!' Jordan complained defensively.

No, probably no one had, Grace realised with the start of a smile. Poor Jordan; goodness knew what he had been thinking of all this time! Oh, dear, it really was quite funny——

'Go on; laugh.' He pretended to be annoyed as her lips twitched uncontrollably. 'I've gone grey worrying about the relationship between the two of you!' He pointed to the few grey hairs he had at his temples, grey that had been there before she even met him.

'Poor darling.' She kissed him there, her eyes dark as she looked up at him. 'Nick is——'

Jordan placed gentle fingertips over her lips. 'You don't owe me any explanations about him. You never did,' he assured her. 'Even if he had been your lover——'

'I've never had a lover,' she told him softly, and watched the blaze of pleasure flare up in his eyes, his gaze suddenly possessive. 'I've never wanted one. Until the night Jessie went into hospital,' she admitted ruefully. 'That night I wanted you very much.' She held his gaze steadily.

He swallowed convulsively. 'I wanted you too, Grace. But I didn't want it to seem as if I was taking advantage of the situation.'

She moistened her lips with the pink tip of her tongue. 'And now?'

'Now I——'

'Ah, here you are!' Nick burst unceremoniously into the room, his face alive in a way Grace couldn't remember seeing for a very long time. 'I've been to see Amery, and it's all settled. He—— ' He broke off, finally seeming to sense that he had interrupted something, his gaze narrowed on the two of them as they stood so close together. 'What's going on?' he asked suspiciously.

'I——'

'Let me, Grace,' Jordan requested softly, his gaze on the other man unwavering, his arm firmly about her shoulders. 'Nick, I would like your permission to marry your niece.'

Grace gasped at his directness, although knowing him as she did she should really have expected little else.

Nick dropped down into one of the kitchen chairs, totally stunned. 'When did this happen?'

He shook his head in confusion. 'The last time I saw the two of you together you couldn't stand the man, Grace.' He frowned.

'That isn't strictly true,' she smiled. 'I still loved him; I was just very upset with him.'

'And now?'

'Now I just love him.' She looked up at Jordan with adoring eyes.

Nick shook his head, obviously still puzzled. 'Does any of this change of heart have something to do with the second Jaguar we now have parked in the driveway?' he asked drily.

'And this.' Grace bent down to pick up the contract and hand it to Nick.

He read it quickly, looking up. 'The second Jaguar belongs to Rhea's husband Raff?'

'He's a little more than that,' Jordan said ruefully. 'But I think you've had enough surprises for one morning. What was that you were saying about Amery?' he prompted interestedly.

'What? Oh,' Nick shrugged. 'Pretty tame stuff after this.' He put the contract down on the table. 'I went to see Amery this morning just to reaffirm what I said to him last night,' Nick frowned. 'I think I made myself pretty clear.'

Grace looked concerned. 'Verbally or physically?'

'Verbally!' He relaxed slightly, starting to smile. 'The man is pretty cowardly when it comes to standing up to another man. And now that you're going to have a husband as well as an uncle for protection I can guarantee neither Jessie nor you will have any more problems with him.'

Grace gave a shaky smile. 'You don't know how good it feels to hear that.'

'There's something else, Grace...' Nick hesitated.

She looked at him sharply, sensing—she didn't quite know what, but something. 'Yes?'

He turned to Jordan. 'You really are getting married?'

Jordan's arm tightened possessively about her shoulders. 'Tomorrow if I could arrange it!'

Nick gave him a mocking look. 'Not too quickly, if you don't mind; I don't want any scandal attached to my niece's wedding.'

'God, how I wish you had made a remark about Grace being your niece days ago,' Jordan groaned. 'I've suffered agonies thinking the two of you were something else completely!'

'Really?' Nick asked interestedly. 'Well, a little suffering is good for the soul,' he taunted.

Jordan gave an easy laugh. 'I might have expected you to come out with a remark like that!'

Grace felt choked with emotion at the growing friendship she sensed between the two men who were so important in her life. Given time she knew the two men would become firm friends. And they were going to have all the time in the world for that, she thought happily.

'What were you going to tell us, Nick?' she prompted softly, having some idea already, sensing a change in him, a change that had been long in coming but which she felt was here now.

He drew in a ragged breath. 'I've decided to go back to London.' The words came out in a rush, as if he was afraid he might change his mind if he didn't say them soon.

'Oh, Nick, that's marvellous!' Grace moved forward to hug him, tears in her eyes. 'I'm glad,' she told him huskily.

'Yes. Well. I'll leave the two of you to continue telling each other how much in love you are,' he teased to cover up his own shaky emotions, kissing Grace on the cheek and shaking Jordan by the hand before leaving.

Grace swallowed convulsively, watching him go. 'I can't tell you how pleased I am,' she choked as she turned back to Jordan. 'Nick is an artist, you know—of course you know,' she grimaced. 'Your file will have told you that. But——'

'Forget that damned file, please, Grace,' Jordan groaned, taking her back into his arms. 'If I had read the damned thing properly in the first place I could have saved myself, and everyone else, a lot of pain!'

'But you do know about Nick?' she prompted softly.

'Yes,' he confirmed simply.

Eighteen months ago Nick had been about to give his first big exhibition in London, and

Grace's father had been travelling to the show with Nick's wife Sue when a van came out of a turning without even looking to see if there was any other traffic on the road. Grace's father had taken evasive action, but it had come too late, and their car had crashed into the side of the van. Sue had been killed instantly, and Grace's father had died a few hours later in hospital.

Nick had withdrawn the exhibition, shut all his work away here at the top of the house, and hadn't picked up a paintbrush since, hating the world, having decided, Grace felt, that it hated him. But Nick's moving back to London had to be a step in the right direction; the rest would come, she was sure it would.

She buried her face against Jordan's chest. 'We're all starting to live again.'

'This is just the beginning, my darling,' he promised. 'For all of us.'

## EPILOGUE

IDENTICAL red bobble-hats pulled low over their ears to keep out the cold, blue duffel coats buttoned up to the throat, blue jeans tucked into wellington boots. The snowman they were building was being seriously hampered by the smaller of the two boys knocking it down as fast as the bigger one was building it.

Jordan chuckled softly as he stood at the window inside the house watching them, and kissed Grace lightly on the brow as she joined him.

'Do you think we ought to go out and help them?' she murmured indulgently.

Two years of marriage had deepened her beauty for him. She was his world, everything, more even than their son—the little vandal of the piece outside ruining things for Timothy as the elder boy did his best to build a snowman.

At fifteen months old, Donald Quinlan Somerville-Smythe, named after his paternal grandfather, had his whole family under firm control, was adored by everyone, from his parents, to Jessie, to Timothy, to his aunt Rhea and uncle Raff, to his uncle Nick. Another redhead, Donald had been walking since he was ten months old, and Jordan felt as if he had been running to catch up with him ever since!

'I think they deserve each other,' he grinned. 'Timothy had me up at the crack of dawn this morning when he realised it had snowed in the night.'

Grace frowned at the blanket of snow on the ground. 'I do hope Rhea, Raff and the children manage to get here ready for Christmas tomorrow.'

'They'll make it,' Jordan said with certainty, having confidence in his brother. 'Diana and baby Thomas will nag him into it!' he added with relish.

Grace smiled, giving him a sideways glance as she sobered. 'Nick telephoned a few minutes ago.'

He raised dark brows, sensing something was troubling her. 'Don't tell me he can't make it?' He knew how important this Christmas with them all together was to Grace, Nick having made his excuses the year before.

'He's bringing someone with him,' she said, chewing on her bottom lip. 'He wouldn't tell me much about her, except her name is Dani, and she's helping him get ready for this exhibition he has planned for the summer.'

Jordan chuckled softly at her concerned frown. 'Grace, Nick's forty years old; it's time he met someone.'

'Oh, I do so hope he has,' she said worriedly. 'Jordan, I really do think we should go outside and help them!' She made a dash for the door. 'I'm coming, Donald!' she called as she ran.

Jordan turned to watch out of the window as Grace pulled their son from his face-first dive into the snow, the boy looking most disgruntled at the indignity of it all as he was brushed down by a giggling Timothy.

His family.

His Grace.

His saving Grace.

Spoil yourself next month
with these four novels from

**FORMS OF LOVE by Rita Clay Estrada**

*Lost Loves* mini-series

Dan Lovejoy had lost his wife in a tragic accident when he met her double. Only this woman who looked like Kendra wasn't Kendra. Dan couldn't help himself; he started to fall in love with her. But this woman had some very *unusual* secrets of her own.

**CHRISTMAS IN JULY by Madeline Harper**

Ali Paxton Bell had more than Christmas on her mind when Sam Cantrell came to town. Sexy and charming, Sam definitely had a twinkle in his eye. And one hot, steamy night he paid Ali a visit she wouldn't forget in a hurry...

**STRANGE BEDPERSONS by Jennifer Crusie**

Nick Jamieson wasn't the right guy for Tess Newhart. He was caviar and champagne and she was take-out Chinese. He wore tailored suits and she wore faded jeans. He wanted to get ahead and she wanted...him. Great sex wasn't enough to build a relationship on—was it?

**MADELEINE'S COWBOY by Kristine Rolofson**

Madeleine Harmon was finally going to visit the West—take sunrise breakfast rides, have adventures and watch the desert stars. Only she got picked up by the wrong man at the station and found herself taking care of Stuart Anderson's ranch and his lonely young daughter.

# TEST OF TIME
## Jayne Ann Krentz

---

HE MARRIED FOR THE BEST REASON…
They had a lot in common and would be great together in business—and in bed. Marriage to Katy Randall would also help make people forget just how rough Garrett Coltrane's past had been.

SHE MARRIED FOR THE ONLY REASON…
Love. But the growing fear that shook her during the ceremony exploded into heartbreak when she discovered that love was the only thing Garrett didn't want.

DID THEY STAND A CHANCE AT MAKING THE ONLY REASON THE REAL REASON TO SHARE A LIFETIME?

*"A master of the genre...nobody does it better!"*

Romantic Times (USA)